I am going to ge
and for all, no m

And Drew had meant
took one step into his

She was wearing a snug-fitting pair of well-worn blue jeans over black hand-tooled leather boots. Her T-shirt was faded black and sported the name of a rock band he'd never heard of. She wore a wickedly broad smile beneath eyes of mossy-green determination.

"Mr. Robson," she began, without invitation. She sprawled in one of his wingback chairs. "Sorry I'm arriving unannounced like this, but since our last meeting didn't go as well as I'd hoped, I thought a different approach might work."

"It hadn't occurred to me that you'd be crazy enough to come back," he said tightly. "I'm still not looking for anything you're offering."

"But you are still looking for a way out of the hole you're in."

His eyes narrowed as he sat down in the chair next to her, glaring.

She studied him unflinchingly. "Just hear me out. Five minutes. That's all I'm asking. What do you have to lose?"

My pants?

Dear Reader,

Is there anything better than the sparring and tension that emerges when a strong man and an equally strong woman go head-to-head, and sparks fly? Not for me! Meet Jade Morrow and her stubborn client Drew Robson. Drew's company is in trouble, and only Jade knows exactly how to save it. If only Drew would see things her way! Drew gives her a run for her money, she gives him something to think about…and they both give each other the ride of their lives.

Jade and Drew are two of my favorite characters—confident, sexy and larger than life. I hope you enjoy spending some time with them as their story unfolds.

Also, visit www.tryBlaze.com for the latest in the series!

Happy reading,

Cathy Yardley

Books by Cathy Yardley

HARLEQUIN BLAZE

14—THE DRIVEN SNOWE
59—GUILTY PLEASURES

HARLEQUIN DUETS

23—THE CINDERELLA SOLUTION

RED DRESS INK

6—L.A. WOMAN

WORKING IT

Cathy Yardley

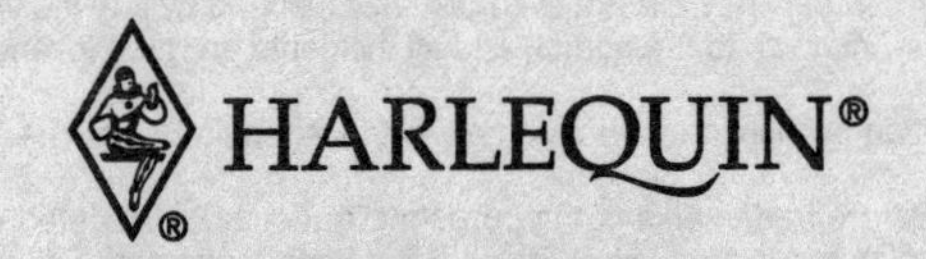

TORONTO • NEW YORK • LONDON
AMSTERDAM • PARIS • SYDNEY • HAMBURG
STOCKHOLM • ATHENS • TOKYO • MILAN • MADRID
PRAGUE • WARSAW • BUDAPEST • AUCKLAND

For Chris Becker…if not for keeping me sane, then for making the insanity a hell of a lot more fun.

ISBN 0-373-79093-7

WORKING IT

This edition published by arrangement with Harlequin Books S.A.

Visit us at www.eHarlequin.com

Printed in U.S.A.

1

"MR. ROBSON IS RUNNING late," the older woman behind the desk said without apology. "He had other business he needed to attend to."

Jade Morrow smiled. "That's fine. I'm in no rush, Mrs.... I'm sorry, what was your name again?"

The woman hadn't given her name to begin with, and Jade knew that was deliberate. Just as she was deliberately pretending she'd missed it.

"Mrs. Packard," the woman finally said. Her tone was like unsweetened lemonade.

Jade kept smiling. "Mrs. Packard, I appreciate the update. I don't mind waiting. I've been looking forward to meeting Mr. Robson for some time now. A few more minutes won't hurt."

"At least a few," the woman said, and Jade could've sworn the woman's eyes gleamed. "Maybe more like twenty."

"Give or take," Jade said, even though her temper inched up. "In that case...could you point me to the ladies' room? I'd like to freshen up. It's hot up here, isn't it?"

"It's a steel mill," Mrs. Packard replied. "An old one, at that. It gets hot." She was wearing a cotton dress with small cornflowers on it, and looked as if she'd just stepped out of a refrigerator, even though it was easily ninety degrees in the cramped "lobby."

"Ladies' room?" Jade repeated.

The woman pointed vaguely down the hallway. Jade decided to find it on her own.

Jade located the rest room, with a hand-written sign that had a crude stick figure of a triangular woman and the word "Ladies" written below it. It was small, but since Mrs. Packard was the only woman she'd seen so far in this part of the plant, Jade figured it didn't need to be large.

Jade checked herself in the slightly cracked mirror. She'd put her hair up in a halfhearted bun this morning, and her forehead was already dotted with sweat. The perspiration was making her already wavy hair go nuts, and curls were escaping from the knot and tickling her neck. Her makeup was starting to melt. She dabbed at the offending smudges. Then she grabbed a small brush from her purse and tugged mercilessly at her hair, almost stabbing her head with the bobby pins to get it to stay. That would probably last a good ten minutes.

She straightened her suit, smoothing the lines of her short skirt. She considered taking off the jacket, leaving her in her sleeveless blouse. With any of her established clients, she would have. Of course, if it were any of her established clients, she'd be wearing slacks, a light tank top and her boots.

It didn't help that the suit was black. She'd meant to go for an impression of authority, power. She felt as though the impression she'd be giving would be heat stroke.

Doesn't matter. One hour. I get in front of the guy for one hour, and it'll be settled.

She felt the little jangle of nerves in her stomach and her pulse elevated a little. She'd gotten this way during high school before big debate competitions. A rush of adrenaline, a tingling in her chest. The sure feeling of bagging another win for the team. In this case, her team was Michaels & Associates Marketing and Public Relations Firm. The win would be getting Mr. Drew Robson to acknowledge his contract with their company.

When you were fighting a battle, and you were stuck, you called in air support, she thought as she slicked on a quick coat of lipstick, blowing a kiss to her cleaned-up reflection.

When you were fighting a difficult client, you sent in Jade Morrow.

She walked back, her high heels clicking on the faded linoleum floor. Mrs. Packard glared at her.

"He's ready to see you now," she said with an undercurrent of accusation.

"Fantastic." Jade flashed another brilliant smile at her, just to annoy. "Thanks."

She squared her shoulders and pushed open the door.

"Mr. Robson," she said, her tone firm but friendly.

He turned, and she couldn't help it. She stopped dead.

Three other account execs had tried to deal with Drew Robson, the new owner of the steel plant and the guy who was refusing to honor the contract his predecessor and father had signed. The first woman had left crying. The next two men had been more persistent, yet neither had lasted longer than a week in trying to pin down their "client." The last one had warned Jade that Robson was the coldest, meanest son of a bitch he'd ever met.

There was just one little fact they'd all neglected to mention.

The cold, mean son of a bitch was *gorgeous.*

He was built like a football player, yoked shoulder

muscles and biceps that made the T-shirt he was wearing pull taut against his torso. His hair was jet-black, glinting like obsidian in the harsh afternoon sun. His eyes were light blue and practically glowed on their own. They stared at her, clearly unamused.

She cleared her throat, wincing at the small sound. "I'm Jade Morrow," she said. Her voice bobbled slightly.

One of his dark eyebrows quirked up. "And you want…?"

You, she thought, taking in the planes of his face, the chiseled cut of his body. *How about an hour, to start?*

Her smile was warmer for the thought, just a little frivolous joke to put things in perspective. He was cute. That was a point in his favor—it had thrown her off.

She was living proof that looks were deceptive.

"Sorry. I'm with Michaels and Associates…"

"Oh, God. I thought I'd finally gotten rid of the last of you." His jaw clenched, and she watched in fascination as the muscles there rippled. "I don't have time for this."

She kept walking toward his desk. He was getting less cute by the second.

Think of the money, she ordered herself. Drew's predecessor, his father, had signed a contract for one hundred thousand dollars' worth of public relations services from Michaels & Associates. It wasn't their largest account, not by a long shot, but the elder Mr. Robson had suggested there would be more—to the tune of a few million dollars, spread over a few years. Steady, rich work, the type her firm loved best.

Obviously his son didn't share those optimistic sentiments.

Charm first. Save the rough stuff for later. She smiled warmly, a counterpoint to his dark scowl. ''I understand that your contract with our firm was something of a surprise.''

''I didn't sign anything with your firm,'' he growled. No kidding, the guy actually *growled.*

Her smile stayed steady. ''No, but the previous president did.''

''The previous president is currently on a beach on some island that lacks extradition laws,'' Drew shot back. ''Maybe you should try getting the money from him there.''

Well. He wasn't pulling any punches. Now her smile was a little more natural...and fierce.

Game on, Jade.

''Yes. I understand your company has been going through some financial difficulties,'' she said, her voice deceptively mild. ''Embezzlement, right?''

He glared at her.

''It's not widespread knowledge, but it's accessible enough to be dangerous—especially once word gets out on how financially unstable the company might become. My firm could spin that so it's less damaging,'' she said, and as she predicted, he exploded.

''I'm not having you 'spin' a damned thing.''

''That sort of thing looks bad, especially for anyone looking at a financial statement,'' she said, her voice still even. For all his scowling and posturing, the guy was leading with his chin. He was a lot of bluster. She could handle him. She paused a beat, then said quietly, ''It's not going to look any better if word gets out that you're not honoring contracts that your father signed.''

She'd floored him with that one. He stared at her,

his mouth drawn in a grim line. "Well. I guess that firm of yours finally sent in the big guns."

She couldn't help it. She grinned. "What makes you say that?"

"The others didn't resort to blackmail."

The grin slipped away. "It's not blackmail. It's the truth. Your company has a contract with my firm. You need to spend one hundred thousand dollars in one month."

"So come back in a month."

She rolled her eyes, groaning to herself. "It doesn't exactly work like that, Mr. Robson," she said. "It takes planning. We need to set objectives, see what your company really needs. Then we'll set up definable goals, then outline how to achieve them. Then my firm will implement the plan and report back to you."

He glimpsed up at her, shaking his head and muttering.

"Come on now," she said, feeling irritated herself. The guy was trying to blow her off, obviously, and she had caught him off guard. But this was actually going to help him. What did he think he was accomplishing? "You didn't think you'd just write a check in a month, and get, what, one hundred thousand 'units' of P.R.?"

Now he looked up at her…and for a second, her breath caught in her throat. What she'd taken for anger when she walked in had been mere annoyance. Now, he was actually angry.

It was impressive, and not a little bit scary.

She took a deep breath. Without waiting for him to ask, she sat in one of the chairs across from his desk, crossing her legs and smiling. *The best defense is a good offense.* "We're getting off to a bad start. Why don't we start over? I'll give you options for what you can do to spend the money, and an action plan that will take up a minimum of time and effort on your part. Simple, and painless."

He muttered something that sounded a lot like, *I'll give you an option of what you can do.*

She leaned forward. "Okay. Why don't you tell me what I can do, then?" When his gaze shot to her, she smirked. "To help you. Obviously what we're doing isn't making you happy—which is odd since we haven't done anything for your company—but you've got a contract. You could pay it all off and we could do nothing, if that's what you'd prefer. But it seems ridiculous to pay for a service you're never going to take advantage of. It's not like we could harm..."

"I suppose it might be worth it just to pay the bill and not have to listen to your voice," he mused.

That one was a direct hit. She narrowed her eyes at him before she could stop herself. She took a deep breath, got her bearings. Grinned. "You give me something to work with, I'll make sure I only communicate with you via e-mail. It's all about keeping the customer happy. Trust me. I can be very accommodating."

"I see."

He stood, looking as if he was unfolding himself out of the chair. With her seated, he towered over her. He was wearing jeans, and filled out said article of clothing very well. She forced herself not to gape.

"And just exactly what do you do to keep your customers happy, Ms. Morrow?"

His tone was so brisk, it took her a second to realize he was making an insinuation—and a nasty one, at that.

Now she got up, making sure she did it slowly and deliberately. She was five foot nine, and that was before she strapped on her sexy stilettos. Still, it surprised her to see he was still taller. Most men weren't. She met his glare with a heated look of her own.

She sighed. She was disappointed that of all the tacks he could have chosen to piss her off, he'd gone for the obvious one.

"Let me get this straight." She kept her voice low, just this side of husky. "What you're asking is how far will I go to make sure my clients are…satisfied?"

If anything, his eyes went colder. He nodded.

"And what I'll offer you to make sure you're…" She smiled, letting her tongue just barely lick the corner of her mouth. "Happy?"

"I think I can already put that together for myself." He crossed his arms. "And…"

"I can tell you exactly what I'll offer," she said, and leaned forward. She had a good body, and from the quick dart of his gaze, she knew he knew it, as well.

He was listening. Hell, he was riveted.

"I'll offer you…*a chance at evading a lawsuit.*" Her tone went from sexy seductress to angry collector in a heartbeat. "I'm not here for my health, Mr. Robson. And despite what you're trying to imply, I didn't think I'd earn our hundred grand with a quick horizontal mamba. I'm here to offer you a chance to work with one of the best P.R. firms in Michigan. I'm here because I've done research, and since your father skipped off with close to a million dollars of your company's money, you could use good P.R. more than ever. I'm here because we can help your company." She crossed her arms, mimicking his stance. "I'm here to *help.*"

"Like hell," he said, and his voice lashed out at her like a strap. "I'll tell you why you're here, Ms. Morrow. You're here because my father stupidly signed the contract with your company, and then bugged out, leaving me holding the bag and forcing me to put up with you idiots. Now, I have to use money that could be used to renovate this plant on a bunch of services I never agreed to. If I even thought your services were worth it. Which I don't."

She gaped. He came around the desk with the dangerous grace of a wolf, standing just inches in front of her—towering over her again. She looked up into eyes like blue ice.

"You make your money lying to people and trying to get them to believe it's for their own good," he said, his words clipped. His anger probably made the blast furnaces in his factory look chilly. "You want me to say everything's fine with a big fake smile, put a good face on the fact that thousands of people may lose their jobs if this plant doesn't start making some big cash, and soon. You want me to believe that you can increase my profits with a goddamned *press release.* And, to top it all off, you come in here wearing a skirt so short you could wear it as a headband, and supposedly you're just offering your business skills?"

She took a small step back in the face of his verbal barrage.

He followed her, six foot five inches of angry, muscular male. "You go back to your high-ranking P.R. firm, and you tell them they send another damned suit over here to get me to play ball, I'm not going to be so *polite.*"

He stalked over to the door, opening it and looking at her pointedly.

Her head swam. She'd faced tough clients before, early in her career, but they were usually oily, sleazy, too cheap to dole out the money that the P.R. they'd asked for had given them. She managed to get around each and every one of them. Later, it usually meant cajoling a tough client who had cold feet. Sometimes it took a lot of debating...and a little bit of conning. Once, it had taken a shouting match. But she'd never faced such naked hatred—or such passion.

The other execs had said Drew Robson was a bastard. They hadn't mentioned that he had a reason to be. Up to the smart-ass comment about the skirt, the guy had a pretty good reason, at that.

"You gonna stand there looking confused," he drawled, "or are you gonna run along now?"

Her gaze snapped to his. He smiled, all teeth and sarcasm.

For a fraction of a second, her temper leaped to the fore.

I should put this damned skirt on my head and quote some sales figures on how our firm has turned my other clients around. If he thought she was trying to use her body to get him to agree with her, she might as well use it to her advantage, right?

Regaining her sanity, she walked with as much dignity as she could manage out the door, pausing in front of him.

"This isn't over," she said, more because she didn't want him to have the last word than because she felt the burning desire to deal with the gorgeous, infuriating man.

Even then, she didn't win.

"With you people," he said, in a voice ripe with frustration, "it never is."

DREW STOOD OUT in the parking lot, dribbling the old basketball he kept in his office. He was glad he'd gotten a new basketball hoop on the factory wall. He'd remembered playing ball here since he was in junior high, waiting for his father to finish up work. Drew arched his back, sending the ball sailing toward the chain net. It swooshed through with a satisfying clink. He retrieved it, his body going through the motions automatically.

Mr. Robson, this is Fleet Steel Ore. You're behind on your payments.

Drew closed his eyes, paying attention to the thump of the ball against asphalt, trying to drown out his thoughts. He'd been fielding calls all day, trying to put out fires, trying to calm down creditors.

Mr. Robson, please call us immediately. Your company is one hundred and twenty days past due…

Mr. Robson, we don't want to involve a collection agency…

Drew, we were old friends with your father, but closing in on ninety days, our accounts receivables department doesn't really believe in friendship…

Drew threw the ball. Swoosh-clink. Retrieved it. A slow dribble back to his starting point.

Trust me. I can be very accommodating.

He held the ball for a second, then rolled his arms a little, trying to work the kinks out. His shoulder blades felt as if they'd been fused together at the neck. He'd taken to playing basketball to try to relax, and if he needed to do one thing right now, it was to relieve some of the tension roiling through him.

The tension had increased even more sharply after he'd met her. Of all his creditors, a tall, leggy, curvy redhead was not one he needed to dwell on.

"Hoops already? It's only six o'clock. I didn't expect you'd be out here until eight."

Drew wiped the sweat out of his eyes with the back of his hand before looking over. His chief financial officer, Ken Shimoda, was in shirtsleeves, his tie in his pocket, his briefcase in hand. Ken was a fixture at Robson Steel, much like the basketball hoop. Drew couldn't remember a time when Ken wasn't there.

"Rough day," Drew said, shrugging. He did a few quick bounces. "I needed a little basketball therapy. You up for a quick game of one-on-one?"

"Maybe ten years ago," Ken said, smiling ruefully. He was twenty years older than Drew, but lately he looked much older than that. Of course, Drew thought, they probably both looked older these days. Every day he felt as if he'd aged ten years, lately. "No, I'm headed home. I told my wife I'd be back by six-thirty."

Drew arched an eyebrow. "Too many late nights?" Drew's last serious girlfriend, Sheryl, had commented on that. Often. At least, before she'd left. He hadn't had the time or the energy to find another girlfriend since.

"She understands that late nights are a requirement of the business," Ken said, and in that second Drew envied the hell out of him. Ken had been working till about eight or nine every night for the past three months. Drew knew this because he usually said goodbye to the man as Ken was walking out, leaving Drew to work another hour or so.

Drew didn't have anybody who'd care if he worked until one in the morning...except maybe Mrs. Packard, who would undoubtedly comment that he looked tired. It wasn't quite the same.

"You're a lucky man," Drew said.

Ken shrugged, then smiled. "Well, tonight's our anniversary. She's a patient woman, but even she's got a breaking point."

Drew dribbled the ball again, sent it arcing toward the basket. It rolled off the rim and into the net. "Enjoy yourself." He smirked at Ken. "And if you're tired tomorrow, and have to come in late because you've been celebrating too much, I'll understand."

Ken laughed good-naturedly. "You'd understand more if you got a woman of your own."

"Good point." Drew lined up his next shot.

"Speaking of women," Ken said conversationally, "who was the tall redhead I saw strutting out of your office this afternoon?"

Drew's shot went wide, bouncing off the rim with a loud ringing sound. Drew grumbled as he chased the ball down, trying to ignore Ken's laughter.

"It's like that, huh?"

Reluctantly, Drew pictured the woman he'd been trying in vain to put out of his mind for the past few hours. The second he'd looked up at her, watching her bear down on his desk, he'd felt a jolt of attraction that he hadn't felt in a damned long time. He seemed hyper-aware of everything about her. The garnet shade of her hair, the fullness of her lips, her legs that seemed to go on forever. The way the first button of her blouse was undone had probably caused the ruination of stronger-willed men than he. She had a face that was too sexy to be angelic, with a devilish quirk to those full lips of hers that instantly made you suspect trouble was coming, and more important, that you'd enjoy every minute of it. Those misty greenish-gray eyes must've been what they had in mind when they named her Jade. Another couple of moments and he would've seriously considered bagging the rest of the day and asking her to dinner—or asking her to anywhere else she might be open to going.

He frowned. Then she'd had to ruin it all and say where she worked.

"It's like nothing," he finally responded to Ken. "She's one of those bloodsuckers from that P.R. firm Dad hooked up with. I swear, I have no idea what he was thinking when he signed that damned contract."

"That firm's supposed to be a big deal on the West Coast. Your father thought they could help turn the company around, get out the good word to investors. Build up our image. At least, that's what he told me when he went through with it." Ken sighed. "You know your father."

Drew dribbled the ball hard enough to have the sound of rubber echo in the lot. Yeah, he knew his father, all right. "I got my opinion of their work across pretty firmly this time. I don't think we'll be seeing her again."

He didn't know whether to feel relieved or disappointed by that fact.

"Are you going to ignore the contract, then?" Ken sounded shocked.

Drew scowled at Ken. "Of course I'm going to honor the contract. You know me better than that."

Ken visibly relaxed. "Sorry."

"That's okay." The fact that Drew wasn't quite sure how he was going to pay off the contract...well, that was why he was out here playing basketball. He'd work on it tonight. He'd come up with something.

"Well, as long as you're going to pay it anyway," Ken said hesitantly, "maybe you should go ahead and work with them."

Drew was surprised enough to stop, resting the ball

on his hip. ''It's bad enough I have to pay them. I can't afford to waste time working with one of them. That investor meeting we've got next month is the most important thing. I'm still pulling numbers on that. It's too big a deal for me to lose focus.''

''Yeah. But, Drew, investors look for presentation,'' Ken countered. ''Your father said that maybe the P.R. agency could help with that, too. You've got to admit, your father was a good judge of presentation and sales.''

Drew didn't say anything.

''He was a consummate salesman.''

Drew's eyes blazed. ''He was a liar and a thief.''

''I'm not trying to say he wasn't,'' Ken said, holding his hand up protectively. ''I'm just saying he had a real talent for sales. And, I might add, a good rapport with the sales force.''

Drew knew where he was going with this. ''Half the force was giving away everything but the keys to the inventory to make their quotas. What was I supposed to do? I had to fire them.'' Drew sighed. ''At least the new guys are guys I can trust. They're smart, they've got integrity. They'll pick up the rest in time.''

''That's just it. We don't have time, Drew.''

Drew felt his grip on the basketball increasing. He was surprised the damned thing didn't explode. ''I know that, Ken. And after the meeting with the investors, I'll focus on it, I swear. But I've only got two hands and twenty-four hours in a day.''

''It's going to be June next week, Drew.''

''Yes, I know,'' Drew said, ''but...''

Suddenly, it struck him. Of course he remembered June. His father wasn't able to make his high school graduation or his college graduation, because both were in June. And June meant the annual road trip through the Southwest, when his father would go visit their biggest customers, schmoozing them, getting their orders for the following year.

"No," Drew said. "I don't have time for this."

"You can't afford to ignore this," Ken said sharply, surprising Drew. "I'm your CFO. I know what the financial picture looks like. We don't get larger sales for next year, if we keep losing customers, getting the investors' backing isn't going to mean squat. I was hoping one of the salesmen would be up to speed, but nobody's ready. It has to be you."

Drew closed his eyes for a moment, the headache pounding at his temples was getting even more severe. "You know, there was a time when the only thing I ever wanted was this factory." He opened his eyes, looking at it. "I just wasn't expecting it to be like this."

"It never is." To his credit, Ken sounded apologetic. "I hate to put it this way, but unless you go on this sales trip, it won't be your worry anymore. You'll just have to worry about getting a new job." He paused. "Of course, most of the town of San Angelo will be out of a job, as well."

"I know what the factory means to the town, believe me," he said in a low voice. "Did you really think you had to guilt me into going?"

Ken didn't say anything.

"I'll go. Just get me the list of customers and whatever background you have. When do I have to leave?"

"Next Monday." Ken sighed. "I really hoped one of the sales guys would be ready."

"It's okay." Even though it wasn't. "Don't you have an anniversary to get to?"

Ken looked at his watch, swore. "All right. I'll be in early tomorrow. We'll start working on it."

"Good night, Ken."

Drew dribbled the ball, hard enough for his arms to ache. He wasn't sure how long he could keep this going. Thanks to Ken's comforting talk, Drew's attempts at relaxation had ground to an ugly halt. Something had to give, he thought, lining up his shot. If something didn't change, he didn't know what he'd do. What he needed was some help. No. What he needed was some money, and some help. In fact, what he really needed...

Inexplicably, he thought of Jade's green eyes and wickedly sexy smile.

The ball bounced off the rim with a clanging ring.

He sighed, grabbing the ball and heading back to the factory. He might as well get some more work done. His game was pretty well shot.

"JADE, I only have one thing to say about it. And that's *no.*"

Jade sighed, forcing herself not to sprawl in the plush chair that flanked her boss's huge glass-and-metal desk. "Betsy, this would mean a lot to me."

Her boss, Betsy Diehl, surveyed her solemnly from her own leather executive chair. She was one of the newest partners at the marketing firm of Michaels & Associates, and she'd been Jade's boss for about two years now. Jade had been apprehensive, at first—lots of people had nicknamed her "Raw Diehl"—but the relationship had worked out. Jade valued her boss's honesty and brutal pragmatism. Betsy expected a lot, and she pushed hard, but Jade felt as though Betsy honestly understood what it was like to struggle. Betsy had worked hard to get where she was, or so she had told Jade, going from poor circumstances to her current respected position as a marketing genius. She'd been written up in industry magazines. She'd co-authored a book. Today, Betsy was wearing her steel-gray hair in a sophisticated blunt-cut bob and a stylish eggplant suit that screamed Rodeo Drive. She looked like a woman who other people looked up to...a woman who took crap from no one.

She was exactly what Jade wanted to be when she grew up.

"Why does this account mean anything to you?" Betsy's voice was cultured, as if she was chastising a member of her garden club rather than her direct report. "You've got a full load as it is."

"Nothing pressing," Jade said. "I've got all of my key accounts taken care of, and it's not like I'd be ignoring them. I would love to take Robson on as a challenge, but you know I don't turn my back on my work."

Betsy's nose wrinkled with displeasure. "Robson is a little nothing account. Sure, some of the other partners thought that it would turn into something, but—"

"I think we shouldn't write it off just yet," Jade interrupted, causing Betsy's frown to deepen. Jade bit back on an impatient sigh. "Sorry. I'm just really excited about this account. It's a little hard to explain."

Probably because I'm not entirely clear on the reasons myself.

"It can't be the money," Betsy scoffed. "Because a measly hundred thousand is hardly worth getting out of bed for."

Jade smiled at the comparison. "No. It's not the money."

"Is it the challenge?" Betsy's eyes narrowed. "I know you, Jade. If somebody told you that you couldn't climb Mount Everest, the next thing I'd see is a framed photo in your office of you on some snowy peak with a broad grin. Probably giving the cameraman the finger."

Jade looked away, laughing nervously. "I'm not that bad."

"I heard about this Robson character from the other execs," Betsy warned. "I never should have let that pass your desk, but you've still got that reputation as a closer..."

"I like that reputation." Jade grinned. "I'm one of the best."

"Yes. But, Jade," Betsy said, her voice going gentle and patient, "that hasn't exactly gotten you the promotion you've been hoping for, now, has it?"

Jade's grin slid. She stood, started pacing a little. "I know. And I know you think I should be working on higher profile accounts. But we haven't had a high-profile account come my way in months."

"We just have to keep working on it," Betsy said. "Be patient."

"I've been patient for five years," Jade said. "If they're not going to let me prove myself on a big account, then I was thinking, maybe it's time to show them what I can do with a small account. An impossible account. One they've written off."

Betsy sat up. "So that's what you want with Robson." Her tone sounded impressed. "They watched some of their top account executives fail, and then you go in...hmm. Interesting."

Jade saw her advantage, pressed it. "I know I can turn this around," she said, her voice low and impassioned. "You should see this factory. All of the workers seem to love Drew Robson, and the Robson family. He's got a fiercely loyal staff. And he..."

She stumbled on her words. He was amazing, frustrating. But he was also dedicated to saving his company, its workers, and the town. She had felt turned on—the guy was impossibly good-looking, and she wasn't blind—but she had felt something more. She'd felt inspired.

"He's the heart and soul of that place," she said. "I win him over, and the rest will fall into place."

Betsy pressed her fingertips against the broad surface of her desk. "How long do you think this will take?"

Jade felt a glimmer of hope burn in her stomach. "I'm not sure. Fairly quickly...no more than a few months." She got the feeling if she didn't turn things around for Robson, his company might not be around for much longer than a few months anyway. Now was not the time to mention that to Betsy, however.

"A few months. And how much of your time?"

This was a little trickier. "As I said, I wouldn't be ignoring my key accounts. Most of my work with my current clients is just maintenance, anyway."

"And new accounts?"

Jade winced. "I'd have to ask for a break from new account work for a while," she admitted. "Just until I got Robson back on its feet."

"I don't like it," Betsy said. "I value your help with my new account pitches—there isn't anybody at Michaels and Associates with your flair for presentations or proposals."

"I promise, I'll still be able to help you with those," Jade said hurriedly, sitting back down in the seat with a thump. "You won't notice a difference in my work habits."

Betsy sighed, sitting back, obviously evaluating. Jade held her breath.

"Tell me something." And now Betsy's eyes were shrewd. "This *is* just for the promotion, right? There's nothing else here I don't know about?"

Jade stared. "Sorry?"

"You're not going altruistic on me, are you?" Her voice rolled out in sonorous waves. "I mean, charity has its place...but I'd hate to see you pinning your hopes on some poor little company that doesn't have a chance no matter how good you are. There's taking on a challenge, and then there's career suicide."

Jade's spine stiffened. "I like helping people."

"So do I. So does everyone," Betsy said smoothly. "But sometimes you take things on to help people. And then, sometimes you say no because you're only hurting yourself."

"This isn't like that," Jade said, crossing her arms. She realized how defensive her posture was and forced her body to relax. "I just really think I have a shot with this. It's an untapped opportunity. And, yeah, showing the partners how well I can do in the same company their hotshots failed in will only help my cause. Now can I work on the Robson case, or not?"

Betsy smiled. "I've had a lot of people work for me over the years, but you're special, Jade. You rather remind me of myself...when I was your age, of course."

Jade smiled back, highly complimented. "Would you have taken on the Robson case?"

"Probably." She took a deep breath. "Okay. You can take on this little pet project of yours."

Jade beamed. "Great. I'll get started right away—"

"Not so fast," Betsy interrupted. "There are a few provisions on letting you do this."

Jade nodded, still elated. She should have known her boss would do this—nothing came easy when you were working for Raw Diehl. But then, few things Jade took on were easy. She prided herself on that.

"First of all, you're going to keep working on all of your accounts. One slip-up on any of them, and you're off the Robson account."

"Agreed."

"Second, you're still going to help me with those new account pitches."

Jade groaned internally, but kept her game face on. "No problem."

"Third…you're bucking on this to get you a promotion, Jade. That means that you're going to have to prove yourself to the other partners and to myself. You have to get Robson to pay the bill. From the looks of it, that means pulling the company out of the fire single-handedly. That's an awfully tall order."

"I know."

"I'm going to have to go to the other partners and explain why I'm not putting you on other accounts, and why you're spending your time and our resources helping what could be a delinquent customer," Betsy said, and her gray eyes were like flint. "That means that I'm going to have to do some fast talking and make some concessions."

Now Jade felt a cold prickle of apprehension dust her spine. "I don't want to put you in a bad position," she said.

"I've been on the hot seat before, don't worry," Betsy said with a negligible wave of her hand. "But in order to say that you can shirk the new account work, especially for a long shot...well, if it goes under, we're both going to look bad."

"I understand."

"So, I'm going to propose this—if you get the Robson account, you finally get the promotion to account supervisor, with the opportunity to buy into the partnership—" Betsy paused "—but if the Robson account doesn't pay, or if anything goes wrong...then you're going to have to forfeit any promotions for the entire following year. And you'll have to give up some of your key accounts. It'll be like starting all over again."

Jade swallowed hard. "I see."

"Now, are you sure you want to risk this?" Betsy's face was concerned. "Or do you want to just be patient, see how it goes at your next review? That's only four months away. It might be different this time."

It might be different this time. How many times had Jade walked into her boss's office with that thought? And walked out empty-handed? Still, maybe it was safer...

She thought, suddenly, inexplicably, of Drew Robson. With his flashing, light blue eyes full of righteous fury. He would've been safer staying at some other job, but instead he'd taken the helm of a sinking ship, determined to do everything he could to save it. He would never take the easy route. He wouldn't go quietly.

She wouldn't do less.

"I'll take the risk," Jade said instead, standing and shaking Betsy's hand. "Thanks for letting me have the chance."

"I shouldn't be surprised. As I said...you're special." Betsy shook her head. "I'm sure that if anybody can do it, it'll be you, Jade. Good luck."

"Thanks."

"And don't forget about my new account work."

"Yes, ma'am." Jade winked, causing Betsy to laugh.

As Jade walked out of Betsy's office, she felt a burst of excitement—quickly coupled with a burst of nerves.

I've got the opportunity, she thought. *Now...I just have to make it happen.*

And making it happen meant tackling the lion in his lair yet again. She went to her desk, picked up the phone and opened her organizer. She dialed, tapping her pen against her desktop impatiently.

"Robson Steel."

"Ah, Mrs. Packard, so lovely to speak with you again," she said quickly. "I need to set up an appointment as soon as possible with Mr. Robson. When can you schedule me in?"

2

DREW FLIPPED THE LAST slide over in his presentation, forcing himself not to run a finger under the collar of his starched white shirt. He'd tied his tie too tight. Damned thing felt like a noose.

"So, gentlemen, investing in Robson Steel over the next four years could mean additional profits and an obvious significant return on your investment. It would be revitalizing the community, retaining jobs, and our streamlining would help the environment by reducing wastes by an additional ten percent. It's the ecological, political and economical choice."

He paused, then shut off the projector. "Uh...thank you."

He looked over at the other end of the conference room, where Ken was sitting, pretending he was an investor. Ken didn't say anything.

"So how'd I do?" Drew finally growled.

Ken frowned, shaking his head and rubbing at his temples. "Drew...I work for you, and *I* wouldn't invest after a presentation like that."

Drew yanked at his tie, taking a deep breath as it loosened. "Listen, I'm doing the best I can."

"Don't say that," Ken groaned. "That means it's all downhill from here."

"If you hadn't worked for my grandfather, I'd kick your ass," Drew said, wadding up the tie and throwing it across the room. Ken let out a dry, sandpapery laugh when it hit him in the chest.

"Your grandfather," Ken said with a sigh. "He was the same way. Couldn't charm his way out of a paper bag, but by God, the man knew steel."

Drew sobered quickly. "Yeah. Yeah, I know." Drew smiled. "You know, after all these years, I still miss him."

They were silent for a moment.

"Still, you've got four weeks," Ken said, clearing his throat. "Your grandfather could devise a solution for any problem on earth when it came to steel. You'll figure out something."

"Sure I will," Drew said, feeling his stomach begin a slow boil of nerves. No pressure, or anything. *I laugh in the face of pressure. Ho, ho, ha, ha. Whee.*

Mrs. Packard knocked at the door of the conference room. Considering she usually looked as though she'd just been permanent-pressed, her frazzled state was unnerving.

"What is it?" He stared at her. "An invasion?" Maybe those creditors had gotten tired of the phone calls. Could you repossess a steel press?

"That *woman* is back," she said, sounding out of breath, as if she'd been fighting off infidels at the door. "And you won't believe what she's wearing."

Drew felt his stomach clench at this announcement. The way that Mrs. Packard said "woman," in a tone she usually reserved for such terms as "Jezebel" or "libertine," meant only one thing. The tall, redheaded P.R. barracuda was back. And from the sound of things, she was loaded for bear.

"She was quite insistent that she see you, even though I told her you were busy." The fact that the woman actually defied his stern-faced assistant showed that she was brave. Or foolish. Or possibly both. "Shall I throw her out?" Mrs. Packard looked as though she'd relish the chance.

Ken chuckled a little more easily this time. "After a statement like that? I want to see what she's wearing."

"And won't your wife love it when I let that one drop at the company picnic," Drew said with a humorless grin. "Don't worry. She won't be here for long. I'll handle this, Mrs. Packard."

Mrs. Packard looked momentarily disappointed, then nodded. "I'll show her in."

When she left, Drew looked at Ken. "Okay. Out."

"Come now," Ken protested. "What's the harm in an old man admiring a rather amazing—"

"It's going to be quick, and it'll probably be messy," Drew interrupted. He already remembered just what amazing attributes the woman possessed. "I don't want you interrupting."

Ken stood, then wiggled his eyebrows. "Interrupting what…and how hasty are you planning to be?"

Drew cursed himself silently. "*Interfering*. I meant, interfering."

"Of course you did." With one last sly grin, Ken wandered out.

Drew threw his suit coat over the back of a chair and rolled up his sleeves. She was tenacious, he'd give her that much. But tenacious or not, he'd send her right back to her fancy, schmancy P.R. firm. Crying, if need be. He didn't relish acting like this, but he knew how these P.R. people worked. The first guy Drew had spoken with from Michaels & Associates probably would've misted up if he thought it would seal him a sale.

Drew heard the clack of footsteps coming down the hallway before he saw her. He set his face in a firm, determined frown.

I am going to get rid of this woman once and for all, no matter what she looks like.

And he'd meant it, too. Right up to when she took one step into the room and his jaw dropped.

She was wearing a snug-fitting pair of well-worn blue jeans over what looked like black hand-tooled leather boots. She was also wearing a faded black T-shirt that sported the name of a rock band he'd never even heard of. Her red hair exploded around her head like fireworks. She wore a broad smile beneath eyes of mossy-green determination.

"Mr. Robson." Without invitation, she sprawled herself in one of the conference room chairs. "Sorry I'm arriving unannounced like this. I've got a proposal I think you'll be interested in, and I seemed to have difficulty setting up an appointment, for some reason. Not that I'm implying anything. I'm sure you wouldn't have given that…uh, your assistant specific instructions not to put me on your calendar."

"I would have if it had occurred to me you'd be crazy enough to come back," he said tightly. "And don't make yourself comfortable. You won't be staying long."

"Now that's where you're wrong," she said confidently, propping her feet up on the desk and crossing her legs at the ankle. She looked like a cross between the CEO of a multimillion dollar company and a roadie for Lollapalooza. "I made a mistake with you. I thought you were looking for polish, and some charm…and let's face it, a little polite strong-arming. I understand now that it was a total misjudgment on my part."

"I'm not looking for anything you're offering," he pointed out.

"Exactly. But you *are* looking for a way out of the hole you're in."

His eyes narrowed and he sat next to her, glaring. "I used to bounce in a club for a while. Don't make me escort you out, Ms. Morrow."

She sat up, meeting his gaze with an unflinching determination. "Just hear me out. Five minutes. That's all I'm asking."

"No."

"You're trying to save your company," she said, her voice low and impassioned. "I can help you do that."

"Bull." He reached for her arm. "Now come on…"

She held his wrist, stopping him. He wasn't pushing, but she wasn't struggling, either. It was just a gentle grip, her fingertips brushing the flesh over his pulse.

It stopped him more than a fist would have.

"You need an inflow of cash. Quick. That means investors," she continued. "Investors like companies with buzz around them, you know that. You start to get your name—in a positive light—in the trade mags and other papers, and you'll be better able to…"

"We've been to investors," Drew said, his voice tired, trying to end the conversation. He didn't know why he was letting her pull him into this. "We're running out of time. This isn't just me trying to shut you up, this is a fact—we don't have the time you're talking about to make a successful go of it."

She frowned. He noticed that she hadn't released his wrist.

"So what happened?" She finally pulled away from him and, for a second, he felt bereft. He hid the confusing emotion by putting his hands against his temples, rubbing against the now-ever-present brewing headache.

"I don't see the point in telling you." He didn't mean for that to come out so curt, but it was too late to take it back.

He noticed that she didn't look cowed. Nor did it look as though she was leaving.

"I don't *know,* all right?" He took a deep breath. Maybe if he just said it quick, she'd leave. "Our numbers are bad, but not that bad. Of course, as you mentioned, it doesn't help that the previous president embezzled almost a million dollars and fled the country."

"It doesn't help that you're young, either," she mused.

"Thirty-four isn't exactly right out of school."

"You didn't get an M.B.A. until you were older, either," she added, frowning. "That's not a bad thing."

"I sure as hell don't think so," he said, trying hard not to bristle at her casual assessment. Then he scowled. "And how the hell do you know when I got my M.B.A.?"

"You're my client, Drew." She paused, shooting a friendly, almost sexy smirk at him. "You don't mind me calling you Drew, do you? Because for the next few weeks, we're going to be working very closely together. Calling you Mr. Robson is going to be a pain in the ass."

He couldn't help it. He smiled back. "Sure. Call me Drew. But as far as being your client..."

"When I work with a client, I make sure I know

everything relevant about the business and the people I'll be working with,'' she said. Her voice was now all business, not even a hint of flirtatiousness. ''I've done a lot more research on you since our first meeting. As I've already said, it was an error in judgment on my part. It won't happen again.''

He couldn't help it. He looked her over, from her curls to the scuffed tips of her boots. ''I have to ask. What about the getup?''

She laughed, a warm, rolling sound that hit him like a fist in the gut. ''I figured this was the only attire I could wear that would convince you I wasn't trying to use my body to get your business.''

His own body involuntarily tensed at the lazy, sexy drawl of her words. The woman would have to be wearing a potato sack to make her body unappealing. But it was obvious that she'd worn this as a direct response to his skirt-as-short-as-a-headband comment.

''So, you came in work clothes, did some homework, and you're trying to convince me that what you do is valuable,'' he said, trying to regain some of his previous anger. It would be easier to kick her out in that mind-set. The problem was, his heart wasn't really in it this time. He'd been happy to the first time she'd come around. She was sexy as hell then, too, but she'd looked like a banker, or worse, a salesperson. Then she was trying to either con him or to blackmail him. Now she looked like somebody he could talk to…and she was trying really hard to listen to him. She was saying she could show him a way out. And for a second, he wanted nothing more than to talk to her and to let her do her best.

He shook his head.

He had to kick her out. He couldn't afford to do anything else.

She stared at him for a second, sighed. "You don't believe me, and I don't blame you."

"You don't blame me." This made him pause. Then he leaned back in his chair. "But you're not going to stop pestering me about this, are you?"

She smiled. "Now...what kind of person would you think I was, if I drove all this way just to give up that easily?"

He couldn't help it. He laughed, before choking it down to a quick, throat-clearing cough. "Well, as you can see, I'm pretty busy today..."

He shouldn't have said it. She glanced around and quickly saw the last presentation slide he'd left up after his mock "investor presentation" with Ken. She was out of the chair in a flash, going to his pile of slides.

"Hey!" He got up to stop her, but it was too late—she was plowing through them.

"This? This is what you're going to present to a group of investors?"

"Give me those." He tugged the slides out of her hands, not needing to feign annoyance at her tactics. His voice turned sharp. "Like I said, I'm busy. Which means you're leaving."

"You realize, of course, that you're burying them in information," she said with a sweet smile. "Nobody's going to cough up money at the end of something like that. You'll be lucky if they're still *awake* at the end of something like that."

"What, you want a check for that brilliant piece of advice?" he snarled, then winced.

"Well, I don't think it's worth one hundred grand,

but..." She stopped, her green eyes going wide. "You know, that's it."

"What's it?" Talking with the woman was like watching television with a bored teenager armed with the remote.

"I've got an idea on how I can help you. *And* how the firm can earn that hundred grand." She bit her lip thoughtfully, something that made her look devilish...and cute, although women like her usually hated being called cute. Sexy, exotic, dangerous, perhaps, but never cute.

"What are you doing tonight?" The question was offhand, and she wasn't even looking at him. Still, the rough-husky sound of her voice tugged at him.

"Guess it depends on what you have in mind," he replied reflexively. "No. Forget I said that. I didn't mean that."

She didn't, and wouldn't. He'd bet his car on it. Her grin was pure mischief.

"I'm working late," he said, his justification sounding lame to his own ears.

"You'll still be working," she said. "Working with me. Can I borrow those slides?"

"No, you can't," he said, putting them behind his back. "What the hell are you talking about?"

"Michaels and Associates does P.R., naturally...but we also do coaching, for sales, media, presentations," she said, her voice growing more excited. "It's a perfect plan. I'll go into it more tonight. Just give me a few hours. We could have dinner. Business dinner, nothing funny," she said firmly. "I don't want any more crap about how I 'take care of' my clients. I run strictly by the book."

He looked at her again, this time making sure she

noticed his slow perusal of her form. "You don't look like the by-the-book type."

"Look all you like," she said, her voice smug. "By the time I'm done with you, you're going to be so busy you won't even be able to see straight. I'm hard on my clients, but it's worth it. And you're going to be one of my clients, Drew Robson."

"Whether I want to be or not, huh? That's pretty tough talk." He took a step back, when what he really wanted to do was step closer. She smelled good. Sort of vanilla-y, which was sexy but at the same time appetizing.

I need not to be thinking of my sales coach as appetizing.

He winced.

Correction. I need not to be thinking of Jade Morrow as my sales coach.

She followed him, not giving an inch, her arms crossed. "Listen. I know you don't want me here, and that's fine. As much as I love a two-hour drive from L.A., coming to your plant in the middle of nowhere isn't fun for me, either. But I will keep coming here, every single day, and picketing your parking lot if I have to. I'm very serious about my job. As far as I'm concerned, you're a client of Michaels and Associates, and you're a client of *mine.* And yes, I'm going to help you whether you want it or not."

Her eyes were blazing. He sighed.

"I don't have time for this."

She still didn't say anything.

"Fine. One hour. But I have a lot to do," he said irritably. He was giving in. He was *caving.* What happened to the persona that was able to intimidate burly steelworkers on the plant floor? He was a hard-ass. He was a rough boss.

He was, apparently, a marshmallow.

"When?" Her expression was bright and optimistic...and just a little bit smug. "And where?"

"I have stuff to work on—I suppose I could break at seven," he said. "And what's wrong with here?"

"Too much your turf," she said firmly. "Business dinner. Let's go somewhere else."

He shook his head. "I don't think that's a good idea..."

"Of course you wouldn't, but you're coming around," she said. "Come on. Neutral turf. Just tell me where to meet you. And hand over the slides."

He sighed. "All right. Seven o'clock at Grady's."

"Perfect." She waited a beat. "Slides?"

He looked down at the pages of plastic in his hands. He'd have to scrap them anyway, as Ken had said. "They're confidential," he said, instead. She might be sexy as hell, but that didn't mean he had to trust her.

She rolled her eyes. "You signed a contract to pay us...and *we* signed a confidentiality agreement." Her tone said, *Like I'd break that?* She let out a little huff.

Slowly he handed over the slides, watching as she tucked them under her arm.

"All right. Seven it is then," she said, walking toward the door. Then she stopped, looked over her shoulder for a second, her hips tilted, her expression one of sexy invitation.

"Yeah?" he said when she just stared at him.

"I will say one thing about your sales presentation," she said with a half smirk. "That suit works for you."

With that, she winked and walked out, leaving him

zinging with sexual awareness—and crunched with frustration.

This is such a bad idea. He didn't have the time for even a flirtation with his sexy sales coach, much less…

He groaned to himself.

Sales coach. Damn it, she was brainwashing him already.

JADE SAT at one of the booths at Grady's bar and grill, just off the freeway. She had the slides laid out on the portion of the table that wasn't occupied by the huge steaks they'd just been served.

"Now, if you'll look at this slide here…"

Drew frowned at her. "What?"

She muttered to herself, then raised her voice. "I said, if you'll look at this slide here…"

"What?"

She glared at him. "Drew, did you *know* there was going to be a local band playing here tonight?"

He grinned. "Local bands always play at Grady's. Thursdays through Sundays."

She leaned back, not willing to let him see her more frustrated. "And I suppose this is the only restaurant in town?"

"Well, there's Pietri's, but he's closed for renovation right now," Drew said, his eyes glinting. "And you were the one who wanted to go out."

Yeah, she'd been the one who'd wanted to go out. She'd wanted to get the upper hand on neutral territory. She should have known better. This entire *town* was his territory. She'd done more research that afternoon—the slides had gone a long way toward showing her what his company did. She also discovered that his steel plant provided most of the jobs in the small town of San Angelo. Since they'd sat for dinner, she'd counted no less than twenty people who'd come over to say hi or to have a word with Drew—and express concern about the future of the plant.

They'd also given her the once-over, being the outsider that she was. She got the feeling that they didn't see Drew outside the plant much—or out with women, for that matter.

It really shouldn't have made her feel good to know this, but it did.

"Listen to me," she said, leaning a bit closer to him. "You're throwing around too many figures here and not enough sales points. Why should they help you?"

He had leaned in to hear her, as well, and she could smell the spicy cologne he was wearing. "Because we're a great steel mill," he said defensively. "We're—"

"You, you, you," she interrupted. "They don't *care* about you."

He looked at her, his blue eyes sparking. "Then why should I do the thing at all?"

There was something about him angry that just made something inside her churn with emotion. To be specific, frustration.

"How did you get this far when you're constantly leading with your chin?" she asked more to herself than him. However, the band had decided to close out their set, and in the relative quiet she could tell Drew had caught her comment.

"I thought you were going to try *helping* me," he said with sarcasm. "But gee, I can't thank you enough for dinner with such a charming companion."

"You're picking up the tab," she said before she could stop herself. Then she took a deep breath.

"Okay. Let me start this over. Investors are like anybody else. They're motivated by self-interest. If you want them to give you money, you have to show what's in it for *them.*"

She was going to continue, but he was staring at her with a strange expression—she would've almost said sadness. "Do you really believe that?"

She blinked. "Do I really believe what?"

"That everybody's in it for themselves."

She stared at him.

He had changed out of his suit—she wondered if her comment had anything to do with that decision—and was now wearing a T-shirt, like herself, and a pair of jeans. He had the shadow of stubble grazing his jawline, and his office must've gotten characteristically hot because he had the slightest sheen of sweat at his temples. He looked rough, rugged. Possibly dangerous, in all the right ways.

And he was an *idealist.*

A six-foot-five, black-haired, blue-eyed, gorgeous *idealist.*

She resisted the urge to tug her hair by the roots. This was going to be rougher than she'd thought.

"I'm not saying that the investors are bad people," she said slowly. "And I'm not saying that you're just trying to suck up to them, either."

"Really?"

She was going to have to teach him not to drawl like that, all sarcastic and biting. She straightened her shoulders.

"I'm one of the best P.R. and media coaches in the business. I could show you reams of data that show what I've done for my clients." She quirked an eyebrow at him. "Would that have made a difference?"

She smiled when he scowled.

"No. I need to show you what's in it for *you* and for your company."

"You make it sound like I'm just doing this for me," he grumbled, and she leaned closer to hear it over the tunings of the next band. "A lot of people are depending on me. A lot of jobs. You see all these people."

She glanced around, nodded. "I'm not saying that you're selfish, Drew," she said, a little softer than she intended, causing him to lean even closer to hear her. "I'm just saying that when you know what the other person needs, you can convince them that you can help them. That's all."

He didn't move, even after she stopped speaking, and she tilted her head. She was only inches away from his face. "I really am trying to help you, Drew," she said, now almost a whisper.

They stayed that way for a long moment. Then the band started with a jarring clang of noise and they jumped apart.

"Let's get out of here," he said, taking a look at the bill and throwing some money down on the table. She just nodded, feeling shaken.

Taking a step out into the evening air, she took a deep breath. It had gotten hot in there, hotter than she'd realized. Of course, it wasn't just the temperature, she realized as she watched the flex of his muscles as he walked in front of her.

She was losing focus. Not a great idea…not when she had so much riding on this.

He walked her to her car, an old Ford Mustang painted the same fiery red as her hair. "This your car?"

She smiled. "That's my baby."

He grinned back at her. "I suppose a woman driving a car like this can't be *all* bad."

"Thanks." She took a deep breath. "Enough beating around the bush. I can help you. You're going to need help with this presentation to your investors. If they cough up the money, then you'll have money to pay me *and* do renovations to your factory. That's not self-interest. That's just plain logic. I help you...you help me. That's business."

His eyes went dark and he looked thoughtful.

"Listen, I know how much you hate the sound of that. You're doing this for the town. When I'm on your team, then that's what I'm doing it for, as well. All right?"

He still didn't say anything.

She leaned against her car, crossing her arms. "Man. What do I have to do to convince you that I'm not just feeding you a line here?"

He stepped close to her.

She held her breath.

"I understand what you're saying," he said, his voice low and husky. "Really. I do. But...okay, to hell with it. If I screw this up, I *won't* be able to pay you. Period."

He sounded as though someone had twisted a knife in his stomach. A man like him, admitting how bad off he was, had to be one of the more shameful situations she could've put him in. She felt an instant sympathy for him, and put a hand on his shoulder.

"You're not going to screw up," she said softly. "I know it."

"Oh, really?" He was trying to get that sarcastic tone back, but it wasn't quite working. "And how do you know that?"

She grinned. "Because nobody loses on my watch."

He smiled…and leaned in.

For a brief, brilliant moment, her mind froze. She wasn't sure if she wanted him to move in the rest of the way or if she wanted him to take a step back. Or if she wanted to just move in herself.

Instead he froze, too, inches away from her. They stood there, staring, and she could see the glinting of his eyes, almost black in the moonlight, the shadows making the planes of his face even harsher.

"Okay," he said, his voice rasping over her skin and causing her to shiver. "I'll do it."

God, she hoped so. She was afraid of how hard she was hoping. "Do what?" she finally croaked.

He took a step back. "I'll go along with what you suggested. The sales coaching thing. With you."

She felt… Well, she supposed it was relief. Step one was over. She'd got him to agree to work with her.

Her lips tingled with thwarted anticipation, and she forced her nerve endings to just calm down. *We won, you idiot. Stay focused!*

"So." She cleared her throat, standing straight. "That's fantastic. We should start right away. I mean, you've only got—what?—four weeks. That's not a lot of time, but if we work hard…"

She saw him smiling slightly and shaking his head. "What?"

"There's a little problem," he said, and he sounded just as frustrated as she felt. "I can't start right away. In fact, you're probably only going to have about two days or so to get me, er, coached."

"Two days?" She didn't mean to yell, but the surprise tended to bring out the volume in her. "What are you, nuts?"

"I think your temper is beginning to grow on me," he said with a grin.

"I think your sense of humor is going to kill me," she bit out. "I also thought that you were being straight with me."

The humor left his expression. "This isn't me yanking your chain. Seriously. I have to go on a three-week sales trip—a road trip, to some of our more rural customers. They're bigger spenders, and we need those orders now more than ever. I *have* to go."

"That's what you have salesmen for," she said, knowing that the argument sounded petulant. But, *jeez,* two days wasn't enough to coach anybody who was going in cold. Even as confident as she was, she wasn't crazy enough to believe that!

He sighed. "Let's just say I'm the closer on this deal."

She closed her eyes. He *would* have to put it in terms she understood.

"So." He chucked the bottom of her chin, the grin back in effect. "See you in three weeks?"

"I can't possibly work like this," she said.

"That's all I've got." He motioned to her car. "Not that it hasn't been a fun evening and all, but don't you have a two-hour drive ahead of you?"

"Yeah," she said. "When are you leaving?"

"Monday," he said. "First stop is Montecito…a few hours from here, near the Nevada border."

"Maybe you could…I don't know…*call,*" she said, racking her brain. Two days. There was just no way this would work.

He smiled. Indulgently, she thought. "Sure. I'll try."

"This isn't going to work," she muttered as she opened her door and climbed in.

"Don't worry," he said, shutting the door behind her and waiting for her to roll down the window. "Nobody screws up on your watch, right?"

The curses she threw at him were drowned out by the roar of her engine. He grinned and leaned down.

"I'll call," he said, just inches away from her face. Then, with a lightning-fast grin, he pulled away.

She watched him as he walked to his own car, getting in, driving away. Fortunately he didn't notice that she leaned back against the leather upholstery of her seat, almost melting into it. She was short of breath. The guy was a walking, breathing, sexual punch in the gut. And she'd felt the hit, all right.

It was a first in her experience. And it was utterly humiliating.

She finally pulled out, heading toward the highway. Now that he wasn't in her physical proximity, she could focus on what was even more disturbing than his powerful sensual appeal. For example, the fact that she now had only two days to do what a miracle worker couldn't pull off in a week. And what sort of screaming idiot goes on a three-week road trip just before a big investor meeting, anyway? She should just walk. Tell Betsy that she'd made a huge error in judgment, plead for her to forget about their little agreement, and go back to waiting for her performance review. Better still, pretending that she'd never even *heard* of Robson Steel, the town of San Angelo, or Mr. Sexy Pants Drew Robson himself.

She took a deep, cleansing breath.

Nobody screws up on your watch, right?

She wasn't walking away. And apparently, Drew Robson wasn't the only screaming idiot in town.

After several choice curses and a few daydreams of

strangling Drew—among other things; she was only human, after all—she finally settled down and shifted into problem-solving mode.

It wasn't impossible. Few things were. What did she really need, anyway? She needed more time to teach a man who was infuriating, smug, and utterly appealing how to sell.

While I'm at it, might as well tackle that whole World Peace thing, she thought, shifting gears. At least she had two hours on the road. She tended to think better when she was on the road, anyway.

She blinked.

On the road.

She grinned, the car's roaring engine seeming to cheer her thoughts. Three-week road trip. Now *there* was a solution.

"I'M GLAD you're going through with this, Drew. It'll mean a lot. And I'm sure you'll get more comfortable once you get out on the road."

Drew tossed his luggage into the trunk of his Chevy Impala with a little more force than necessary. Ken had been talking to him since Drew had walked through the door this morning. Drew was pretty sure he'd get more comfortable as soon as he was behind the wheel of the car and away from Ken's compulsive encouragement.

"You went over the list of clients, right?"

"Yes, Ken," he dutifully replied as he put his garment bag next to his big Samsonite. He was going to be on the road for three weeks. He felt as if he'd packed for a war.

"Did you bring samples?"

"Brought the product brochures," Drew replied,

looking at Ken skeptically. "I'm not bringing a two-ton oil cap with me. I don't think my car's rated for that kind of weight."

"Oh. Of course." Ken smiled sheepishly. "I'm sorry. I'm nervous. This is so important for Robson Steel."

"Believe me, I know that," Drew said. Ken was standing next to the car, flanked by Mrs. Packard, who was too cool a customer to wring her hands. Still, her staccato-sharp voice was shooting questions at him each time Ken stopped to take a breath.

"You've got all of your maps?" It would've sounded more maternal if she'd sounded less angry. "All the addresses?"

"Right in the passenger seat, Mrs. Packard." She'd neatly printed all of the driving instructions. He was surprised she hadn't installed GPS in his car one afternoon while he wasn't looking.

"I've included a lot of information on the customers, the most I could get my hands on," Ken said apologetically, looking at Mrs. Packard a little warily. "You should have at least the night before to go over the papers. And you're bringing your laptop, right?"

"Yeah, I've got the laptop." He put the laptop case next to the garment bag. Thank God he had a huge trunk. At this rate, he'd probably be putting Ken in the trunk and strapping Mrs. Packard to the roof. "I've got the background, I've got the maps, I've got the product descriptions. My cell phone battery is charged, I've got my spare and the charger with me. I've got about forty pairs of clean boxers with my name written on them. Anything else?"

Ken grinned. "You only brought forty pairs?"

"You'll want bottled water for the trip," Mrs. Packard said. "It's a long drive. It's easy to get dehydrated."

Drew rubbed his eyes with the palms of his hands. Kids going away to college didn't get grilled like this.

Mrs. Packard looked up at the sky. "Weather's not looking good," she said. "You'll be careful driving."

It wasn't a question. He nodded anyway, fighting the instinct to say, "Yes, ma'am."

"Well, I guess you're as prepped as you're going to get," Ken said, shaking Drew's hand. "You've been working like a demon all weekend. I think you're going to rack up some serious sales."

"From your mouth to God's ear," Drew said, only half kidding. He'd boned up on all the details, yes. But he'd also worked to keep his mind off of Jade. The way she'd talked to him, both confident and still sweet. How she'd said that he wouldn't screw up. That was something that haunted his dreams…her putting her hand on his shoulder, looking into his eyes.

Of course, in his dreams she'd done more than just comfort him.

He closed his eyes. He had three weeks on the road to get her out of his system. Then he'd be so cross-eyed from his trip, he'd have two days to focus on getting investors to save his company. He'd be too wrung out to worry about a sexy temptress distracting him from what was important.

He was just about to slam the trunk shut when the sound of a car speeding into the parking lot distracted the three of them.

"What is *that?*" Ken said, startled, as a cherry-red, old-model Mustang all but screeched to a halt by Drew's car.

Drew knew the car. And he knew the driver.

Jade got out of the car in a swirl of dust. She was wearing comfortable-looking khakis, a black tank top and sneakers. ''Great! I'm not too late.''

It was the first time since Drew had met Mrs. Packard that he'd ever seen the older woman floored. Ken wasn't even dignified about it—his mouth was literally open.

''Too late for what?'' Drew felt compelled to ask.

Her smile was bright—and he knew that glint in her eye by this point. That was determination. ''For the road trip, of course,'' she said, opening her trunk. He watched her pull out two suitcases and a laptop case.

''Oh, no,'' he said. Foolish, but he stood in front of his trunk with his arms out, ignoring her frown. ''You're not coming with me.''

She looked over at Ken and Mrs. Packard, her face set. ''Would you please excuse us?''

Ken goggled, then tugged at Mrs. Packard, who glared at Jade and distinctly murmured, ''Well, I never.''

Jade shrugged. ''And you never will if you keep wearing that support hose,'' she murmured back.

If looks could kill, Drew thought, then Mrs. Packard was doing the visual equivalent of pistol-whipping his new sales coach.

Jade turned back to Drew. ''You've got investors to persuade, remember?''

''And a sales trip,'' he added. ''There's no point in renovating the plant if I've got no orders to fill.''

''So we multitask,'' she said, putting her suitcases down by his feet. ''I go with you. I see how you do on sales presentations. I coach you from there. I coach you on the road, during dinners. If you need it, I make hypnotic suggestion tapes for when you sleep.''

"What, you're not going to just chant over me?" She couldn't be serious. She couldn't possibly be serious.

She winked at him. "Only if it's necessary."

His mind reeled. "I can't...I mean..."

"You'll probably hate me. But I'm not going to let you screw up on my watch." She nudged him out of the way. Surprised, he let her, watching as she put her suitcases companionably next to his, shutting his trunk herself. "Now. You driving first, or am I?"

"You're not driving," he said, still feeling numb. This wasn't happening. This couldn't possibly be happening.

She grinned. "All right."

And before he could stop her, she'd shut her own trunk, set her alarm, and climbed into his passenger seat.

He stared at her, then over at Ken and Mrs. Packard. Mrs. Packard had turned a brilliant shade of red. Ken looked torn between amusement and abject horror.

"She's not going with me," he said to them, then walked over to her, opening the car door. "You're not going with me."

She looked at him over the dark green tint of her sunglasses, that grin of hers sexy and impudent. "Sure I am."

"No, you're not." He gauged just how quickly she'd be able to get a hold of things if he decided to yank her from the car. "What do you think you're doing? I've got a sales trip, for Christ's sake. I don't have the time or the energy for this!"

Now she looked serious. "What you don't have the time for is prepping for that investors' meeting," she said. "This will create time. Trust me."

Trust her?

Her green eyes were beseeching—and strangely compelling.

"One week," she said in a low voice. "If you still think I'm not doing anything productive, I'll find my own way back to Los Angeles. But I need a chance, damn it. And at this point, you don't have a lot of options."

He stared at her for a long minute. Her face, the one that so many people would just write off as pretty, sexy, stunning, held more than just good bone structure and porcelain skin. He could see past it to the steel underneath. She was a sledgehammer wrapped in a mink stole. She was strong, and smart, and he wasn't getting her out of his car with a crowbar.

For whatever reason, he found that more than anything persuaded him.

"One week," he repeated, then shut the door. "Ken, Mrs. P., I'll call you from the road."

He left them staring in disbelief at the car as he got in the driver's seat, shut the door and started the engine with a low rev.

"One rule," he said as Jade buckled up. "No radio commando. I get to choose all the music."

"No problem," she said with a laugh in her voice. "You're the client."

3

JADE AND DREW SAT at a roadside diner, somewhere in the middle of nowhere on the way to Montecito. That was just what the sign over the dingy eatery said, too: Roadside Diner. After surveying her choices, she settled on a burger and fries with a chocolate milkshake. Drew had the same, except for the milkshake. She got the feeling it was a little too frivolous for the man, who was frowning enough to crease his skin.

"You keep making that face, it's going to freeze that way," she said sweetly, pushing her straw around in the thick ice cream.

"I never should've agreed to this," he muttered, not looking at her. "We just drove three hours and you didn't stop talking *once*."

She tilted her head to the side. "I'd talk less if you participated more," she pointed out.

"I was thinking. I need to think about stuff," he said, glowering darkly. "Unlike some people, who just blurt out anything that enters their head."

She batted her eyes, taking a sip of the milkshake. She was getting under his skin. That was a good start.

The waitress, a black-haired woman in her twenties, came over and plunked the plates down in front of them, then turned to walk away.

"Excuse me," Jade said, trying to stop her, "could we get some ketchup?"

The woman glanced at Jade, shrugged, and shuffled back to the kitchen.

Jade let out a low sigh. Apparently it was an off day—she was having trouble getting through to anyone. Of course, being stuck in a car and trying to pry open a clam like Drew Robson was bound to frazzle anybody. She turned back to her main concern. Drew was tucking into the burger with single-minded fervor. She took a bite. It wasn't bad, but it wasn't good enough to explain his focus on it. She knew he was eating in the hopes that she wouldn't get him to talk.

Well, she thought. He's wrong there.

"So. You're trying to rescue the factory from your father's mistakes," she said casually. "You're overly honest, where he was pond scum. Stop me when I'm wrong."

He stopped, his jaw clenched on a bite of food. Then he swallowed slowly and shrugged. "I wouldn't say I'm overly honest."

He wasn't contesting the pond scum comment, which was meant to get a rise out of him. That wasn't good.

"I see. Don't tell me...he was a really good salesman, huh?"

His eyes narrowed. He'd stopped eating, she noticed, and was toying with a French fry. "That's what they tell me. I've never worked with him."

Something else she'd have to investigate. "Charming?"

Drew shrugged. She took that as a yes.

"Good-looking, too, huh?"

Now his eyes met hers. "What makes you say that?"

"You had to get *something* from him."

He looked puzzled for a minute. Then slowly, finally, he smiled in return. She felt the effect of it right down to her curling toes. "Is that a compliment?"

"It's an observation," she replied, feeling her heartbeat skip a little unevenly. "The point is, you're practically phobic about this whole sales process. I'm just trying to figure out why."

The smile vanished as quickly as it came, and she momentarily felt bereft at its absence. "So you're something of a shrink, now, too."

Now it was her turn to shrug. "The key to being a good salesperson, or a good public relations person, is being able to understand people." She paused a beat. "Not to be offensive, but right now you're not that hard to read."

He was riled enough to answer, which was the point. "It's not that I don't like selling things. I like sales. That's what keeps the company going," Drew said. "It's just...techniques, pitches, crap like that. I believe in the plant, and that's what I talk about. If they need us, they'll buy something. That simple. I don't convince people to do something they don't want." His pointed stare implied that she did.

She sighed. His sounding so earnest was part of the problem. "I'm not saying you should...excuse me," she said, then paused, stopping the young waitress as she shuffled past the table. "Ketchup?"

The woman shrugged yet again, then headed back toward the kitchen.

If she forgets this time, I'm going to...

To her surprise, Drew stopped the woman, as well, waiting for her to look up from her order pad and directly into his eyes. "I'm sorry. Could you get mustard as well as ketchup? I'd really appreciate it."

His voice was like warm honey. The waitress's eyes widened. So did Jade's. The request was in a low, undemanding tone, but his smile was wide and friendly, and his look was engaging.

"R-right away." Now she wasn't shuffling anymore. The waitress practically sprinted to the kitchen.

Drew turned back to Jade. "Sorry. What?"

Jade blinked at him. "Do that again."

"Do what again?"

"What you just did with the waitress."

"You want me to ask *you* for mustard and ketchup?" His voice was amused. "Okay. Got any mustard and ketchup on you?"

The waitress showed up before Jade could answer, putting the condiments down with a loud thunk. "Here you are," she said, never even looking at Jade.

Drew rewarded her with a smile, similar to the one he'd sent Jade earlier. The waitress was obviously similarly affected, Jade noticed. The fact shouldn't have irritated her, but unreasonably, it did.

"Thanks," he murmured, and the woman straightened.

"You need anything else," she said with a wink, "you let me know."

Jade could just guess what need the waitress wanted to help out with—and it wasn't on the menu.

He turned back to Jade, not noticing the hungry gaze of the waitress. "Guess I don't need any ketchup from you, after all," he said, opening the bottle and pouring a small pool of the stuff by his French fries. "Was there a point to me asking that, by the way?"

Jade waited until the waitress reluctantly retreated to the kitchen, then turned to him. "I'm not talking about asking for ketchup. I'm talking that charm you just broke out with. You know. What you did to the waitress."

Now he looked honestly bewildered. "I didn't do anything."

"Oh, *please.* That Paul Newman stare, your voice going all low and Barry White-esque..." She lowered her own voice. "'Could you get mustard as well as ketchup? I'd *really* appreciate it.' If that's not charm, I'll eat my luggage."

"That was just being nice," he said irritably, dredging a fry in ketchup.

"Ha. If I could be 'nice' like that, I'd own half of California and a good chunk of Texas," she said, stirring her shake. "*That's* sales. I couldn't get the woman to give me the time of day, and now she's ready to jump through flaming hoops to get you dessert. What does that tell you?"

He grinned, looking up at the ceiling thoughtfully. "That you annoy more people than just me?"

She growled at him.

"Possibly it's because I'm cuter than you are."

"Keep burying yourself," she said between clenched teeth. This wasn't helping him. He was just resisting the issue at hand. "Okay. Are you nice to your customers, then? Friendly, stuff like that?"

He stopped snickering and sobered. "Of course I am. I mean, it's a bit different..."

She pounced. "Why?"

"I don't want her to buy tons of steel products from me," he said, rolling his eyes as if the question itself was ridiculous. "I didn't want anything from her but ketchup."

"Which I'm sure she'd be disappointed to hear,"

Jade said offhandedly, then said, ‘‘but the fact is, you did want something from her.’’

‘‘So, I’m just supposed to say ‘I want an order from you, I’d really appreciate it’ and that’s it? They’ll buy from me?’’ He rolled his eyes. ‘‘Well. I’m certainly getting my hundred thousand dollars’ worth of coaching out of this. You’re basically saying I should do what I’ve been doing.’’

Jade gave in to the impulse and tugged at her hair, letting out a high-pitched squeak of frustration. ‘‘What I’m saying is, if you put sales points in that tone of voice, you’ll be able to sell anything to anyone. You tell them how what you’re doing will help them, you tell them why you’re the best man for the job and follow it all up with that...that—’’ she made a motion with her hand ‘‘—that damned sexy honesty of yours, and you’ll slam-dunk it. I’m not asking you to lie. I’m not even asking you to pressure. I’m just saying for you to be a little different in how you say things...and to stop acting like I’m either the enemy or somebody completely useless!’’

She realized she was attracting the attention of the only other patron of the diner, as well as the waitress and the cook. She quieted down, muttering into her milkshake, ‘‘That’s all I’m saying.’’

He was staring at her, those light blue eyes of his hypnotic. He was intense, there was no question about that. He looked as though he was really thinking about what she said. There was such a drawing power in him. He might think he was cut and dried, completely devoid of charm, but she knew better. When he wasn’t thinking about it, he was one of the most compelling men she had ever met.

Then he opened his mouth.

"Damned sexy, huh?"

She growled, then closed her eyes. Counted to ten. Then she looked at the waitress, who was staring at the table like a predator. "Check, please?"

HAD DREW BEEN ALONE, he probably would have ridden with the window down, his arm getting tanned by the late afternoon sun and chapped by the hot Nevada wind. But he had Jade in the car...a blessedly quiet Jade, who hadn't spoken to him since they'd left the dingy little diner off the highway. He had the air-conditioning going, yet he could still feel the heat waves coming off of her. Some of it was irritation, he realized, trying not to grin. Still, some of it was just her, pure and simple.

She's certainly one of the hottest women I've ever met, no question.

He looked over at her. If it were any other woman, he'd have sworn she was pouting, angry at him for not listening to her, trying to prove her point and "punishing" him by ignoring him. That wasn't Jade, as far as he could tell. He could just see the curve of her high cheekbone since she was turned to the window, and her lower lip pouted in fullness, not temper.

She was considering her next move...and he felt sure there would be a next move. She wasn't giving up or giving in to emotion. She was trying to figure out another way around him.

He grinned, turning his full focus back to the stretch of highway in front of him. He had to say that her determination, while annoying, was also kind of arousing. She was a strong woman. He liked strong women.

A few miles down she finally broke the silence. "When do we get to the hotel?"

"I figure around seven or eight tonight," he answered, shrugging.

He could feel her gaze on him. "Really? I didn't realize it was so far away."

"It's not," he replied. "We're stopping at Martinez Motors first."

He turned to see her gaping at him in horror. "You're kidding."

"No, I'm not." He watched as she went pale. "What?"

"You've been driving about six hours, and now you're going to walk straight into a meeting?"

"I've known Alejandro's family for years," he said. "When I was in college, I worked for Robson during the summer, and I occasionally drove some deliveries to Martinez Motors. I even did a little work with them when I was at a competing plant. They know me." He smiled, thinking of the large, family owned operation. "This isn't going to be a problem."

"Exactly how big a customer are they?"

"Medium big," he hedged, then said a little more emphatically, "their loyalty is the important thing. Trust me. They're some of the most down-to-earth, real people I know."

Which was why he'd planned the trip with them as the first stop.

"You could have mentioned this at lunch," she said, her tone tart.

Now he looked straight at her, grinning. "Would that be before or after you remarked on my Barry White sales abilities?"

She didn't even grace that with a reply. To his surprise, she unbuckled her seat belt and squirmed in her seat, reaching into the back.

"Hey, watch it!" He dodged her shapely hip as she fumbled, obviously tugging at something. "I'm driving here, remember?"

She pulled a bag out of the back seat and sat back down, buckling up. She started rummaging through it frantically. "Martinez Motors, you said?"

He looked at her suspiciously. "What are you doing?"

"Trying desperately to do some research on the first client sales meeting you're holding," she said. "We don't have another one today, do we? Some other meeting I don't know about?"

"You don't even need to be involved in this," he said sharply. He tightened his grip on the steering wheel. "In fact, I don't see how you being a coach has anything to do with you knowing everything about my customers."

She sighed. "I'm sure you know everything there is to know about the customers, but you're the one who has problems with sales. I need to know as much about the situation as I can. And I'd like to know what your strategy is, how you plan to sell them."

He sent her a bewildered glance. "I don't need a strategy with Martinez Motors," he replied.

She paused. "You don't have *any* strategy? No sales points?"

"I told you, they've worked with us for years."

He turned to see her arch one graceful eyebrow, then she quickly started flipping through the folder in front of her.

It occurred to him that now was probably the best time to get some ground rules laid out. He knew she wanted to show him how to be a better salesman. He figured that just meant she'd be waiting quietly in the background while he spoke with his customers and contacts, and then she might say some pithy comments afterward. Now, he realized that wasn't very likely. While he doubted she'd just come out and correct him, he also realized that she'd probably stumble in, thinking she knew about steel or about his customers. She'd probably try to show him how it was done.

He should have realized it sooner, he thought. Jade was not a quiet-in-the-background kind of woman. She was an active, aggressive, get-it-done-at-all-costs type of woman. In other words, she was the last thing he needed to talk to Alejandro, the kindly older man he'd known for years. Alejandro would react poorly to some flashy L.A. public relations expert who thought she knew how to push product. If anything, she'd probably make Alejandro think twice about what Robson was doing…and whether or not Martinez Motors should be a part of it.

Jade might sink this deal.

He was coming up on the exit for Martinez Motors. He'd have to do something about this, and soon.

They pulled up to the factory. There were still cars in the parking lot, and he spotted Alejandro's car in its reserved parking space.

"I don't want you talking at all during this," he said quickly, then got out of the car.

It didn't look as though she heard him. "Give me a second," she said instead, reaching over to pop the trunk. She got out, shutting the door. "I need to freshen up a little. I still think we should have at least stopped in the hotel first. I probably look like a mess."

He made the mistake of inspecting her appearance. She did look a little wrinkled, and her khaki pants and black tank top were a shade too casual for any normal business meeting. Still, her clothes emphasized her form, without being overtly sexy. In fact, it emphasized her beauty somehow. Nobody could call her flashy in that outfit, and yet anybody with decent eyesight could tell she was a looker no matter what she wore.

He noticed when her green eyes surveyed him in turn. Her full mouth puckered slightly with disapproval. "You're looking pretty scruffy, too, you know."

He bristled before he could stop himself. He looked down at his own gray Dockers and short-sleeved shirt. "This is your sales advice? I should dress up for people I've known for years?" He shook his head. "I already told you. I know the Martinezes. Dressing in a suit wouldn't make a bit of difference. They aren't going to care what we look like."

Especially you, he thought. Because I'm going to make sure you're not really a part of the meeting.

She looked dubious. She pulled a hairbrush through her luxurious curls, quick and business-like, then got a compact out of her purse and dabbed at her face with a few quick, artistic smudges. She looked good to him, but watching her smooth lipstick over her lips made his own mouth go dry. She looked at him, her eyes sharp. Then, she winked. She traded her sneakers for a snazzy pair of low boots and pulled out a blazer.

He rolled his eyes, gesturing to his watch. "Any time milady is ready," he muttered.

"You might not care if you look like you got dressed in the dark," she said, stowing all her stuff away and smiling at him, "but some of us believe in first impressions."

"This isn't a first impression for me, remember?"

"It is as president of Robson Steel."

He threw up his hands, ignoring the way she sashayed past him. He did have to admit, she looked good.

When doesn't she?

They got to the lobby of the building, similar to Drew's own. He smiled at the receptionist. "Hi. Rosa?"

Rosa, a young girl in her twenties, squealed and ran from behind the counter, giving him a big hug. "Drew! We didn't know when you'd be here."

He caught Jade's look of surprise from over Rosa's shoulder. "You didn't schedule this?" Her tone seemed to hold only curiosity, but he could tell from the widening of those mossy-green eyes of hers that she was shocked—and a little disapproving.

"I told Alejandro I'd be here this week," he said. "I know Alejandro's schedule. This is Alejandro's niece, by the way."

"Ah." Jade smiled at Rosa before shooting another look of surprise at Drew.

Rosa let go of Drew and looked at Jade. "Who's this? Your girlfriend?"

Jade blinked at Rosa.

"Ah, no," Drew said, thinking fast. This was not going to work well at all. He couldn't talk to Alejandro with Jade sitting there…with the possibility of her piping up and angering the older man.

He watched as Jade's disapproval melted into a warm, wide smile. She held out her hand, and Rosa took it. "I'm Jade Morrow," she said. "I'm…"

"She's…uh, a student," Drew interrupted.

Both Rosa and Jade turned to look at him, Rosa with a smirk, Jade with a look of utter shock.

"Yes. She's thinking of going into the steel business, and she's working with Robson. As an intern." He felt like he was babbling, so he reined it in. "That's all."

"An intern?" Rosa looked at Jade. "Really?"

"Apparently," Jade said, and Drew winced.

"Business or engineering?"

Jade paused for the briefest fraction of a second—and Drew thought the whole thing was shot.

"Business," she finally replied smoothly. "I'm going for my M.B.A. Mr. Robson here has been kind enough to let me tag along on some of his sales calls."

"Sales call?" Rosa laughed. "Good grief. I thought this was just a visit."

"Is Alejandro free?" Drew prayed he could see him right away.

"Sure. He's on the factory floor. I'll go get him." Rosa went to the phone, and he heard her over the intercom. "Tio? Drew's here in the lobby." She hung up the phone, then frowned. "I'll go make sure he gets here."

With that, she left Drew alone in the lobby with his very peeved sales coach.

Jade took a step closer to him, and he could smell her vanilla perfume. "Business student?" Her whisper was a cross between disbelief and anger.

"Alejandro's a friend. If I tell him I hired a P.R. person and a sales coach, he'll think I've lost my mind," he replied in a low voice. "It won't help, believe me. In fact, I think it'll be better if you don't sit in on this meeting."

Her eyes snapped with fire. "You might've mentioned this in the car," she said. Her voice sounded perfectly calm, that smooth, smoky alto that he'd been drawn to since the first time she spoke to him in his office. "Then you could have left the radio on and cracked a window for me so I got enough air!"

"Listen, Jade, you work for me, remember?"

"I'm supposed to work *with* you," she retorted. "And I—"

"Drew!" A voice interrupted them. "It's been too long."

Drew turned with relief to see the Hispanic man walking through the door. Alejandro Martinez might have aged, but he still moved like a young man—energetically. "Alejandro. It's been way too long." He gave Alejandro the handshake-half-hug that men had perfected since the advent of football.

"We've wondered how you've been," Alejandro said. "I figured you were too busy, taking over at Robson Steel. How is it going?"

"We're managing," Drew said. "It's been tough, no question, but we'll get through it. It'll just take some hard work."

"I'm sorry," Alejandro said, noticing Jade. "Who's this, Drew? I didn't mean to be rude."

Jade's smile was like a sunrise. "I'm Jade Morrow. I'm a, uh, business student. Mr. Robson's letting me tag along to learn about the business. Sales calls, especially."

Alejandro looked at her intently, then looked at Drew. "How altruistic."

Drew felt himself flush a little, like a little kid caught scaling the refrigerator. "Yes, well, Jade's really incredible. She wants to learn everything there is to learn about the business, you know?"

Suddenly he had a flash of brilliance. "I was wondering...do you think someone could take her on a short tour of the plant?"

Jade's full mouth set in a grim line. "I'm sure that would be fascinating," Jade countered, "but I thought it'd be more educational to sit in on the sales call..."

"It's hardly a sales call. It will just be two friends catching up," Alejandro said, and Drew felt a wave of relief. "Rosa? Could you give Ms. Morrow a quick tour?"

Rosa smiled. "Sure, Tio. Ms. Morrow, follow me. Hopefully I'll be able to answer any questions you have."

Stymied, Jade sent one last caustic look at Drew. "Thanks, Rosa. That's very nice of you." She looked at Alejandro. "And it was very nice meeting you."

"Likewise," he responded. Drew watched as Rosa escorted Jade out of the room. "Wow. That is a whole lot of woman you've hired there, Drew."

Drew shook his head. "You have no idea."

Drew followed Alejandro into his office. It was small and an utter mess. Drew grinned. "Nothing's changed since the last time I was here."

"We're that kind of business," Alejandro said with a casual shrug.

"We've been doing business together for a long time," Drew said, sitting down. "I'm glad that Robson Steel's been able to count on Martinez Motors, and I hope you've been able to count on us, too."

Alejandro sat in his seat with a heavy sigh. "I think I know where you're going with this, Drew."

"I figured we'd get the sales order out of the way, and then we could catch up, maybe go for a little dinner. The whole family."

"Drew...I can't."

"Well," Drew amended, "we don't have to do dinner..."

"No. I can't put in an order for next year with Robson Steel."

Drew stopped. "Pardon?"

Alejandro fidgeted with a small piece of machinery that was being used as a paperweight. "Drew, we've been good friends for a long time. I was friends with your father, as well."

"You're not ordering with another vendor because of Dad, are you?" Drew's voice was harsher than he'd intended.

"It's not that," Alejandro said. "Well, not personally. But Robson is in trouble. Everyone knows this. As much as I want to help you, there's a good chance you'll go under. If I place an order with you and you....well, you know. I'd be stuck until a new vendor could supply me, and they'd put all their regular customers as priority. I can't afford that."

Drew blanched. "I'm doing everything I can to turn it around, Alejandro. We won't go under. Not if I have anything to say about it."

"That's just it," the older man said kindly. "You won't have anything to say about it. Not in the end."

Drew took a deep breath. This wasn't happening. This just wasn't happening. "It would really help the factory. We *need* this order."

"I can't tell you how sorry I am that I can't promise it to you." And to his credit, he really did look apologetic. "If you stay in business, if you can get the factory back on its feet, I'd be happy to sign back up with Robson Steel." He paused. "Just not now."

Those final three words hit Drew like a hammer. He closed his eyes for a second, then nodded. "I understand."

"JADE? What's this I hear about you being out of the office for three weeks?"

Jade was sitting in her hotel room at the Sleep EZ Motel just outside of Montecito, Nevada. The room was done in shades of mustard yellow and avocado green. She was sitting on the edge of her bed, which felt lumpy as old oatmeal. All of this wasn't helping her mood one bit. Now, her boss calling her on her cell phone was just icing on the cake.

"Betsy, you said I could go after the Robson Steel account. I'm doing sales training instead of a media campaign. That's how we're going to get the hundred thousand."

Betsy paused. "That's a good one. Nobody else thought of that."

Jade grinned smugly. "I know."

"Still, why are you out of the office?"

Jade closed her eyes. "I'm training sort of on the fly. I'm doing a road trip with Drew Robson."

"Really?" Betsy's voice was inquisitive. "I see. And how's it going?"

Jade let out a breath. "Well...it hasn't been optimal." Understatement of the year. "But I think once we work out some communication issues, we'll be doing well."

"In other words, he's being completely irrational and not listening to you," Betsy paraphrased, a laugh in her voice.

Jade let out a weak chuckle. "Well, at least he's trapped in the car with me for a few hours a day. I figure it's sort of like brainwashing."

"In the car? You don't mean you're doing a real road trip?" Betsy's voice crackled with static. "Who does that anymore?"

"You wouldn't believe the little towns we're hitting. If we flew, apparently it'd take just as long to drive from an airport," Jade said. Of course, the fact that she doubted Robson Steel wanted to spend the money on all of that plane fare didn't help, either, but she wasn't about to tell her boss that.

"Jade," Betsy said, her voice wheedling, "are you *sure* that you want to go through with this? It just seems like you're betting awfully hard that this man and his company will get you what you want. I'd hate to see you throw away your career at Michaels and Associates for a losing proposition."

Jade had been thinking the same thing, but hearing Betsy say it... "I'm not," Jade said. "I've just been fine-tuning my approach."

"If you say so. Like I've said, you remind me of me when I was your age," Betsy said. "You'll get whatever you put your mind to."

"Thanks," Jade said.

"Just keep checking in, okay?"

Jade laughed. "Will do. 'Bye."

Jade disconnected, then stared at her surroundings. She was in a teeny town, miles away from any kind of metropolis. And just next door was the name to her pain: her client, Drew Robson.

She couldn't believe that he'd pulled that stunt at Martinez Motors, sending her off with Rosa while he cut his deal with Alejandro. She'd been seething, but realized it was partially her fault. She hadn't been clear enough about how she saw their working relationship actually working. But she wouldn't make that mistake twice. When he'd collected her in the lobby, she knew more about motors than she ever thought she'd want to. She also realized that she needed to take her new client in hand and start setting out a few ground rules. He wasn't the type of man who would take every word that fell out of her mouth as gospel truth of selling. He wasn't the type of man who would trust his future into her hands, either.

She sighed. Come to think of it, he wasn't like any other type of man she'd run into…in this business or any other.

She'd tried to talk to him in the car on the way back, but she'd still been trying to figure out her approach—how to convince him. And he had been sullen and unwilling to communicate, anyway. She had some suspicions there. He said that he'd talk to her later, but he needed food and rest.

She'd let him rest long enough for her to get some food. Then, he'd have to deal with her.

Forty-five minutes later she knocked on his hotel room door, a six pack of beer in one hand, a pizza balanced on the other. She finally kicked at his door when he didn't respond.

"All right, all right," she heard the muffled reply from the inside of the room. "Just a minute."

She was going to be calm. She was going to outline exactly what her problems with his methods were, and then discuss how they could work together. They'd eat pizza, drink beer, and hash this all out before they got back into that car tomorrow.

He opened the door. He was wearing jeans, no shirt, and he was rubbing a towel against his wet hair. "All right. Jeez. What?"

Lots of tanned torso. Little drops of water beading on smooth, toned muscle. You could iron on the guy's stomach.

For a minute Jade's mind went completely blank.

"Helloo-ooo?" Drew waved a hand in front of her face, completing her humiliation. "You wanted something?"

Well, not when he put it that way. Jade ignored the way her stomach jittered and her pulse elevated. It might help if her client weren't so damned gorgeous, that's all.

She cleared her throat. "Pizza delivery. Oh, and beer. Hope you like Corona."

He sniffed the aroma of the pizza, and sent her a little half smile before obscuring his face with the towel as he rubbed at his hair vigorously. "That's nice of you."

"I'm not nice," she said. "In exchange, you have to listen to me. More to the point, we need to work on some communication issues."

He paused, and she could hear the weary sigh muffled through the terry cloth. "Why am I not surprised?"

She put the pizza down on the dresser, then grabbed a slice and a bottle of beer for herself before settling into the room's solitary chair. She watched as he pulled the towel off, his hair damp and tousled. He hung the towel on the rack, and she could see the play of muscles across his back. She saw in the mirror that his jeans were unbuttoned, even though they were zipped. He'd obviously tugged them on in a hurry when he'd gone to get the door.

Wonder if he had time to put on underwear?

She was not a woman who blushed, but her temperature definitely rose. She sternly instructed herself to focus on his face when he turned around. She hated it when people had conversations with various parts of her body instead of looking into her eyes. She imagined that even men felt the same way.

Drew, on the other hand, had obviously caught her quick visual audit of his body. She caught her breath. His smile was quick, sexy, and his eyes seemed to darken a little.

"See anything you like?"

She ignored the sudden tightening in her chest. When he put his mind to it, he could be downright mesmerizing. If she was any other woman, she'd probably be sitting on his bed and taking him up on the unspoken offer in his eyes.

She frowned. She wasn't any other woman. He was about to find that out.

She popped the top off of her beer and shrugged. "I see a man who bamboozled me out of being present at today's sales call, so no, I can't say I'm too fond of what I'm looking at right now." She took a pull off of the beer, then stared into his eyes. "How did that go, by the way?"

He scowled, reached for a T-shirt and yanked it over his head. "I don't want to talk about today," he said, reaching for a beer. "I don't even want to *think* about today."

"You didn't get the sale."

He glared at her, then grabbed some pizza. "No. I suppose that makes you happy."

"Why would I be happy? If you don't get sales, I don't get paid. Neither of us win." She ate some of her pizza, and he did the same, frowning at her over every slice. Finally she leaned back. "We've got to get on some kind of even ground, Drew. I know you don't think I can help you. And I have to agree—I can't help you if you won't let me."

He sat on the edge of the bed, frowning. Then he put the beer down on one of the night tables, and stretched out.

She forced herself not to stare.

"I don't think this is going to work out," he said. "I mean, I didn't think it was going to work out before, and I *know* it's not going to work out now."

"You don't know that."

"There wasn't anything you could have done today," he said sharply, his eyes alight. "If this is the way things are going to go, I don't know that there's anything *I* can do. Can you understand that?"

She stood, looming over his reclined position. "I understand that you're punking out and giving up," she said in an even voice. "After all of your talk about your factory and your town, I thought frankly that you had more in you than this."

That got him. He was on his feet in two seconds, again surprising her with his catlike speed. "Don't you ever imply that I don't give a damn about my factory and my workers," he said, his voice like ground glass.

"Then show me you give a damn," she said, not backing down an inch. "If you think that nothing I do is going to make a difference, if you think you're screwed anyway, then let me try! I can't hurt anything else. I can only help."

He was inches from her, and she could see his chest heaving. His fists clenched. "My father signed up with your firm to make himself feel important," he said. "He was like that. I thought maybe you could make some suggestions to help me. I was grasping at straws—I must have been out of my mind."

"You know I can help you," she said. "You're just scared of letting me try."

‘‘Why? If I really thought you could save these sales, I’d let you run the whole damned thing!’’

She felt like shaking him. He was stubborn, too stubborn.

‘‘Fine. Let me have the next one.’’

He blinked at her. ‘‘What?’’

‘‘You think I can only mess things up. You think you’re already screwed. Let me have the next sales call.’’

He laughed harshly. ‘‘You don’t even know anything about steel.’’

‘‘That’s what you’re there for.’’

He threw up his hands. ‘‘This is why I know you can’t help me. You think that you can just stand there and mouth a bunch of sales platitudes and they’re just going to roll over and give me money? You’ve got to be delusional!’’

‘‘Let me try, damn it.’’ She was right up against him. If it were a Western, someone would be running to get the sheriff.

‘‘Fine. You want a shot? In two days, I’m supposed to meet with Norinal Machines. And it’ll be all yours.’’

She narrowed her eyes. He was giving in—but there was a catch. She could tell. ‘‘Seriously?’’

‘‘And I won’t help a bit,’’ he said.

‘‘I still get the customer files?’’

He motioned to his laptop case. ‘‘All yours.’’

‘‘Fine.’’

‘‘If you don’t get it,’’ he said, crossing his arms. ‘‘You’re out of here. Rent a car, get a map, and don’t stop till you hit Los Angeles.’’

She smiled fiercely. ‘‘And if I do get it…you listen to me. You start working with me, for real.’’

He shrugged. ‘‘Deal.’’ He put his hand out.

She took it, feeling the grasp of his hand, warm and rough against her own. She was staring at him. The intensity of his gaze was overpowering. He looked so fierce, so determined.

''Good luck,'' he said, his absence of confidence more than apparent.

''I don't need luck,'' she whispered. She noticed he hadn't let go of her hand.

He leaned in, and for a moment she held her breath. She was still furious with him, anger pouring through her, making her heart race. But there was still, under all of it, that attraction—that dumb stupid chemistry that seemed to erupt every time she was near him. It took everything she had not to lean up, not to ravish that stern mouth of his. She didn't feel like this often—actually, she hadn't felt like this before in her life.

''You'll need luck now.'' He whispered it, so close that she could feel his breath against her neck.

She stood on tiptoe, feeling her breasts brush inadvertently against his chest. ''Just give me the customer files,'' she whispered back, ''and we'll see how it really goes.''

When she pulled back, he looked shocked. Dazed. Inches away from her.

Then he walked to his bag and pulled out the files. She accepted them silently, then left.

4

WHAT THE HELL were you thinking?

He'd been thinking that he didn't need her help, until her impassioned plea for a chance, and her quiet demand for respect, had triggered something in him. She was easily one of the sexiest women he'd ever met. But her personality kept continually surprising him. She obviously had integrity to go with that razor-sharp smile and savvy. She certainly deserved more than she was going to get out of this deal.

He sat next to her in the plush, obviously newly redecorated lobby. She looked cool, calm and collected, with a plum suit and a brilliant white shirt. She looked both professional and feminine, alluring and competent.

She looked back at him, caught him staring, smiled. "Remember...this one's all mine."

He nodded. "Wouldn't have it any other way."

Of course, he knew something she didn't. She didn't have a chance today. And after today, she'd be out of his hair, and more than likely out of his life.

Finally he'd be able to focus on saving his quickly failing business...rather than focusing on the brilliant, beautiful, gutsy woman, who was starting to haunt his dreams and fantasies with an intensity bordering on obsession.

Norinal Machines was only a client because his father and then his salesman made outrageous concessions to keep them. That would stop today. Of course, he could probably use the cash, but he couldn't afford all the free giveaways that went along with it.

Jade was smiling to herself as she looked over the customer file. If possible, it looked thicker than it had when he handed it over to her. Maybe he should have looked at it a little more closely…

He looked away. No, he knew better. This was a lost cause. If she could pull this one off, then she'd be a miracle worker.

You said you'd give her a chance.

He looked at her again. It wasn't his fault that her chance was the one customer he was guaranteed to lose.

"Mr. Robson? Drew?"

Both he and Jade stood. The purchasing manager at Norinal Machines, a middle-aged man dressed in business casual khakis and a buttoned-up light denim shirt, was walking up to them. "Hi, Skip," Drew said, holding out his hand.

"Great to see you," Skip enthused, shaking Drew's hand emphatically. "The annual Robson Road Trip… Just like your old man. Tradition, that's what makes your company great. Speaking of your dad, how is he doing these days, anyway?"

Drew winced. Before he could answer, Jade demurely cleared her throat, giving him an opportunity to change the subject. "Oh, Skip, I wanted to introduce you to a consultant who's working with Robson Steel—this is Jade Morrow. Jade, Skip Morganstern."

He watched as Skip did a quick perusal, pausing on Jade's long legs and ample breasts. And for a brief second he imagined himself giving Skip a nice right hook for his trouble.

"Ms. Morrow," Skip said with a broad smile. "This is a welcome surprise."

"I hope you don't mind me sitting in on your sales meeting," Jade said, her voice light and...flirtatious? Drew stared at her. And what was up with her asking permission? She was about as tentative as a cannonball.

"Not at all," Skip said magnanimously. "Come on in to my office."

Drew followed as Jade kept up with Skip, asking questions the entire time. Skip was practically bursting the buttons on his chest as he pointed out every bell and whistle the company was famous for. "We've just got a really large contract from the government," Skip said. "We're heavy players in this industry."

Drew rolled his eyes surreptitiously behind the man's back. They were fairly large, when it came to Robson Steel. But in the industry? They were barely a blip on the radar screen. The man was obviously just trying to sound important to Jade. And from her corresponding remarks, it sounded as though she was impressed.

And what was going on with that, anyway? She was smart. Couldn't she see that the guy was full of it?

They stepped into Skip's office and sat down. Skip and Jade kept going for a few more minutes. Finally, when they stopped to take a breath, Drew broke in.

"I'm glad we were able to set up this meeting," he said, bracing himself. Everything would pretty much be going downhill from here, he thought. "I know Norinal Machines has placed relatively small orders with Robson Steel in the past, and you were used to working with my father, but..."

''Drew, before we go into all that...about next year's order.'' Skip's voice had grown sly, sort of a just-between-us-guys inflection. ''I don't know about this year's order. I mean, things are a lot different than they were last year.''

You can say that again. Drew gritted his teeth. ''What, exactly, is the problem?''

''You've probably noticed the new lobby. Hell, even my office is redone,'' Skip said with a smile. ''We're moving up. We've got to be more careful than ever about who we use as vendors.''

''Oh, really?'' Drew's voice was dangerously low. The guy didn't even notice, just kept going, leaning back in his squeaky-new, black-leather chair.

''We understand that there's some difficulty at your plant. Some *financial* difficulty,'' Skip continued smoothly. ''That's a bad sign, Drew. Think about it from our side. You have some trouble on the line, you run behind schedule, and that leaves us here at N.M. high and dry. I can't afford that with a big government contract coming. We're going to need somebody reliable.''

''Of course,'' Jade said sympathetically.

Drew stared at her. This? *This* was how she thought about helping him?

''I see you understand our position,'' Skip said, with only the faintest trace of a leer. ''It's a tough business world out there. It's nothing personal.''

Drew felt his temperature rising steadily. ''We've never missed a shipment,'' he said, his tone turning curt. ''We've always been more than reasonable...''

''Now, now! As I said, it's nothing personal,'' Skip reiterated, looking nervously at Drew, then turning to

Jade. "We just need to review our options. We'll be talking to other vendors, as well."

"That makes perfect sense," Jade said.

Drew was ready to strangle them both.

Now, Skip, obviously feeling confident with Jade in his corner, turned back to Drew...and his smile grew sly. "Of course, we'd love to continue working with Robson Steel. You produce excellent quality merchandise. And you have been pretty timely, no question about that. Maybe, with the right inducements, we could work out a deal."

Drew was just about to tell him what he could do with his inducements, but Jade leaned forward in her chair. "May I ask a few questions?"

"Of course," Skip said, although his attention seemed more riveted on the open top button of Jade's blouse than on her queries.

Scum. Total scum. Drew suddenly felt dirty about the way he'd looked at Jade. But it was different. He knew that Jade was more than just her looks—she'd yanked the rug out from under him enough times to know. What was the likelihood Big Smile Skip would be able to see further than her bra size?

He clenched his jaw, waited until his voice could remain even. "Listen, I think..."

Drew had been about to interrupt, but Jade's look surprised him into silence.

Respect. She'd wanted respect, a chance to show what she could do. He leaned back in his chair, forcing himself to hold his tongue.

Unless the guy ogles her again. Then, I don't care what she says. I'm clocking him.

"I'm new to this industry, so I just wanted to ask a

few simple questions. First of all, you make airplane and tank parts, right?''

''Just a few of the smaller components for a variety of different machines,'' Skip said with a tone of barely noticeable condescension. ''I'll be sure to get you a product brochure.''

''That would be great,'' Jade said with a sunny smile. Still, Drew couldn't help but notice a quick flash of her eyes.

About time, he thought.

''Or maybe we could even talk about it at length later,'' Skip said suggestively. ''How about...''

She stopped him. ''Sorry, you did just say you'd gotten a government contract?''

Skip smiled again—Drew used to call it a salesman's smile, but he got the feeling Jade would take offense. Well, Drew had warned her about this one. Still, she was trying.

''We sure did,'' Skip bragged. ''Our biggest contract to date. It's been a banner year for Norinal Machines.''

She smiled in return.

I think I'm going to gag, Drew thought sullenly. It was bad enough that they weren't going to get a sale from this. Did he have to sit through this rigmarole?

''Would this be the contract that was reported in the most recent *International Steel News* article?''

Now both Skip and Drew were staring at Jade. Skip's wanna-be seductive grin fell a few notches. ''Um, yes. I suppose it was.''

''I'm new at this, as I mentioned.'' Jade's face was the picture of innocence—damned woman was all but batting her eyes at Skip. ''But didn't that article say this is the first big contract that Norinal ever landed?''

Drew couldn't help it. He grinned as Skip spluttered

and tried to redeem himself in Jade's eyes. "Now, you have to understand, we're moving up now and..."

"I'm not trying to cast aspersions," Jade said in a comforting voice. "The report was pretty complimentary otherwise. But it did mention that it's a delicate time for Norinal Machines. Any problems with the contract and it could wipe you out completely. It also mentioned that you'd leveraged everything to get the contract, and now...well, I suppose that would suggest you're in some financial straits."

Skip looked at her, obviously shocked.

I guess your newly redecorated office isn't enough to win the lady over, Skip. Drew grinned broadly.

"I'd hardly call it financial straits," Skip said, crossing his arms. A little vein was sticking out on his forehead, Drew noticed.

"I imagine financial reports can be deceiving. And those sorts of articles are designed to put a bad face on things, especially for smaller companies trying to get bigger."

Drew felt less triumphant. She was being nice to the guy—too nice. Skip was, let's face it, a jerk who was just about to try to hamstring Robson Steel for preferential treatment. What was she getting at?

"I'm glad you understand, Ms. Morrow," Skip said, his voice grateful.

"Of course. Robson Steel has been getting some bad press lately, as well," she said neatly. "And you, of all people, should know that they've lived up to their commitments of timely orders, rush orders, all with that same quality."

"Ah, yes, of course," Skip agreed.

"And if you changed over to a bigger supplier," she said, and Drew saw her eyes go a little lower-lidded, "you might be ignored, and your shipments might be put in jeopardy because you weren't...shall we say, the biggest fish in the pond?"

Skip's eyes widened as the truth of her words hit. "I...hmm. You might have a point there."

"I'm just saying...smaller companies ought to stick together." Her lips curved into a friendly smile. "That way, the growth of one helps the growth of the other. It's in both Robson Steel's and Norinal Machines' best interest to continue working together."

Skip stared at her, then straightened. "And of course, Robson Steel has always had a great working relationship with us. We'd hope to continue with that tradition..."

"We won't be able to give you all the discounts and freebies you've been promised in the past," Drew said in a flat voice.

Jade shot him a quick glare. He ignored it. This was just a waste of time. Skip would just insist on the usual kickbacks, and Drew wasn't about to give in on that one.

Skip's eyes turned mutinous, and his mouth pulled into a small line. "Well, I still think..."

"The advantages of the working relationship are more than just a few discounts, though, don't you think?" Jade's smile was ingenuous, and Drew watched as Skip was temporarily derailed. "You've bought only relatively small shipments from Robson Steel in the past. Now, you've got a big contract...and you're going to want the best products in the most reliable and quick timeframe. So why would you want to press for a few concessions that really don't mean much, now that Norinal Machines is in the big leagues?"

Skip seemed to mull it over. Then, to Drew's surprise, he started nodding.

''I think,'' Skip said, still looking at Jade and almost ignoring Drew completely, ''that we'll be able to work something out.''

JADE SANG ''We are the Champions'' in the shower, loud and proudly off-key. The Nevada heat had practically wilted her in her power suit, but in the air-conditioned cold of the conference room at Norinal, she'd scored her first big win for the Robson account. Drew had walked away with a two-year contract to continue providing for Norinal Machines, with no discounts or freebies...and it was a larger order than Robson had ever received. Thank God that steel magazine had a Web site. She'd managed to do a fair amount of research in a short amount of time. She doubted the rest of their clients would be that easy, but the point was, her methods *worked.* Now she had proof.

Drew had certainly been floored. He had barely said a word to her the whole way back from Norinal Machines to their hotel. He'd said he needed a shower, even though he'd looked a lot cooler than she'd felt. He was also a lot more subdued than she was. Of course, he wasn't the one who had just landed the sale.

She'd forgotten how juiced up she got after a win.

So she'd agreed that they both clean up, but insisted that they meet for dinner and get back to work...his next customer was small, but it was probably the perfect testing ground for him to try out a few techniques. Nothing drastic. Still, she was really looking forward to seeing what he could do once he got a few basic sales skills down.

She got dressed, still humming, doing impromptu little dance moves in her happiness. It was coming together. She was doing it. Robson Steel was going to be a success, and Drew was going to get just what he wanted—a thriving company. And she was going to be an account supervisor. It was better than Christmas.

She walked down the hallway to Drew's room, wearing a sundress and sandals, her still-damp hair up in a loose bun. She knocked. "Drew? You ready for a little dinner and a little conversation?"

He took a long time opening the door, and when he did, she was surprised to find he wasn't ready. He was still wearing the same khakis and shirt, and if anything, he looked ill.

She stepped in, letting the door shut behind her. "What's wrong?"

"I don't feel like dinner. And I really don't feel like conversation." His tone was curt, and his arms were crossed. His light blue eyes were bright with intensity. "Maybe we should just pick up in the morning."

She frowned. Drew's vibe of displeasure was overwhelming. She supposed she could let him stew in it...but damn it, she'd done well today. Besides, retreat wasn't exactly a Jade Morrow trademark.

"You don't look too happy for a guy who just landed a two-year contract," she said.

"I didn't just land a two-year contract." The sharp angles of his face seemed even harsher in the poor hotel lighting. "You just landed it."

She waited, but he stopped there, just staring at her. "You're welcome?" She tried smiling.

He glared at her.

She sat on the edge of the bed, letting out a huff of irritation. "Okay. Spit it out. What is up with you? I did what I promised. I showed you that my techniques work. You said that you'd give me a chance. Is this your idea of backing up your word?" She quirked her head, studying him. "Because if it is, you suck at it."

"Your technique?" He rolled his eyes. "I suppose that's your version of asking for mustard and ketchup—use that *damned sexy honesty,* and the guys will do anything you ask, huh?"

She blinked at him. "Oh, no. Tell me you're not going there."

"You were doing everything but pouring that guy coffee. You were hanging on his every word," Drew said, and Jade felt the pit of her stomach turn to ice. "You were cooing over the guy like he was some kind of star quarterback and you were a cheerleader. So yeah, you landed the sale. The thing is, I don't know how you plan to 'teach' me your techniques when I don't have a D cup!"

She stood, adrenaline pumping through her system like a flash flood. "You son of a bitch. You think that I only got that sale because of my looks? Because I've got a good body?"

He sent a searing look over her, surveying from head to toe. "I'm just saying you did what you had to do to prove me wrong. You did what you had to do to get the sale."

"I did what I always do to get the sale," she countered, her hands clenching into fists.

"I'm sure you did," he replied. His tone was not complimentary.

She wanted to hit him. She wanted to slap that look of anger and derision off of his chiseled face. "Let me see if I understand this," she said, her voice low and icy. "I gave you a sale today. But not because I did research, made a logical argument, or used any sales techniques like showing why we were preferable or knowing what the customer needed, or anything that could be taught. I only got him to agree to a two-year deal because he liked how my cleavage looked.'' She took a deep breath. ''Is that what you're saying?''

He didn't say anything, but she saw his jaw muscles clench. He stared at her. Then, finally, he spoke up.

''Tell me. Honestly. You may be good at what you do, but if you were ugly, or a man...I just don't know.''

All thoughts of restraint—of sanity—left in that instant. ''I see. Well. Let me share something with you, Mr. Robson.''

With that, she grabbed the front of his shirt and half tugged, half pushed him, until he lost his balance and fell onto the bed. She saw the look of surprise the second before she pounced on him, all arms, lips and anger.

It was a sensual attack. It wasn't sexual, it wasn't even hot. It was angry, and bitter, and intense. He was accusing her of using her body to get what she wanted...using her looks to ''get away'' with something he couldn't. She'd heard the argument before, either whispered behind her back or snidely hinted at to her face, in more situations than she'd care to remember. Now, from a man she was trying so hard to help, it was more than she could bear.

I'll show you how a woman uses her body to get what she wants.

She attached her mouth to his, her lips heated, her tongue probing. She wanted to make him want her, force him to feel something. She wanted to hurt him the way he'd just hurt her. She was feral, a primal force. She felt as if she could kill him with passion if she weren't careful.

She didn't want to be careful.

He hadn't reacted at first, was simply stiff in shock as she started. But slowly, insidiously, she could feel his body reacting. His muscles, tensed almost for battle, eased, allowing her to mold herself to him. She straddled him, one hand gripping his shoulder, the other cupping the side of his face, holding him to her. His back bowed slightly, and as she stayed with his mouth, she felt her body press harder against his, her breasts crushing against his chest. She could feel more than hear his rumbling sigh.

She didn't know when the attack shifted. She was getting confused. She was angry, and hurt, and distraught. But when his lips started playing against hers, matching fierceness for fierceness, when their tongues tangled and his hands clutched her hips and she felt him grow hard between her legs, she started to feel other things. She felt her body start to instinctively react, growing hot…anger turning to pure arousal. And more than that. She felt yearning, wringing through her. She felt like crying. She felt like screaming. Instead, she just kept kissing him, their bodies stroking against each other as each moved. She buried her fingers in the hair at the nape of his neck as she pulled him to her, closer. His breathing was uneven, ragged as hers.

She felt his hand smooth down her hip…and reach for the hem of her skirt.

Jade. What are you doing?

She pulled away, almost throwing herself off of him.

He sat up abruptly, his eyes looking dazed. "Jade, wait…"

"*That* is what my body is capable of." She put a

hand to her chest, feeling her heart beating wildly…and feeling the ache behind it, as what she'd just done started to sink in. Sexual frustration warred with shame. "If I'd wanted to use my body to convince that guy Skip, I could have gotten him to order *ten* years' worth of steel, Drew. I could have gotten him to invest in your company. I could have made him do *anything.* So tell me again. Do you really think I used my body to get what I wanted?"

He stared at her, his breathing still rasping. "Jade…"

She pointed at him. "You're just like all those other jerks who think that I've got a pretty face and a hot body and nothing else. You think I'm incapable of getting anything without using my looks. News flash, Drew. I don't play that way. I don't *need* to. I'm not going to pretend that I don't know what I look like. And I'm not going to change how I look and wear sackcloth just to prove to idiots like you that I've got a mind, too. And whether you want to admit it or not, my mind is what got you the sale this afternoon, Drew!"

Drew's blue eyes were dilated, so large they almost looked black. "Now wait a minute…"

"Don't. Just…don't. This conversation is finished." With that, she turned and stormed out, back to her own room. She had just about unlocked the door when the tears started. She locked it behind her.

What the hell have I done?

She had tackled a client. She'd made an ass of herself. She'd lost the account, and her promotion, and what the hell, let's just throw in some self-respect while we're at it, huh?

She felt sick.

She paced for a minute, her breathing shallow, her stomach queasy. She needed to talk to someone. Obviously not Betsy—with news like this? Jade couldn't believe what she'd just done.

No. This called for someone closer than that. She picked up her cell phone.

After four rings she heard the answering machine pick up. "You know who you've reached...and you know why I can't answer the phone. Talk to you later."

Jade waited for the beep, then took a deep breath. "Hailey? I figure you're bartending tonight, but whatever time you get in, could you call me? I really need to talk. If I don't answer, check your e-mail. It's important."

She hung up. She should have known Hailey would be at work. Unfortunately, there wasn't really anybody else she felt she could talk to.

She climbed onto the hotel bed, turning on the television with the remote and staring at the screen blankly. She would have to figure out how to get to the nearest airport. She would have to figure out how to explain this to Betsy. She would have to figure out how to save her career. She would have to figure this out alone.

She had gone through worse alone, she thought as channel after channel flashed across the television screen. She would get through this.

DREW PACED THE CONFINES of his hotel room, holding his cell phone. "Ken, she's got to go."

He heard Ken sigh over the crackle of static. "What happened?"

Drew flashed mentally to seeing her descend on him, before his eyes had closed and his body had drowned in sensation. He couldn't talk about that, not to Ken. Hell, he could barely get a grip on it himself.

"I just don't think she should be here. If we've got to pay the contract, we'll pay the damned contract, but I don't need to hear a bunch of bull about creative listening or sales techniques or anything. It's just crap. I don't need it."

Ken paused for a second. "So. No sales."

Drew cleared his throat. "We got a sale," he admitted reluctantly.

"Really?" Ken's voice immediately went from grim to elated. "How good?"

"Two year. From Norinal." Drew shook his head. "But that's not the point. The point here is..."

"Two years?" Ken interrupted. "You're kidding? Oh, wait. Norinal. Those are those bandits the sales guys had to bribe. How much of the store did we have to give away to get that one?"

Drew was really starting to feel uncomfortable—and irritated. "Ken, would you focus here?"

"That bad, huh?"

"We didn't give away anything. No freebies, no discounts. It's a straight two-year deal."

"No kidding. Is it a small order?"

Drew gave him a number, and ignored Ken's low whistle. "Ken, would you focus?" he finally snapped.

"Why aren't you happier about this?"

"I'm glad we got the sale," Drew said. "I wasn't even expecting it. I just wrote it off."

Ken was silent for a second. Then he said slowly, "I almost hate to ask, but...did the woman who now 'has to go' have anything to do with the sale?"

"That's not the point here. She's got to go because she doesn't have anything useful to teach me."

''Come on, don't be so hard on yourself,'' Ken said, completely misinterpreting his comment. ''You could learn the sales stuff, if you really wanted to.''

Drew rolled his eyes in exasperation, but before he could correct his CFO, Ken plowed forward.

''I'm surprised that you let her work with you this long, honestly. And I'm glad she helped land the sale. In the first place—well, damn, you know we need the money. But you've always had a chip on your shoulder. I honestly figured you'd have her on the first bus out of town at Montecito.''

''It's not because she's a woman,'' Drew said, wondering sickly if it was. He knew that he thought she'd played up to Skip. He'd been furious, and he hadn't wanted to think why. Was that it, though? Was he just a bigoted...

''No, not because she's a woman,'' Ken said with a small laugh. ''Because she's a consummate salesperson. The only person I've ever seen that was smoother than her when it came to closing the deal was your father.''

Drew felt his chest clench. ''What?''

''You always hated it when your father got into salesman mode. You always thought the product was enough.''

''I still think that,'' Drew muttered.

''Yeah, well, the product is what keeps the sale. But sometimes you need more than that to get in the door. I think your coach just proved that—a two-year with Norinal with no freebies? That's unprecedented.'' Drew could hear Ken's impressed tone over the phone. ''So do me a favor? No more talk about getting rid of her. I think she could be the best thing that ever happened to you, and more important, to Robson Steel.''

Drew winced. He'd been balking at her techniques, and her sales techniques. And he'd felt something else—close to jealousy—when she'd talked to Skip. He wasn't going to think about that now. But Ken was showing him that it wasn't Jade that was the problem. It was him, Drew, that was gumming up the works.

Too bad he hadn't talked to Ken before he'd shot his mouth off.

"Well, I won't bring it up," Drew said, then realized—Jade might have other ideas.

"Good. Because without her help, I don't know if we're going to make it."

Now Drew really started to feel his nerves fray a little. "What if she just decides not to stay, though?"

Ken laughed. "Are you kidding? That woman's a pit bull. It would take an army to get her to back off."

"I don't know."

Ken's laughter stopped abruptly. "What did you do?"

Drew closed his eyes. Ken knew him too well. "We had a fight after the sale."

"*After* the sale?" Ken's voice cracked. "What, are you nuts? You should've been down on your knees thanking her! What in the world were you fighting about?"

"It's not really important. Well…I might have made some comments on how she handled the sale. I made some comments." Drew paused. "Bad comments."

Ken didn't say anything, but Drew knew he was waiting.

"Like comments about her being a woman and getting the sale," Drew finished.

Another moment of silence from Ken, then, ‘‘As in, I-should-be-getting-the-lawyer-on-the-phone comments?’’

‘‘I don’t think it’ll come to that.’’ Especially not after her chosen method of retaliation. He could still feel her, all smooth skin and hot, mobile mouth. He didn’t know that he’d ever forget that sensation.

‘‘Can you patch it up?’’

‘‘I don’t know. It was a really bad fight.’’ Drew thought about it. ‘‘I don’t know if she even wants to talk to me.’’

‘‘Tough shit.’’ Ken’s voice turned gravelly, less like the benevolent executive he’d become and more like the factory worker he’d grown up as. ‘‘Grovel if you have to. But if she’s going to save Robson Steel, you can afford to lose a little pride. The factory, Drew. That’s the only thing that matters.’’

‘‘All right, all right. I’ll take care of it.’’

‘‘Good. Tell me how it goes. And for God’s sake…keep it together.’’ With that, Ken hung up unceremoniously.

Drew took a deep breath and walked out of his room, heading to Jade’s door.

‘‘Jade?’’ Drew knocked on her door, calling softly. ‘‘Jade, please let me in. I need to talk to you.’’

He thought he heard her stepping up to the doorway, probably peering through the peephole. He held his breath. Then he heard the latch slide, and she opened the door.

‘‘It’s late, Drew.’’

She was wearing a long T-shirt and a pair of sweats. Her hair was pulled into a makeshift ponytail, and she wasn’t wearing any makeup. The slight dusting of freckles that her makeup normally covered was peeking out at him from underneath green eyes that looked way too tired.

"I know. I'm sorry," he said apologetically. "I didn't wake you, did I?"

She didn't answer. He didn't think she'd been sleeping, either. She had dark shadows under her eyes. Maybe she'd been crying. He felt his stomach churn. God, he hoped she hadn't been crying. Making a woman as tough as Jade Morrow cry was practically a felony. If anything, he felt worse.

"I just want to talk to you," he said.

Her eyebrow went up; she still held the door.

"And apologize. I really need to apologize, Jade."

She sighed, then walked into her room. He followed, shutting the door behind him.

She sat on the edge of the bed, then looked at him expectantly.

He cleared his throat. "I was angry that you managed the sale," he said without preamble. "I was angry that I'd screwed things up so badly. And I'll be honest—I didn't like the way that guy was looking at you or talking to you. And you didn't seem to mind at all. In fact, you..." He paused. "I *felt like* you were using it to your advantage."

"If I felt insulted every time a guy gave me a once-over, I'd be permanently pissed off, Drew," Jade said, her voice weary. "If he'd gone further than that, I would have stopped him cold. But he was just trying to show off, show he was better than me. And show that he was too important for Robson Steel to play straight with. I didn't take it personally. Instead, I let him keep his pride, while showing him that if he didn't go with Robson, odds were good that he'd be screwed and he'd be kicked out of his newly redecorated office by the end of the year."

Drew winced. Yeah, she'd done that. Neatly. Professionally.

"I am sorry," he said, and he meant it.

She kept quiet for a moment, then looked at him, her eyes enormous, with a sheen of moisture that she quickly blinked away. "I've taken a lot of crap from clients. Ordinarily, it doesn't affect me this way," she said, and he was amazed at how casual her voice stayed, at odds with her expression. "I let you get to me. It won't happen again."

He wanted to sit next to her, to take her into his arms, to comfort her for the hurt he himself had caused. But he thought it would just damage matters more. "I was a jerk," he said instead. "I was a complete ass. I felt stupid and threatened, and I just went after the easy insult. I didn't want to admit that you were right."

She cocked her head. "Are you admitting I was right now?"

He nodded. "You got that sale on your own," he said. "You did it with finesse. Hell. You did it with *class*. I could definitely take lessons from you."

She smiled weakly. "Well. At least that's a step in the right direction." She stood up, walking over to him, and put her hand out. "Then let's make a bargain of our own. For the next three weeks we have left, you listen to me. You actually *work* with me. None of this patronizing, none of this pretended open-mindedness. You're going to work harder with me than you ever have with anyone in your entire life."

He took her hand. "Deal."

Her grip tightened, surprising him. "And if you ever, *ever* insinuate that I'm using my body or my looks to land a sale,'' she said, her voice still casual although the fire in her green eyes was anything but, ''I will make you the sorriest man alive.''

He nodded. ''Deal.''

''Great.'' She let go of his hand, then motioned to the door.

''Ah, there's one other thing,'' he said.

''What?''

She was looking less hurt. He wondered if he was going to make things worse—but damn it, it was something that had to be dealt with. They were going to be on the road together, and working in pretty close quarters, for the next few weeks. Better to talk about it now and get it over with.

''The kiss, Jade,'' he said. He couldn't help it, his voice thickened a little.

She sighed. ''Now that's something I need to apologize for. I've never...'' She cleared her throat and looked away from him for a moment. Then she looked at him, the clear, direct gaze he was used to. ''I have a policy of not getting involved with my clients. I certainly have never harassed one before. I sincerely apologize.''

''I sort of brought it on,'' Drew muttered.

''There is absolutely no excuse,'' Jade replied. She obviously felt guilty...her face had gone pale. ''I can assure you of one thing—it won't ever happen again.''

The wave of regret that that announcement caused hit Drew with a wallop. ''I, uh...well.''

What was he going to say? *I didn't mind at all. In fact, I was hoping we could try it under different circumstances. How's next Tuesday for you?*

''Let's just pretend it didn't happen,'' he said finally. ''Start over. Clean slate.''

She smiled and he could see the tension release from her. She almost sank onto the bed. "Clean slate."

The fact that she felt better made him feel better, at least. Well, part of him felt better.

She got up, walked over to the door and opened it. "You'd better get some sleep. Tomorrow's going to be a long drive, and we're going to be starting your coaching for real. Your brain is going to be tapioca before I'm finished with you."

He grinned. "I'm not afraid of you."

"You will be," she said, winking.

He paused in her door frame. He was going to kick himself for this, but… "Before we go completely clean slate, I want to make one comment. Then it's behind us for good."

She looked as though she was bracing herself against the door. "Yes?"

He thought twice about it, then went ahead and said it. "I believe you."

"You believe me, what?"

"The way you kiss," Drew said quietly, "you could've gotten anybody in the world to do anything you wanted."

He waited, studying her reaction.

Then, slowly, she smiled.

"Since our clean slate starts tomorrow, I guess I can add this," she said, her voice going smooth and tinged with laughter as she nudged him out the door. "You should see me when I'm really trying."

She closed the door, leaving him in the hallway, grinning…and, not surprisingly, turned on as all hell.

"Well, you asked for it, you idiot," he muttered to himself, then went back to his empty room with a rueful grin.

5

IT WAS THREE DAYS P.K., or Post Kiss. They'd visited two small clients who had duly re-upped their order for the following year with little or no persuasion on Drew's part. Jade had been introduced as a consultant and colleague. She'd been talking with Drew about business every single day in the car, but once they got to their hotel, they usually went to their respective rooms. Often they were right next door to each other. She wasn't sure if the kiss had anything to do with the decision to keep to themselves every evening, but they were running out of time. She had his agreement to work with her, and she couldn't afford to waste a minute.

She stared at his hotel room door, taking a deep breath.

I can't remember when I've been this nervous before.

She meant that, too. Her palms actually felt a little sweaty. She'd certainly never felt this way meeting with a client before.

Of course, I've never actually kissed a client before, either.

And she'd never kissed a client, or kissed *anybody,* who came remotely close to Drew Robson.

She replayed the kiss at odd times. Like she was in high school, mooning over the first guy she'd ever kissed, she thought with derision. There would be a lull in their intensely focused conversations, and she'd find herself staring out the window, brushing her lips with her fingertips. Remembering the feel of his lips against hers, the way he turned what was meant to be a harsh, punishing action and coaxing her to relax. He'd all but seduced her with the brush of his lips, the feel of him, the taste of him as her tongue stroked against his. Then they were on the bed, the hardness of his chest beneath her. The hardness of *him* between her thighs, making her want to scream with wanting.

It was insane, to say the least. No wonder she was hesitant to go to his hotel room, for whatever the reason.

Just put it out of your mind. This is too important.

She put her hand up to the door.

Game on, Jade.

She knocked.

He opened it almost immediately. He was wearing his usual jeans and a T-shirt, and his hair was mussed. His eyes were candle-bright as he surveyed her. "Hi, there. I thought you were room service."

"Nope." She forced a smile. "If you've got the time, I thought we'd go over the next customer file, and maybe tie in how your sales strategy is going to apply to your investor meeting."

His grin was quick, and she warmed to it. "Now, how could I turn down an invitation like that? Ugh."

"It won't be that bad," she said, feeling comforted. He was being casual about everything, as if they'd never had their, er, "incident." She was just being weird about the whole thing. She needed to relax, just get past it.

"What'd you order?" She settled herself in the

chair. The hotel was almost exactly like the last hotel they stayed in, she noted...the same Navajo-white walls, similar tacky bedspread, even the same televisions that were often chained to the tables. Or worse, the remotes chained to the nightstands.

"I got the caviar," Drew joked, leaning against the dresser. "They're throwing in a grilled cheese sandwich for free."

She chuckled. "I had the goose liver pâté and a tuna melt."

He grinned. "Bright lights, big cities, gourmet food...how are you ever going to adjust to life in Los Angeles?"

"It'll be a letdown, but somehow I'll manage."

He studied her thoughtfully...then, unfortunately, he moved over to the bed, throwing himself across it. He rested his chin on his hands, looking at her. "Do you like it? Los Angeles, I mean."

She wished he wasn't on the bed. She crossed her legs primly, ignoring the slight ache just looking at his lean form stretched out on the mattress. "Ah...L.A.? I like it, I guess."

"So you're not from there, huh?"

"No. I grew up closer to San Diego." She'd brought a diet cola that she'd bought at the vending machine, and she walked over to his bucket of ice, studiously avoiding looking at him as she poured her soda into a glass. "Nice, but boring. I went to school in San Francisco, then moved to L.A. when I got the job. That's about it."

"They're all very different cities. Do you have a favorite?"

She frowned. "I never really thought about it that way. I had fun in college. I used to have fun in Los

Angeles, but now..." She shrugged. "When you're in an office, I guess it doesn't really much matter which city you're in."

She hadn't really meant to say that last bit, but now that she thought about it, it seemed true enough. "Why don't we get back to..."

He stopped her with a quiet question. "Is there just work in your life, Jade?"

"That's kind of a personal question, isn't it?" She laughed a little, to take the sting out of her comment. She was working hard to build rapport with him. Still, considering how personal they'd gotten with that kiss the other night, she wasn't sure she wanted to start sharing too much.

"Tell you what," he said with a conspiratorial wink. "I won't tell anyone, and then you can ask me a personal question."

"Quid pro quo, huh?" She looked at the sheaf of papers and file folders she'd brought in with her. "I think we ought to focus on your client tomorrow instead. Jacoby Construction? Ring a bell?"

He groaned, burying his face in a pillow. "You're a machine," he said in a muffled voice. He unearthed himself enough to look at her, his blue eyes full of mischief. "You've got to do something for fun."

"I discipline businessmen. Usually with a whip," she said wryly, wiggling her eyebrows. "Come on, now. Stay focused."

"That brings up a question," he responded, and now she groaned. "Why P.R.? I imagine you'd be good in any kind of business. Why would you get into something like public relations?"

"I don't think I like the way you say 'public relations.'" She laughed, shaking her head. "It's as if you're saying, 'gee, you're a nice girl. Why are you turning tricks for a living?' or something."

"Well, it just seems like..." He stopped. "Why don't you tell me how you see public relations, then. I'll stop while I'm ahead."

"Finally, the man wises up," she said, taking a sip of her soda and sitting back in her chair, tucking her feet up under her. "I got into public relations because I like the media. When I first was in school, I thought I'd be a newscaster or a journalist or something." She laughed. "Can you imagine? Jade Morrow with your nightly news."

He smiled, his eyes glinting. "I bet I'd catch the five, seven and nine o'clock showings," he murmured.

She warmed, and looked away for a second, trying desperately to get her bearings. "Uh...anyway, I worked in the public relations department of this little publisher one summer. They didn't have any money for advertising, but they believed in what they were doing so much, they got tons of publicity and word of mouth. They really were fantastic. I found out I liked that much more than reporting about murders or just looking good on television. So I got a few jobs, wound up working for Michaels and Associates, and the rest is history."

"That's how you got me." His grin was devilish.

She smiled. "Yeah. That's how I got you."

"I don't know. I guess I thought it might be a family business thing," he said, rolling over onto his back and contemplating the ceiling. She felt a twinge...and before she knew it, she had stood up and walked over to the bed. Gingerly, she perched on the edge of it.

If he makes any sudden or remotely sexy moves, she reassured herself, *I'm out of here.*

But he didn't. He just lay there, with his arms behind his head, staring up at the ceiling with eyes as blue as a summer sky.

"I've wanted to be in steel since I was old enough to go to the plant."

"How old was that?" She scooted back just a few inches, so she wasn't slipping off the bedspread.

"I don't know. Around four, I guess."

"Four?" Just another few inches. She could smell his cologne...something spicy, exotic, an unusual counterpoint to his black Irish looks. "That's unusual, isn't it?"

"I'd like to say I was a steel prodigy," he said, glancing at her finally, "but honestly...I think most boys love the idea of heavy metal and furnaces and loud machinery."

She laughed at his candor, leaning on one arm...getting just a little bit closer to him. "I guess your family must have been proud."

He shook his head. "My grandfather was ecstatic. I think my father...well, I don't know. He was sort of competitive. We never really saw eye to eye."

"That's why you worked somewhere else," she mused.

He looked pained for a second. "Yeah. I felt like a traitor the whole first year I worked for one of our competitors. Still, it was good training. And I guess I knew, deep down, I'd be back at Robson. Only when I got there, I knew I'd be running the place." He grimaced. "I just had no idea it was going to be under these circumstances."

"I'm sure it was a disappointment," she said.

He glanced at her, shaking his head. "I'm not disappointed that it couldn't give me a fortune or anything. I just didn't think I'd be in a position where I might not be able to save it.''

She stared at him for a second. He meant it, every word. He wasn't bitter that he wasn't head of a successful company. He was afraid he couldn't give enough to it.

Her heart warmed. She reached out, stroking the hair out of his eyes, letting her fingertips trail for a second across the smooth skin of his forehead.

''Your plant is very lucky they've got a guy like you in charge,'' she said quietly.

He smiled. She didn't know how a man of his size, practically a giant, still had the heart to smile like that—almost innocently. She wanted to melt into him.

''They're lucky I have you working for me,'' he replied in his low bass voice. ''Not everybody has a bona fide, kick-ass sales coach like I do.''

She shook her head, pulling her hand away. ''And a fine job I'm doing, letting you slack off on the job,'' she said, her voice shaking a little bit. ''We, uh, better go over those customer files, huh?''

''Quick question,'' he said.

''I've let you ask enough questions,'' she evaded, starting to move off of the bed. But his hand on her wrist stopped her. It was a gentle touch, but warm. Very warm. Reluctantly she looked at him.

''Your family,'' he said. ''Are they proud of you?''

She blanched, almost falling off of the bed in her haste. ''I suppose so. It's not something we talk about. Why do you ask?''

''You asked me if mine was.'' He stared at her. ''And you know what my dad is like. That's the biggest problem I have here, I think...getting past that. Embezzlement, leaving the company such a mess. Every time I walk into a meeting, I feel like I've got something to prove.'' He looked at her, his expression quizzical. ''I wondered if you'd even begin to be able to understand what that's like.''

She thought of her parents. ''Honestly, no. My parents…well, they were both busy. It wasn't unusual for Dad to work eighty hours a week at the investment firm, and my mother was a trial lawyer…well, they were busy. But they didn't take anything from me,'' she said hastily. ''They were both…''

She was about to say *supportive,* but found that she couldn't. ''They paid for my education. We're not exactly what anyone would call a close family, but not everybody is.''

He sat up and was staring at her…seeing past her evasions, she felt. ''It must have been lonely.''

She shrugged. ''My best friend Hailey was there. I spent a lot of time with her family.'' She smiled, thinking of the raucous crowd of them at her high school graduation, then at her college one. ''I didn't mind.''

''I see.'' He paused a beat, then said, ''So. Both of your parents were workaholics.''

She nodded. ''Yeah, I suppose you could say…''

Suddenly, she stopped.

When you're in an office, I guess it doesn't really much matter which city you're in.

''What are you getting at?'' She stood, spun, her fists on her hips. ''I know I focus on work, but…''

''Shh.'' He stood and, to her shock, actually put a finger on her lips. She didn't know whether to bite him or to kiss him. He pulled his hand away. ''I'm sorry. I didn't mean to…damn it. I *did* mean to pry.''

''Why?''

"Because I like you, Jade," he said. "And I didn't think I would."

She didn't know what to say to that, so she didn't say anything. "Well..." She sighed. "You might call me a workaholic, but I still think we need to get cracking on that customer file."

"I don't think you're a workaholic. Well, you might be, but I'd be the pot calling the kettle black if I said you were." He smiled. "I'm sorry, really. Friends?"

His smile was winning...but there was something in his eyes that said he'd just started scratching the surface. The client-coach relationship was definitely getting murky—exactly what she *didn't* want.

"Friends," she said instead. "Now can we..."

He surprised her again, this time by stroking her arm, one quick, friendly motion. "All right, all right, you slave driver," he said, his voice joking, his eyes serious. "Where were we?"

We were about a foot from your bed and headed straight for it.

She cleared her throat, sat and grabbed the file folder nearest to her. "We were going to go over your sales points."

And, she thought, we were going to get away from anything remotely personal that would make me feel any closer to you than I already do.

THEY'D BEEN DRIVING all morning and working all afternoon, and Drew was bone-tired from both sitting in the car and racking his brain. He'd spied the junior high school as they were pulling into the motel. More important, he'd spied the basketball courts that were in walking distance. It was now about nine o'clock at night. The school was deserted but the lights stayed on. He bounced his old basketball methodically.

She's really an amazing woman.

He arched his back, then tossed the ball. It ricocheted off of the rim and he trotted over to where it was bouncing.

It was a delicate business, getting to know Jade Morrow. Kind of like waltzing over a minefield. Ever since her impassioned plea, and his subsequent apology, they'd been nervous around each other. That was lessening, but he still wanted to know more about her. Whenever he pressed too close, though, she'd cut him off, burying him in sales details.

He never lost sight of the reason she was there: to help Robson Steel and to help him win over the investors. But the more she taught him, the closer they became. He was learning to trust her. With that came a burning need to know her, who she was, where she came from. Why she was so determined and, when she thought he didn't notice, why she had such an aura of sadness and loneliness. Maybe he was imagining it, but every time they strayed from the sales coaching path, he got more and more of a sense of that underlying feeling.

He wanted to know more about her. The need drove him.

The attraction had been there from the beginning, but as he got closer to her, it had intensified to a fever pitch. It was worse to be in a motel room with her. He often would talk to her stretched out on his stomach to hide the ever-present erection that developed whenever she was in the same room with him. It was insane, he thought ruefully, going for another shot, this time sinking it. It was ludicrous. But he wasn't going to argue with it.

He wanted Jade Morrow more than he wanted almost anything.

He shook his head, taking a deep breath of the cool night air. They were in Colorado, with its cool, rich tree smells...a sharp counterpoint to the desert scents they'd breathed in Nevada and New Mexico. It was a long, tiring trek. He enjoyed the scenery, especially with Jade oohing and aahing over it in the car.

Jade. He bounced the ball. It always came down to her.

You're not going to get anywhere with it. He needed to focus on the job at hand. There was a factory, there was a town that was counting on him. He'd called in, and while Ken was happy about the sales numbers, he was also concerned. Drew could easily tell. Still, the road trip, with a different bed every night, the variations on a theme motel roulette, endless stretches of highway...he felt as if the whole thing was removed from reality. Here, there wasn't a plant headed for bankruptcy, or Ken coldly reminding him of his family duties and responsibilities to Robson Steel and San Angelo. Here, there was only the road, the sales calls...and Jade.

He dribbled, ran for a lay-up, sending the ball spinning from the backboard through the hoop with a loud swish.

Forget Jade. Tire yourself out. Get some sleep.

"Nice shot."

He spun.

Jade was standing there, her fingers laced in the chain-link fence. She was wearing a pair of shorts and a tank top, her legs long and luscious. She was wearing tennis shoes.

"The car ride has been hell on my back," she said with a rueful grin. "I needed the exercise, so I went for a jog. Then I thought you looked familiar."

"Yeah. I felt the same way," he said, sternly telling his body to calm down. He was just wearing a pair of sweats, his shirt tucked into the elastic waistband. If he started getting hard, she was sure to notice.

She walked toward him, her eyes speculative. "Mind if I try?"

He bounced the ball to her. "Do you play?"

She grinned. "I was almost this tall by the time I was eleven," she said. "What do you think?"

He stepped away from the basket. "Be my guest."

She stepped up to the painted line that marked the key, with all the intensity of Michael Jordan. She didn't even spare him a look. She leaned back, then sank one of the sweetest hook shots he'd seen in a long time. He whistled softly.

She sent him a quick, saucy smile. Then proceeded to do three more baskets, in quick succession, from various places around the court. He was torn between admiring her fit, lithe body, and admiring her playing. He figured it was about fifty-fifty.

She wiped at her forehead with the back of her hand, her body arching a little bit, her head tilted back, her eyes closed. Her full mouth curving in a smile.

His body went hard in a rush. *Make that eighty-twenty in favor of her body.*

He grimaced and ran after the ball, bouncing it, facing away from her, trying to get himself back under control. "Well, sure, it's easy to sink baskets when there's nobody in your way," he said, trying to distract her.

He glanced at her over his shoulder. She was grinning, but her eyes were lit with battle. "You wouldn't be talking trash if you played me," she said. "One-on-one. Come on."

"I'm not playing one-on-one with you," he said, and suppressed a laugh. "You're a *girl.*"

She strode up to him, taking the ball, her hair bouncing wildly. "Now you're gonna get it."

He'd hoped she'd say that. Too bad it was the wrong context.

He faced her, confident. She dribbled the ball, her eyes never leaving his. Then she made a quick break, faking him out, and headed for the basket for a quick lay-up. He heard the swoosh, barely, over her shouted, "Yes!"

"One point for me," she said, hardly even winded. She bounced him the ball. "Your turn, slick."

"We're going for—what, fifteen?"

"Twenty," she said with a shrug, then smiled.

He thought briefly about letting her win, then smirked. The way she played, he wasn't going to let her win anything. She would probably come close to winning all on her own.

He grinned. Of course, he'd made All State in high school and was the star player on his team. And yeah, he'd been tall early, as well.

"You're not so tough," he said, grinning, trying to engage her. She was a master at psyching people out—that was sort of what he was paying her to do, he realized.

"Don't need to be tough to beat a guy like you," she countered with a wink.

"Hope you brought your pen and paper," he said, getting into the swing of it. He tried faking her out, but she was on him with lightning reflexes. They weren't touching, but they never broke eye contact. He could feel her, just a foot away, tuned to his every movement.

"Why?" she said. She was breathing a little more heavily now, as she chased him in a tight circle by the hoop, blocking his shot.

"Because I'm taking you to school." With that juvenile taunt in the air, he did a quick turn, sending the ball in an arc for a neat three-point shot from the side of the court. "Sweet. I'll just take one point for that, since we're playing schoolyard rules."

"Tied," she said. "But not for long."

What followed was less half-court basketball and more one-on-one war. The taunting didn't let up, and began to get inventive. She guarded, he faked. He was only three points up on her. He would have been scoring more, he realized, if he wasn't so distracted. He was trying to guard her, but she'd back up and he'd feel the brush of her backside against his groin. He'd get overwhelmed by the sensation of it, pulling away…she had to notice. Not that she showed it. Instead, she'd take the opening and make another point.

This woman is going to kill me, he thought, watching her do a small victory dance as she got a point closer to his score. *But what a way to go.*

"That's seventeen for me," she panted, resting her hands on her knees.

"Yeah, but I'm at nineteen," he said. "I make this shot, I win." He dribbled, judging the distance between him and the hoop…and her, standing there with determination. "You know, you never did say what the stakes were."

"You're just asking because you're winning," she said, laughing. "For the moment, anyway. Why? What do you want?"

He kept dribbling, biting back an improper response. "Hmm. Tempt me with something. I want to make this basket worth my while."

"You tempt me with something," she replied. "That way I'll have the incentive to grab that ball and get this game back."

He smiled. "What do you want?"

"If I win," she said slowly, "you buy me ice cream. Chocolate-chocolate chip. Double scoop."

"You're a cheap date," he said with a grin.

"The most dangerous place on earth for you to stand is between me and a bowl of ice cream," she said with a mock frown. "So what do you want? Or should I say, what are you willing to lose?"

"Huh. Well, when you put it that way…how about a kiss?"

She straightened, her eyes widening. "Excuse me?"

Damn it. He'd said it out loud.

"Nothing. I don't really want anything," he said hastily. "I'd rather just beat you on principle."

She looked at him suspiciously, then got back in her stance. "Bring it on, pal."

He went for the basket. She dogged his every step. Finally he made a full-speed charge for the basket. She jumped in his way as he was making his shot and he inadvertently collided with her, sending her sprawling to the ground even as he made the winning shot.

"Jade! I'm sorry." He stepped close to her as she turned over. "Are you all right? I'm so sorry."

"Fair shot," she said, rubbing her elbow from the ground. "No blood, no foul."

He gave her a hand, tugging her up gently. He didn't release her hand right away. "Are you sure you're all right?"

She nodded. Then, to his surprise, she took a step closer. The curls around her face were damp with sweat and she wasn't wearing any makeup. Her ponytail made her look younger, less sophisticated. More open.

"So...you're satisfied with just winning on principle, huh?"

He was about to respond when it suddenly went dark.

He looked around. "Damn it. Guess the lights were on a timer." He was still holding her hand, he realized. "Jade?"

She was standing there, as if she was waiting. She let go of his hand...but still stood just a few inches away from him.

He thought about the consequences of what he was doing, quickly ignored them, and leaned forward to kiss her.

It was a gentle kiss...at first. He rested his hands on her hips, leaning down, finding her mouth by sheer instinct. Her lips felt like heated satin as he parted his lips and hers gently, savoring the texture of her, the pressure of her lips beneath his. She made a little sighing sound, leaning into him. Then he was kissing her hungrily, his tongue sweeping in to taste the deliciously complex flavor of her. He crushed her against his chest. He could feel her fingers creep to the nape of his neck, tugging his head down, pulling him closer to her.

His erection was painfully hard between them. He could feel her nipples like pebbles through the thin cloth of her tank top. He groaned, moving her so she dragged her breasts lightly across his chest. She moaned, and his hands tightened, pulling her hips to him. The cool night air, the aroma of darkness and pine trees, and the feel of the hot woman beneath his palms was almost more than he could bear.

"Jade," he groaned, pulling his lips away from her lips to press heated kisses against her neck. "Jade."

He shouldn't have spoken. Just like that, she pulled away, her breathing uneven. "Damn it." She didn't sound angry…well, she did sound angry. But it didn't sound as though she was angry at him. "I shouldn't have done that. *We* shouldn't have done that."

"Like hell," he said.

"I told you I was going to keep this professional," she said apologetically. "I'm sorry."

"I'm not," he said, taking her hand, pulling her back for a moment and kissing her. But he felt her tugging away, and he let go. "Jade, what's so wrong with this?"

"You're a client, for one thing," she said. "And I'm…I guess I'm just confused."

He could make out her silhouette in the light of the crescent moon. Her eyes looked black in the moonlight. "Jade, I don't want to confuse you or do anything you don't want to do. But I have to tell you…I've never wanted a woman the way I want you."

"I know the feeling," she said softly. "That's why I'm confused."

He took a deep breath, then turned away.

"Why don't you take a night to sleep on it?" He couldn't believe he was saying this. He wanted her…he was so close to having her. But she sounded so upset. He didn't want her like that. If he pressed things, there would be recriminations…regrets. He didn't want that.

"We've got an early start tomorrow," she said, her voice still shaky. "I guess I'll go get some sleep."

"Okay." Even though the last thing he wanted to think about was sales, or the plant...or tomorrow, for that matter. "Good night, Jade."

She hesitated for the briefest second, then replied, "Good night."

He watched her walk toward the lights of the motel, and all he could think was, *I'd give anything in the world for her to be walking with me.*

"WE'RE READY FOR YOU, Mr. Robson." Jackie Augustine, co-owner of Augustine's Specialized Trucks, motioned to them with an engaging smile.

Jade watched as Drew took a deep breath, his jaw clenching slightly. "Great. We'll be right in."

"You're going to do great," she whispered just before they walked into the meeting room. "Don't be nervous."

He looked at her, his eyes like arctic pools, a light teal blue. "I'm not nervous. Why? Do I look nervous?"

She fought not to roll her eyes. "No. You look fantastic."

As she said it, she realized she wasn't lying—he really did look good. Not his usual "casual chic," she thought with satisfaction. He was wearing khakis with a light cream denim shirt, only this time he'd added a blazer and a subtly striped tie. He'd also given all his clothes a pass with the iron, she noted. It might seem silly and girlish, and he'd protested, but looks really did make a difference.

He turned and headed for the conference room. The guy had great shoulders. And let's face it...although it was partially hidden by the blazer, the guy had a nice ass. She grinned, thinking, *I hate to see you go…but I love to watch you leave.*

She abruptly caught herself, sobered. It had been hard not to think of him in those terms. She'd always considered him attractive, that was a no-brainer. Scratch that. She'd considered him sexy enough to make her breathless. Still, there was a big difference between window-shopping and actually buying something. She had admired only—there was a line in the sand that prevented her from doing anything else.

Then she'd been stupid enough to kiss the guy, and her common sense? That had flown right out the proverbial window. She'd gone from window-shopping to…well, she figured it was more like a test drive. She hadn't actually *bought* anything, as it were.

Not yet. And considering he was her client, she reminded herself sternly, not *ever.*

She settled herself at the small conference room table. He hadn't hired her to admire his ass and kiss him on darkened basketball courts. He'd signed on with Michaels & Associates because they were the best, and they would help his company. Rather, he'd agreed to let *her* honor the contract with Robson Steel, because he thought *she* would help his company.

Now was her chance to see if her coaching would help, or if she'd have to try something else. And they were both running out of time to try other options.

Drew sat. His face was calm, even if the slight jitters of his hand fidgeting with his gold pen betrayed some of the nerves beneath the facade. "I was hoping we could start with a dialogue," he said, just as she'd taught him.

Let them do most of the talking, she thought, encouraging him with her eyes. He nodded, as if he heard her mental missive and was acknowledging it.

"Why don't you tell me how your relationship with my company has been going so far? What's made you happy, what could use work?"

Jackie looked at her husband, Frank. Frank started talking, using his work-worn hands to gesture. "We like what you've been able to provide for us...we get our stuff, on time. Still, we feel like little fish in a big pond. You're the first head honcho to come out our way in a long time. Usually we get junior salespeople who don't know a thing, trying to sell us stuff we don't need."

"I hate that," Drew said, and the sincerity was obvious.

"Yeah, well, so do we," Frank said, and proceeded at length to go into detail about the parts he needed. Then Jackie tagged in with some observations about the service or lack thereof they'd received from Robson Steel.

"Wow." Drew frowned. "I didn't know this was going on."

Jade winced. She never would've admitted something like that to a customer. At least, not that way. He sounded so...so *hick.* She tried to will him to look at her, but he only had eyes for the two Augustines.

Which is how it should be, she thought. Still, she was there as his coach. He ought to at least be paying attention to some of her cues!

She was quickly starting to feel out of place at the meeting. Drew took off his blazer and slung it along the back of his chair. He also rolled up his sleeves and tugged his tie looser, until it hung from him like a slack rope. He looked like a private school kid, just out of school. His face was furrowed in concentration as he stared at the diagrams that Frank had pulled out over his wife's objections.

"Well, you shouldn't be paying this much for parts, is some of the problem," Drew said, and Jade quailed.

He's screwing this up. Oh, man, is he screwing this up. He was telling them to reduce their order, to start. And now he was pointing out every place his salespeople had ripped them off, and how the reason their orders were late was because they weren't told the right dates to begin with.

This was going horribly, horribly wrong.

"Um, Drew?" She motioned to him. "Can I talk to you for a second?"

He had been deep in thought, and he looked up at her. "Can't it wait? I think we're really getting to the bottom of this here."

She shrugged. "You're the client," she mouthed.

He smiled. "Trust me," he mouthed back, when the Augustines weren't looking.

She felt a little shiver go through her. Trust him? She was in enough trouble with her attraction. If she added trust to the mix, where would she be?

After an hour, they paused to take a break. Jackie went to get some sodas, and Frank left to grab a few more notes. "What are you doing?" Jade snapped.

Drew blinked at her. "What do you mean, what am I doing?"

"You're not selling to these people, you're basically doing a character assassination on your own company!"

He frowned. "You said to acknowledge and accept their problems with Robson," he said in a patient voice.

"Acknowledge, yes!" She felt like strangling him. "Point out even more flaws, no!"

"Well, it's not working for them," he argued. "They never should've gotten a deal like this. I think the salesperson working with them was out of his mind. And I'm not going to lie to them."

"I'm not asking you to..."

"Jade," he said firmly, touching her chin with his fingertips and angling her face up to his, "I'm not going to do anything I don't feel right about. They're a smaller company, and they're struggling. I want to save Robson, sure. But I'm not going to take prisoners to do it, so don't ask me to."

She fell silent, mesmerized by both the heat of his fingertips and the heat of his conviction. He released her face, and Frank walked in.

"Here it is," Frank said. "Do you really think we could streamline the way we get parts?"

"Sure," Drew said, turning away from Jade. And she watched him hunker down with the Augustines.

If I'm not careful, I could be in real trouble here.

Jade hadn't met anybody like Drew, especially not in Los Angeles or in her line of work. He had scruples. He believed in helping people. She was here for a promotion.

But didn't you take this on because you believed in Robson Steel?

No, she thought suddenly. She'd taken it on because she believed in him.

She needed to get a little distance. They'd been on the road for...what, two weeks? That was plenty of time to lose perspective. Maybe she'd tell him that she needed to work on her own stuff tonight. Working with him, driving with him, spending every meal with him was enough to make anybody a little loopy. And when you were spending almost twenty-four hours a day with a guy like Drew Robson, who had enough sexual magnetism to cause fainting spells in a five-mile radius, well…a girl was likely to start thinking things she shouldn't.

She wasn't just any faint-hearted girl, though.

She focused on the conversation. Jackie was obviously bowled over by Drew, as well, although the looks she was sending him were mostly of overwhelming gratitude. Jade felt a little better—and a little guilty, for thinking he was on the wrong path.

"You really care," Jackie said, her voice a little choked up around the edges. "You're not like those other guys."

"Believe me," Jade said. "He's not like any other guy I know."

Drew looked over at her, and smiled…one of those mind-bending smiles.

"Well, I was going to kick you out of here, Drew. We've done some research from some other plants, who offered better prices. But from what you've gone through with us, I can see you really know what you're talking about."

"I appreciate that, Frank," Drew said. "I'm just sorry it took us this long to straighten things out."

"We're going to continue working with you, based on what we talked about today. That does mean a smaller part order and a change in the process."

"That's fine," Drew said. And Jade felt a strong stab of pride. He really meant it. It really was fine…because it was better for the Augustines.

"I will say this, though," Frank said, standing and shaking Drew's hand. "I'm going to tell all of my other suppliers, and some of my friends, about you and your plant. I thought guys like you went the way of the dodo."

Drew laughed. Jade just smiled. She'd thought decent guys were extinct, too. *Who knew?*

After wrapping up the meeting, Drew walked with Jade out to the car, taking his tie off and stuffing it in his pocket. "That was better than I thought it would be."

"You were great, ace," she said, then stopped him. "So. How does it feel to land your first sale?"

His eyes widened. "That's right. I really did nail that one on my own, didn't I?"

She laughed. "Yup. All by your lonesome."

"I wasn't even thinking of it as landing a sale. I just thought about it as fixing a problem," he said. She grinned at the tone of wonder in his voice. Then, before she knew what he was going to do, he swept her up, spinning her as though she were a rag doll.

"Whoa!"

"Yes!" His voice rang out in the parking lot. "Damn! That was easy!"

"Yeah, well, it's not going to be all downhill from here—"

"Have dinner with me."

She stopped, in the middle of her advice. "Sorry. What?"

"Have dinner with me," he coaxed. His eyes glowed and his hands were still resting lightly on her hips. She ought to tell him to stop, but her mouth seemed to have numbed temporarily. "I want to celebrate. I feel like I owe you at least dinner for helping me get to the point where a sales call wasn't like a dentist's appointment."

"Really, y-you don't owe me anything," she stammered, thinking, *His hands, broad-palmed, long-fingered hands are on my hips...* She shook her head a few times to clear it. "Just doing my job, you know?"

He leaned down until he was eye level with her, and damn if he didn't take his hands away. "Please?"

She was hypnotized by his proximity. She could feel the heat of him and all she could think of was the dark, just a few nights before...of his mouth on hers, her lifting up to meet him, the strength of his arms around her, the heat of him in the coolness of the evening air...

"I really... I..." She cleared her throat. "Oh, all right. Let's celebrate."

His smile was like a blowtorch, hot and blinding. "All right. I'll take you back to the hotel to get cleaned up, and then we'll go paint the town. Such as it is."

She nodded, smiling back, but when he released her she almost slumped over, to her intense embarrassment.

Gorgeous guys, she could deal with. Gorgeous, honest, decent guys...well, they were a little more of a challenge.

Guys like Drew?

She watched as he winked at her before getting into the car.

She was in trouble tonight. She had never been this tempted by a client before. And this time, she had the serious suspicion that it wasn't just her body that was reacting.

6

DREW WAS SITTING at the bar of the hotel restaurant. It was a pretty nice restaurant, and it looked as if there was a sort of dance floor off to one side. He was waiting for Jade. He forced himself not to look at his watch.

He'd already taken a long, relatively cool shower, and he was on his second glass of wine...and he still felt like he could wrestle an alligator and win. Then, he'd probably move on to racing a speeding bullet, or pulling a locomotive, or something. He was jumped up on today's sale. Truth be told, he was riding high on more than that.

He looked up and saw Jade walking toward him. Even the way she strutted was sexy, her hips undulating gently, riveting the gaze of every guy in viewing distance. Her hair was up in a loose knot-thing on top of her head, and curls were framing her face. And her face—oh, baby. *Don't even get me started.*

She was sexy, sensual, beautiful.

Then she smiled at him and that comic-book-hero feeling rushed through him in a wave.

There is nothing sexier than a woman who believes in you.

He stood, holding out a hand to her because it felt natural to do so. She stared at it for a second, then put her hand in his...almost shyly, which he thought was cute.

"You look fantastic," he said in a low voice. He wanted to kiss her. Still, this was supposed to be business—although he was hoping that he could convince her to make it a little more than that.

A lot more than that.

"Thanks," she said, her full lips curving into that sexy half smirk. "You clean up pretty well, yourself."

He gave her hand a friendly squeeze, then let go. *Go slow, don't rush her.* He wanted her, that much was obvious. They wanted *each other.*

Sales fact number 1. You've got to work with what the customer wants, then show how you can accommodate that.

She was the one who taught him, he thought, as the hostess led them to their table. It was only fitting that he use the knowledge she'd imparted to win her over. In the long run, he imagined she'd appreciate the irony.

They sat. She was attracting appreciative glances, he knew that. And although part of him really wanted to glare at the other guys, part of him just basked in the fact that even though she was being ogled, her attention was firmly fixed on him.

"Today was great," she said, her expressive eyes filled with appreciation. "I've mentioned that, haven't I?"

"It's always good to hear," he said. "And I had a good coach."

"No, you had a *great* coach," she said, then laughed. "Sometimes my immodesty amazes even myself."

"It's not immodesty when it's true," Drew said, loving the throaty sound of her laugh. "Look at me. Before you, I was wearing T-shirts and begging for deals. After you, I'm landing big deals in a tie." He waited a beat. ''And having dinner with beautiful women to boot.''

''Yeah, well, when you're a successful salesman, you draw chicks like a magnet,'' she said, her laughter a little more...nervous? He made her nervous. He got the feeling that was a good thing. She didn't strike him as the type of woman that was unnerved by most men.

''As much as drawing chicks has always been a secret goal of mine,'' he joked, glad that she grinned at his comment, ''I think the more important thing is, I'm that much closer to saving Robson Steel. And that's the most important thing in my life.''

''I know,'' she said, her eyes shining, her tone much more serious.

''And you do have a huge part in that,'' he said. He lifted his water glass to her. ''To you, Jade Morrow. For being a personal, tough, badass guardian angel. A guy could not ask for more.''

She looked for a moment as though she was going to mist up—her eyes had the glassy sheen of tears that were kept in check. Then she blinked, hard, and forced a laugh.

''Keep it up and I'll start blushing,'' she said, her voice uneven. ''You did a lot of hard work, Drew. And if you didn't love your factory so much, we wouldn't be sitting here. So right back at you,'' she replied, holding her own water glass up and toasting him. ''To Drew Robson, the toughest client I've ever...''

She paused.

''Yes?'' he prompted.

''The toughest client I've ever felt...I've ever *liked* this much,'' she stammered a little, correcting herself. Then she quickly took a sip of water.

He sipped, as well, to quench the sudden heat that was pumping through him.

They downshifted to small talk, having the occasional heated exchange about whether or not the Raiders should have gone back to Oakland, or the various merits of small-town living versus big-city life. Still, every now and then, their toes would brush beneath the table, completely by accident. They'd both reach for the pepper shaker and he could feel the smooth silkiness of her skin underneath his fingertips before pulling his hand away, a quick caress. If asked later, he wouldn't really remember many details of what they talked about. He just liked listening to her, and watching her as she spoke, her hands gesticulating wildly, her expressive face adding a beautiful counterpoint to her arguments.

She was fantastic.

After having coffee, they got up to go. Going by the dance floor, he saw her look at the little jazz combo. She stopped for a second, swaying a little, smiling.

"I don't suppose you dance," she said in a low enough voice that he wondered if it was a comment she'd meant him to hear.

"I don't dance, generally," he said. Yet the idea—being close to her, having her in his arms with a valid, socially accepted excuse... "But if you don't mind your toes being mashed, and you don't mind leading...heck, I'm game."

She laughed, her face lighting up. Then she shook her head. "Nah. It's no big deal. It's been a while since I danced, but—"

Her statement was interrupted by her squeak as he nudged her toward the dance floor. "Don't worry.

Dancing with me isn't what anybody would call recreational or even relaxing."

She was still laughing until he tugged her closer to him, stroking his fingertips up the length of her bare arms until he rested her hands on his shoulders. Then he gently put his hands on her hips.

"Watch your feet, now," he said. She only responded with the barest of smiles. He saw her pulse beat away in the delicate column of her throat.

He wondered when the last time he'd wanted anything as much as he wanted this woman.

The music picked up slightly in tempo, a sexy number, heavy on the saxophone. Smooth, rich music. She closed her eyes, swaying beneath his fingers. He clenched tightly before he could stop himself, then forced himself to relax. They moved in time with the music, too close to stop the attraction, not close enough to really give in to it.

She was staring into his eyes, and he swore he saw the same hunger he felt mirrored in her warm green gaze. Her hands stroked slightly over his shoulder. He was waiting for more…

She leaned forward, slightly, almost imperceptibly. He matched her, moving until his temple rested lightly against hers. Each breath enveloped him in her vanilla scent. She moved closer. He could feel her chest brush against him, maddening caresses. He wanted to pull her to him. He was getting hard just thinking about it, feeling her beneath the slick material of her dress, the way her hips moved…

She pulled away from him.

"I don't feel like dancing anymore," she said in a small voice. He only barely caught it over the demanding beat of the music.

"Neither do I," he said, his voice rough with desire. "Come on."

The two walked off the dance floor. He put an arm around her shoulders. He wanted her. She wanted him. He could let it get complicated later. Now, he just wanted her naked, beneath him, on top of him, beside him.

I want her every way I can possibly get her.

She was silent as they walked through the restaurant, through the lobby, down the hallway that led to their neighboring rooms. His blood was pumping thickly through his veins. They didn't touch, but he was vibrantly aware of her closeness. When they got to her room, she stopped, a flash of nerves and passion crossing her face.

"I..." Her mouth worked a little, silent, as if she were framing words but unable to say them. She looked at him, baffled.

"I want to make love to you, Jade," he said in a low voice.

"I know." Her eyes were huge. "And I want you to, but..."

He didn't wait for her to finish her sentence. It would have logic, and a really strong argument, he felt sure. He just needed a kiss before she let things get rational. He leaned forward and covered her lips with his.

He'd kissed her before, so he was used to the rush of adrenaline just the brush of her satiny lips sent through him. But he had desire before he started, and he used every ounce of it to convey just how much he wanted her. His mouth parted hers, his tongue dipping in and caressing the fullness of her lips, tickling against the brushing of her tongue. She sank a little, and he leaned her against her hotel room door, working more intently. One of his hands held her steady at the gentle swell of her hip, while the other traced up the smooth cloth of her dress, stroking her midriff.

She let out a little gasp, a muffled whimper. Then the Jade he knew acted, as he had hoped she would. Her tongue tangled with his as her fabulously mobile mouth ravaged his. Her hands stroked up his shoulders before her fingers tangled in the hair at the nape of his neck, tugging him closer to her.

Her hips arched forward, the thin fabric of her dress and of his slacks the only impediment to the burning of their bodies. He tore his mouth from hers when she moved her hips a little too intently, and he felt his erection surging against her, pushing hard.

"Room key," he groaned, his breathing labored, before leaning down and nibbling at her neck lightly. He felt the breath of her corresponding moan against his earlobe.

"Hold on." She fumbled with one hand, grabbed the card key, and got the door open. They slowly moved into the room, and she shut the door. It all felt surreal. She leaned up to him, her eyes staring at him warily even as her swollen lips beckoned him.

Slowly, he reached for her. He started with her hips, tugging her the few steps into the small room...leading her to the bed. She sat on the edge of it, and he sat next to her. Her breathing was shallow, and her pulse was dancing crazily in the vein in her throat. She leaned back, arching her back a little, her eyes blazing like beacons.

He needed no further invitation.

He stroked his hand against her dress, as he had in the hallway, but this time he didn't stop at her stomach. He moved slightly up, barely brushing against her breasts, feeling the nipples beneath his palms hardening to pebbles. He then replaced his hands with his mouth, suckling through the fabric. She gasped, her hips arching. She held him to her, and he moved over her, one leg moving instinctively between hers.

She reached for his shirt, pulling it out of his waistband, her curious fingers moving to the skin of his stomach. He gasped a little as she smoothed her hands around to his back, pulling him to her. He was now clothed, but between her legs, cupped by warmth he could feel even with layers between. He kissed her languorously, pushing slightly, tortured by the closeness. She gasped, bucking against him.

He rolled away for a second, breathing hard. Slow. He wanted this to be slow. He wanted this to last.

She arched again…then pulled up the hem of her skirt, revealing a pair of high-cut lace panties. In dark green, contrasted by the thigh-high stockings in black. She still had her heels on.

He smiled, stroking the delicate skin of her thighs, delighting in her low moan as she closed her eyes, turning her head away from him. His fingers traced upward, with long, slow strokes, until he got to the edge of her panties. He moved the wisp of lingerie aside, the dark red curls soft beneath his fingertips. Jade's breathing was fast, and her legs parted imperceptibly. His erection tightened, almost painfully.

He dipped a finger in, feeling the damp heat of her. He stroked in, gently, feeling her erect clit beneath his index finger. She cried out, a tiny noise, and her hips swayed beneath him.

Then he dipped in deeper, and she gasped, her thighs clamping against his hand.

"I want this, Jade," he said fiercely, leaning down

to kiss her thigh even as his hand started picking up speed. "I want you. All night. Every way I can get you. From now on."

She paused, then her eyes flew open, and she stiffened against him. Gently, but firmly, she nudged him away. Then she rolled off the bed, standing, straightening her skirt.

"What?" he asked quickly, standing, as well. "What's wrong?"

Her hair was wild, tangled, and her lipstick was smudged. Her eyes were a smoldering green, warm with passion, and her skin was flushed.

"You have to ask?" Her tone was woeful. "I can't do this. We can't do this," she corrected, her breathing still hitching. "I work with you. I work *for* you. We... I mean..." She made an incoherent gesture of helplessness with her hands. "Think about it."

He closed his eyes for a moment. He'd known this was coming. But he'd wanted her too much to force himself to think about it.

She leaned forward. "If you were anybody else, there wouldn't be a question. But this is all too important. For both of us," she reminded him.

He took a deep breath, trying to calm his pounding heart. "Nobody screws up, right?" It came out as a rasp.

She smiled awkwardly. "Not on my watch."

And there it was. She was afraid of screwing this up. He didn't think it would affect anything, if they kept it simple—kept it to their own bottom line physical desire. But she was afraid they couldn't keep it simple enough to keep from ruining their goals.

He gritted his teeth. Now that she was forcing him to think about it, he wasn't sure he could, either.

She swallowed, and he could see in her eyes she wanted the same thing.

"I'm sorry," she said instead.

"Don't be sorry," he said. "You're right. We shouldn't."

He turned, groin aching, his pulse still dancing a hectic beat in his rib cage. She walked to the door, awkwardly waiting for him.

He paused before reaching for the doorknob. "I'm not mad at you. I understand what you're saying," he emphasized. "But I still have to say this. I'd do anything right now if you'd let me slide inside of you and make love to you until dawn."

She closed her eyes, and leaned forward, just a breath. She could picture it. He knew it.

She opened her eyes. "Are you willing to sacrifice Robson Steel for it?"

Her words hit him like a fist. He involuntarily shook his head.

"I didn't think so. And you shouldn't. We've both got too much to lose." She took a few deep breaths, her hands forming loose fists. Then she looked at him, her tone forced and bright. "Well. I guess this means good night."

She opened the door, her eyes never leaving his.

He nodded. "I'll, uh, see you tomorrow," he said. Then he walked out, took the two steps to his hotel room, and opened the door just as she was shutting hers.

He closed the door behind him, then stupidly smacked it with his hand. The dull ache was just an echo of the throbbing pain of the rest of his body.

I'd sell my soul to get a taste of that woman.

He closed his eyes, rubbing his hand absently.

His soul, yeah. He might lose his head and forget his priorities just to get involved with her. His rational thought might go right out the window. He'd never been this way around any woman.

He wouldn't lose Robson Steel because he couldn't keep his body under control.

He headed straight for the shower, intent on making it a cold one.

He hired Jade Morrow to save Robson Steel. Apparently, she was better than he thought—since she was saving it from even his own stupidity.

Thank God one of us can keep control. He shook his head, turning the shower on full blast. Then, taking a breath, he forced himself to step into the spray.

Too bad the one in control obviously isn't me.

AT TWO O'CLOCK in the morning, Jade had been tossing and turning in the dark for hours. She'd slept lightly. Dreams of Drew, his muscular body sliding into her just as he'd promised, had woken her up with a start. She moaned, finding her hand creeping to soothe the dull ache between her legs. But all she could think about was him, just feet away, on the other side of the wall. Also in the dark.

Also thinking of having sex with me?

She groaned, putting her head into the pillow.

She'd made the right decision. Her head knew that. It was just a matter of time before her body picked up the clue. At least she *hoped* it would.

She'd never wanted any man the way she wanted Drew Robson. Just with kisses, he made her hotter than any man she'd ever been with. When they finally made love, they'd probably set the bed aflame. Or the floor. Possibly even the shower.

She stroked her hands against the flat of her stomach, closing her eyes, thinking of those lightly calloused hands on her, just like they'd been a few hours ago. Before she'd stopped him.

She growled, rolling against the bed. But they weren't his hands. Her body ached at just the memory of his touch. She wasn't going to die if she didn't experience the man.

She just felt like she wanted to.

She squirmed against the sheets, searching desperately for a cool spot. She had gone to bed naked, and she'd managed to kick off most of the covers, but the sheet still made her feel as if she was wrapped in an electric blanket. Even with the air-conditioning blasting, she felt feverish.

She was right. She knew she was right.

She got out of bed, stumbling over one of her shoes. She was tired, grumpy. A glass of water—that's what she needed. Maybe a cold shower. Men always seemed to do that sort of thing, and it was supposed to help. Or maybe she'd just take a nice, long, productive bath.

Her eyes were still closed tight when she felt for the light switch, grumbling when she didn't find it. She heard the door click behind her, and opened her eyes slowly, wincing at the brightness of the light.

She wasn't in the bathroom, she noticed immediately.

She was in the hallway.

All at once, she was wide awake. It was the *last* hotel they had stayed in that the bathroom was on the right. It had been that way for the past three cities, now that she thought about it.

Not this time. This time, she had turned right, gone out the door, and let it lock behind her.

She felt panic grip her. There wasn't even a throw rug she could snatch up to cover herself. How was she going to get to the front desk this way?

She stared dumbly at the numbers of her door…then the numbers of Drew's door.

Before she could stop herself, she knocked, softly. Then a little more insistently.

He opened the door, wearing only a pair of boxers and a surly expression. "What the…"

He got one look at her, and his eyes flew open. She ignored that as she ran past him into his room.

He shut the door as she darted to his bed, yanking the top sheet off and wrapping herself in it. His eyes bugged out slightly. "Um. Hello."

"You won't believe this, but I was trying to walk to my bathroom half asleep to get a glass of water, and I went out the room door instead, and it locked behind me and…"

In that instant, in the dim light of one of the bedside lamps, she got a good look at his boxers. More important, she got a good look at what the boxers couldn't hide…a fair-size erection. Just like the one she'd felt pressing insistently between her thighs, stopped by their interfering clothing. His body was tanned, looking like burnished copper in the low light. He was just as deliciously muscular as she remembered, and his hair was tousled from the bed. His eyes burned with desire.

"I believe you," he said.

She swallowed.

He walked over to her, slowly, almost tentatively. His eyes were fixed on her face. She felt as though her voice was trapped in her throat, as her nipples abruptly hardened and she felt her thighs go faintly damp. She swallowed again, hard, as if she could free the protest she knew she should be making from her throat. He stopped a foot away from her, and she could feel the heat of him, the sheer carnal desire. But he still paused, waiting. For her.

You want this. You want him.

She wasn't going to stop him this time. It was fate. She wouldn't stop what was going to happen. She couldn't.

He reached for the corner of the sheet, and she felt her grip on it loosen, until the long length of cloth slid slowly down her body, pooling at her feet. She was naked in front of him, and she straightened, challenging him.

"You said you wanted me," she said, her chin angling up.

"That hasn't changed." He took in the sight of her body, studying her slowly before locking gazes with her again.

She took a deep breath. Then she put her hands forward, slipping her fingers into the waistband of his boxers. Then, slowly, gently, she tugged them down until they were at his feet. He stepped out of them easily.

They were both naked, surveying each other. She wanted him so badly, so intensely, she was frozen with indecision. There was so much of him that she wanted to touch, taste. She didn't know where to start.

Fortunately, he took the decision out of her hands by stepping forward and tilting her head up, kissing her neck. She sighed, collapsing against him, and the feel of his hot skin against her own was enough to make her heart start hammering. She reached up, clutching at his back as his kisses got more insistent. He turned, and she let him lower her onto the bed.

He didn't stop kissing her. Instead his mouth moved, from her neck, lowering to her breasts. She could every now and then feel the hot brush of his cock against her hip, her thigh, and she moaned as he increased the pressure...and his fingers started to join the act. He was licking her nipples, swirling around each with long, loving strokes. She arched her back, pulling his head against hers. His fingers stroked down her stomach, his mouth following as he moved lower, holding her as he kissed the flare of her hip. Then he moved lower, his fingers tickling the sensitive opening of her, and she threw her head back and moaned, spreading her legs farther.

"Jade," he breathed against her thigh, as his fingers pressed farther inside her, stroking the sensitive folds of her clitoris even as he delved deeper. The sharp insistence against her thigh as he stroked inside her made her gasp with pleasure. Her hips bucked and her fingers fisted in the sheet beneath her.

"More," she gasped.

The suction and the fingers withdrew, disappointing her...until she felt his breath, hot between the junction of her thighs. Then his mouth was pressing against her and his tongue was circling her clit with insistent pressure. She almost screamed as pleasure shot through her like lightning. Her thighs tightened and she moaned loudly as her hips rose to meet the force of his lips and tongue as it moved deeper. She was gasping, twisting beneath his ministrations.

She was close, very close, when he withdrew. "Not yet," he whispered, his eyes a stormy midnight-blue. "I want this to last."

She was on the brink of sanity, covered in a very fine mist of sweat. She could feel fire coalescing in the pit of her stomach, moving up through her chest. The flesh between her thighs ached with unfulfilled desire.

She was a woman who got what she wanted. She sat up, seeing his erection, dark and heavy, jutting at her.

"Condom," she breathed. "I need you inside me. *Now.*"

He smiled, reaching into one drawer of the nightstand table and producing a foil packet. She took it from him, tearing it open with her teeth. She produced the condom, then sat up, pressing him back on the bed. He smiled…until she put the condom on his erection, smoothing it slowly down his hardness. Her fingers circled him, with gentle pressure. He closed his eyes and groaned, his hips rising slightly. She cupped his balls, smiling herself when he made inarticulate sounds of pleasure at her careful actions.

She wanted to do to him what he'd done to her, but she was too hungry, need driving her with a frenzy. She stroked him, lowering her body over his, feeling the scratch of his chest hair against her now insanely sensitive breasts. She gasped, feeling him poised at her now slick opening.

"Jade," he moaned, his hands clutching at her hips, urging her down onto him.

"I want this," she repeated out loud, feeling him press between the folds of her vagina and stroke against her clit. "I want *you.*"

Then she took him in, inch by inch, sliding the length of him inside her. She stretched to accommodate him, letting out a low cry of pleasure when he pressed in all the way. She involuntarily arched up, feeling him against her G-spot, and he pulled her down on to him, making her take him even deeper inside of herself.

"That feels good," she growled, swiveling her hips slightly, experimentally. "That feels so *amazing.*"

"I knew it would feel like this," he answered, his voice strained as she started to move slowly, rhythmically, retreating only to press further onto him, taking him by inches, torturing them both.

He sat up, surprising her. He kissed her deeply as she moved her legs to circle his waist, so she was sitting on his lap. His arms circled her bottom, and he helped her raise and lower herself onto his erection. The friction of her breasts against his chest and his cock against her clit drove her wild, and she couldn't help it…she started to pick up speed, feeling him press against her, causing waves of heat to course through her.

"Oh," she said, tilting her head back as he bit her neck with gentle roughness. "Yes. Please, yes," she said as her hips increased their tempo.

He was raising to meet her, pushing her harder against him. Her legs tightened their grip, and they were moving faster, sliding against each other, as if to become one being. She gasped every time he pushed against her. They were moving quicker, harder, his hands pressing her hips to him, her hands clutching at his back. He kissed her hard, her tongue twining with his as she tightened the grip of her thighs.

She felt the first tremors of orgasm deep and slow, and trembled as they rocked through her. She held him like a life preserver as he bucked against her, his arms wrapped around her waist, pulling her to him as desperately as she herself clung to him.

She didn't want to let go of him, even when he lowered himself back onto the bed, letting her sprawl out over him. Still, she let him withdraw, and she rolled onto her back, feeling dizzy…feeling disoriented.

It was good. No. It was *great.* It was everything she thought it would be and then some.

She closed her eyes, smiling at the quivery feeling of afterglow. He said he knew it would be like this.

If she had known it would be like this, she thought, then she never would have said no in the first place.

"I take it from the look on your face that it wasn't that bad," she heard his deep voice rumble, smug.

She opened one eye, and a quick glance at his amused expression confirmed it. "I hate men who gloat," she said with a quick grin. "Even if they have reason to."

He smiled…then reached into the nightstand drawer and produced a full box of condoms. She now opened both eyes, wide.

He reached for her and started kissing her, purposefully. Even though she ought to be exhausted, her body immediately started to perk up…and started getting turned on. Soon, she was breathless, clamoring for him. She reached for a condom.

"I promise I won't gloat this time," he murmured against her back. Then, to her shock, she found he was hard again as he entered her.

"This time," she whispered, backing against him, feeling the slide and friction of his body against her as he cupped her breasts and pulled her to him, "I'll let you."

DREW WOKE UP to the pitch dark that only hotel rooms with blackout curtains could manage. He'd barely gotten a few hours of dreamless sleep. He rolled over, trying to get comfortable, stretching out his hands across the bed. Instead of smoothing over sheets and tangled covers, his hand encountered smooth, satiny curves.

All last traces of sleepiness left in a blink. Slowly he traced her contours.

Jade. Here. In his bed.

He was immediately flooded with memories of the previous night. He moved slowly, fitting his body to hers and wrapping an arm around her waist as he pressed a gentle kiss to her neck. "Good morning," he whispered.

He could tell by the way she tensed that she was awake. "I can't believe I'm here," she whispered back. She was stiff against him, not pliant and eager as the night before.

"Neither can I," he murmured back, nuzzling her. "But I'm not complaining, either."

He noticed that she didn't respond to that, even after waiting a minute. "Jade…are *you* complaining? Are you sorry about last night?"

She didn't immediately deny his questions, and he felt himself growing more tense as he pulled slightly away. Instead she leaned over, turning on one of the bedroom lights. He grumbled and shielded his eyes, temporarily blinded. When he finally acclimated, she was staring at him, her hair rumpled in sexy red curls, her obviously naked body covered by a sheet she held to her chest. She was surveying him, her eyes filled with doubts.

"I'm not complaining about last night," she finally said, and he felt a measure of relief. "But I'm not going to say it was the brightest move of all time, either."

He felt his jaw clench. "I don't see why it's a problem."

She put one hand up to push curls out of her face, letting the sheet slip enticingly to reveal the swell of her breast. Before he could really admire the view, she had moved her hand back. "This is a real distraction, is the problem. I knew that last night when I turned you away the first time. I'm not going to repeat that argument."

"Well, it's too late to do anything about it now, and I for one don't regret it," Drew said firmly, reaching for her. But she dodged, standing. He held the edge of the sheet, and after a moment of tussle, she finally shrugged, letting it fall away.

Her naked body, in full light, always managed to rob him of breath. He stared at her for a moment. She was truly a magnificent woman. She crossed her arms, frowning at him.

"I know we can't change this, but we have to deal with it now. It's a whole new element," she chided gently. "For one thing, we have to be really careful. We can't let anybody else know about it."

"Damn. And I was planning on telling Ken to take out an ad." Drew shook his head. "Come on, Jade. Give me a little credit."

"You know what I mean." Her green eyes were hot with intensity. "The last thing I want is for somebody to think that I'm...that you just hired me for...."

She gestured to the bed, and he noticed that her eyes were a little misty. She was really floored by this. He'd never seen her at a loss before.

He sat up, putting his hand out to her. She stared at it. Finally he got up and, despite her reluctance, tugged her back into bed and snuggled against her.

"This is serious!" She struggled against him a little, and he held tighter.

"I know it's serious," he said firmly. "I won't tell anyone. And I *didn't* just hire you for your body or for sex. So don't even think it."

That stopped her. She took a little breath and he could feel the uncertainty coming off of her. "Yeah, but other people..."

"I can be discreet," Drew countered, hugging her. "Nobody's going to think anything other than the fact that you're one hell of a sales coach. I can promise you that."

She lay there silent for a long moment...then she turned, putting her arms around him, rubbing against him a little as she hugged back. "Yeah, well...I've never done this before. This goes against so many things that I believe in."

He hugged her a little more fiercely, feeling his chest warm with protectiveness even as his body started reacting to the fact that she was naked and stroking her body against his. He ignored his burgeoning erection for the time being. "I'm not going to say I'm sorry," he said in a low voice, "because I'm not sorry at all for what we did. All I can say is I'm glad you let me, and I'll try not to do anything to screw this up."

"The job, you mean?" She twisted a little to look at him, inadvertently brushing her thigh against his erection. He stifled a groan. "You're going to make sure that the deal doesn't get screwed up?"

For a second he wasn't sure if he meant that, or if he meant screwing up what was happening between them. Because whether she recognized it or not, there was definitely more going on here than a business agreement. Still, he wasn't ready to talk about that—

and he was fairly sure she wasn't ready to hear about it. "Yeah, I mean the contract."

"Good." She took a deep breath, her voice turning brisk. "Because we've got to hit the road in two hours. And we're going to spend the whole ride, and dinner tonight, going over the files for Reardon Oil."

He smiled at her. This was the Jade he knew. Tough as nails. Still, knowing the vulnerability beneath didn't take away from the appeal at all. "Okay. You're the coach."

"So I'd better get...hey!" She tried to roll away, off of the bed, but he wouldn't let her. "Come on, Drew. I need to get cleaned up, packed. I need to call the front desk and get back into my room."

He grinned at her comments as he rolled over, pinning her to the bed. She spluttered, until he settled himself between her legs. Then he saw her eyes widen, and dilate.

"Drew, we have to go," she said, but he noticed that her voice had turned breathless.

"Not for a couple of hours," he said, his own voice husky with want.

"This is exactly what I was afraid of," she said, although her face looked anything but afraid. Her full mouth beckoned him and her green eyes were low-lidded. "We're getting distracted."

"I sure hope so," he said, kissing her and biting gently on her full lower lip. When she let out a little whimper of pleasure, he brushed his penis against her, feeling the dampness of her against his skin. He shuddered. "Let me make love to you."

"Drew," she said. Her voice was torn between desire and responsibility, he could tell. She cleared her throat and stared at him. "We've only got a few sales.

That's not enough to save Robson. Now, more than ever, we've got to work twice as hard. Having sex with me would be fun...but as I said last night, are you really willing to sacrifice Robson for it?''

He froze for a second, poised over her, the rationality in his head warring with the feel of soft, naked woman beneath his body.

For a moment his only thought was, The hell with Robson Steel. He wanted her more than anything he'd ever wanted. One night with her had not changed that. If anything, it had only intensified it.

He stared back at her. ''I see what you're saying. So. Are you willing to just call this a one-night adventure, and just focus back on work?''

He was studying her face carefully, and was gratified to see a spasm of shock cross her face before she schooled her features and shrugged. ''If that's what you think we ought to do,'' she replied, and he was amazed at how calm her voice was, ''then I think you're probably making the wise decision.''

He rolled off of her, and he noticed that she took in the size of his erection, jutting out at her as he stood. ''Well, then. I guess there isn't really all that much left to say.''

She got to her feet, unsteadily. ''Okay. I guess I'll call the front office.''

He wanted her to say, ''No, let's take an hour and finish what we started.'' He wanted her to say that she could handle an affair with him, that the business wasn't that terribly important.

Damn it, he wanted her to care about him more than she cared about the contract.

He blinked as he realized what his train of thought was. Then he turned. ''I'm going to take a shower,'' he said, glad his own voice stayed casual. "Then I'll meet you in the lobby in an hour, and we'll get going. Is that okay?"

She walked over to him and he felt his resolve buckle. "I'm sorry, Drew," she said, putting a hand on his arm.

He gritted his teeth as his body surged with desire. "No problem," he said. "You're right. I guess I should've listened to you yesterday, huh?"

"I am not saying it was a mistake," she said, her voice low and soothing. "I just...the deal, Drew."

He felt his shoulders tighten. The deal. Always the deal. That was what had stopped her last night, after dinner. It was what was keeping him from her now.

"I know. Go call the front desk."

He shut the door to the bathroom behind him, barely hearing her using the phone before turning the shower on full blast and stepping in.

The deal, Drew.

Back in San Angelo, the factory had always been the most important thing in his life. If there was a choice between working late and spending the night with a woman, he'd naturally choose the factory. But Jade wasn't just a woman. And after a few weeks on the road, he realized that she was growing more important to him daily. He'd never met a woman who valued work, and specifically helping his factory, more than he did.

Is that what you really want, though?

No. She had always been the one who had pushed him to focus on sales. She was the one who said let the client get involved, let the client prove your points for you. Well, he wanted to sell Jade on the idea of making love to him—and having it be more than a few-nights' stand. He wanted that very badly. But if he told her outright, she would just keep kicking up resistance. No. He had to *show* her, and get her to realize that she wanted this as much as he did.

He wasn't going to ask her to make love with him again, he thought with a grin. He was going to make her so turned on, she was going to be crazy with wanting to make love with him—and when she ravished him, he wasn't going to fight one bit.

She might be a fantastic salesperson, and an amazing coach, he thought, getting out of the shower with a light step. But he was one hell of a student.

7

''JADE! I'm glad you called. How's it going?'' Betsy's voice was bright and enthusiastic, despite the fact that Jade had called her office at close to seven o'clock and she was still there. ''I just went through a lot of your e-mails, and they had the most bizarre date stamps on them. Like you were sending them out at two in the morning or something.''

''I've been having a lot of trouble sleeping lately,'' Jade told her, pacing in her hotel room, cell phone in hand. ''I figured I might as well take the time to do something productive. All the accounts are doing fine, by the way.''

''So I noticed,'' Betsy said, and Jade couldn't tell if her tone meant approval or something else. ''I'm surprised. Most people don't manage as well when they're out of the office as often as you've been.''

Jade laughed, shrugging. ''I'd telecommute, but I live five minutes from the office. What's the point?''

''Actually, it's good that you're so comfortable working on the road,'' Betsy mused. ''Seeing how well you're handling your normal workload and this special case, all from hotel rooms, tells me you're going to handle increased travel very well. If it comes up, I mean.''

''Increased travel?'' Jade tensed a little, stopping to

lean against the desk. "Something I should know about?"

"Now, I need you to keep this quiet, but I've been approaching the partners about you. Getting them ready," Betsy said, and Jade felt a little warm glow of pride. "Anyway, we've always done well with domestic companies, but we haven't really cracked into the international field. Considering your background in sales presentations, you could probably train some international offices, get them running with new clients. Sort of be a trouble shooter. It wouldn't be all that different from what you're doing now—except you'd be doing it all the time."

"Really?" Jade made sure to infuse as much enthusiasm as possible in the answer, but internally, she felt her heart sink a little. She wasn't sure why. International travel, a promotion, a high-profile job? She ought to be over the moon.

She rubbed absently at her eyes with her fingertips. She was just a little fatigued, that was all. Crummy hotels. Hours on the road. And now, trouble sleeping. She was just a little worn down. And she'd been out of sorts lately.

"Speaking of sales training," Betsy said, and Jade heard the smile in her voice, "How's your long-shot client coming along? Mr. Robson?"

Jade thought of Drew. Immediately her body went hot and achy as the memory of their one night together assailed her.

"He's f-fine," she managed to stammer.

Have mercy, that man is fine.

"Are you actually able to train him?"

"He's doing very well," Jade said, automatically going on the defensive as a reaction to Betsy's amused tone. "He's picked up enough to land the past several key sales on his own. I've been able to finally concentrate on the big Inesco presentation. He's been amazing."

Amazing was an understatement. For the past week and a half he had totally immersed himself in the job at hand. He was a sales junkie, working on client files and sales calls, going over information with her when they drove or had dinner. He had not mentioned anything other than business once in that whole length of time.

He also had not touched her, beyond the most casual of contacts—an accidental brush of arms in a hallway, the quick friction of his chest against her back if he scooted behind her to get to his seat in a conference room. Which was a good thing, she thought. It showed that he agreed with her, that their lovemaking needed to be put aside. It showed that he valued her business acumen. It showed that he respected her decision.

The fact that his not touching her was nearly as maddening as being touched by him was therefore very disturbing...since obviously she was the one who had the problem. He appeared to be fine.

"That sounds promising," Betsy said, oblivious to Jade's ruminations. "Make sure you keep me posted. If you pull this off, the sky's the limit. I hope your passport's current!"

Jade laughed politely, then finally got Betsy off the phone. She sank onto the bed, cell phone still in hand.

She was starting to get obsessed. Cliché as it would sound, she'd never felt like this before. She liked sex, no question. It was a fun pastime, when she didn't have more important things to do. The thing was, up until now, work had *always* been more important. It wasn't even a question of priorities. Now, she couldn't seem to focus. She was getting everything she wanted handed to her on a platter—all she had to do was to keep her head in the game and her body out of it.

She took a few deep breaths, then dialed another number on her cell phone.

"Hello?"

"Hailey." Jade felt a little swell of relief. "Boy, am I glad I got a hold of you."

"I was out of town with the family," Hailey said, causing Jade to smile. The fact that Hailey's family still had group vacations said a lot. "What's up? Are you okay?"

"No, I'm not okay. I screwed up, and I need your advice."

"Tell me everything," Hailey said without hesitation. "Do you need me to fly down there?"

"I'm not in L.A. I'm in..." Suddenly, it occurred to her that she didn't even remember the name of the tiny town they were staying in. "I'm in New Mexico. Somewhere."

"Somewhere, New Mexico? Why?"

"Road trip. I'm working with a new client." She bit her lip. "The client's the problem, actually."

"I should've guessed this would be work related."

Jade smiled weakly. Hailey and her family had never really subscribed to the idea of climbing the corporate ladder. "This is a little different than my usual work problems." She paused a second. "I slept with him. My client. That's the problem."

She heard Hailey's surprised gasp. "Shut up!"

"I swear, I didn't mean for it to happen," Jade justified in a rush. "We'd gone out to dinner and I was able to say no when he asked me that first time but then I was locked out in the hallway naked and he answered the door in boxers and all hell broke loose!"

"You lost me somewhere near 'naked in the hallway' or so," Hailey said with a chuckle. "Okay. First things first. What kind of problem are we talking about?"

"Are you kidding?" Jade rolled onto her back, staring at the ceiling.

"Humor me."

"I work for the guy. He's trusting me to turn his company around. Worse, my company is trusting me to turn his company around, because I told them I could, even though it's an insane long shot. In fact, they're going to give me a promotion if I pull this off. This is too important for me to botch because I slept with my customer!"

Hailey made a noise of sympathy. "I wondered. So it wasn't like a he-was-terrible-and-now-I-have-to-deal-with-him problem."

Jade thought about Drew—about how talented he was with his hands, his mouth. The way his body worked with hers. "No. That is definitely not a problem."

"That sounds promising," Hailey said. "I don't suppose you could go into detail?"

"Let's just say he's good enough to throw my game off," Jade said. Ordinarily she had no problems sharing details with her best friend. But Drew was different, on all sorts of levels. "I can't afford to screw this up. I've already told him that we should just pretend it never happened, and keep going. He agreed with me."

"So where's the problem?"

Jade blinked. Put that way, there shouldn't be a problem. "Well..."

"Jade," Hailey said, her voice suspicious, "there's more than just casual sex with the wrong guy here, isn't there? What's this guy like?"

"He's..." Jade closed her eyes. "He's idealistic. He's really loyal, especially to his factory and his workers. He's dedicated. He's also arrogantly sure he's got the answers, he's bull-headed, and he's a bullet...once he's on course, he just keeps going."

"Huh," Hailey said. "Doesn't remind you of anybody, does he?"

"I don't follow."

"Never mind. The more important thing here is—you didn't once tell me about what he looked like. That he had a great bod. That he's a Michelangelo in bed."

"He does have a great bod," Jade admitted wryly. "And he's an artist in bed, no question."

"And for that I say congratulations to you. But the thing is...you didn't say that right off the bat. So I ask again—what's the real problem here, Jade?"

Jade went still. She knew, on some level, that it was more than the sex. But she wasn't ready for what "more" might entail. The sex was distracting enough.

What if it was more than that?

"You're thinking too hard," Hailey said, cutting into her worries. "I can hear the gears turning from here."

"I'm scared," Jade said softly. Hailey was the only person in the world she would say this to, and it still made her throat choke. "I can't afford to lose this. I've worked too hard for this promotion. And I never screw up."

"Jade," Hailey said, her voice warm. "You won't screw up. And some of us care about you no matter what you do."

Jade thought of Hailey, and her family…and, inexplicably, of Drew.

"Maybe you should follow your heart on this one," Hailey said gently. "Maybe it's not a mistake. Maybe it's a risk worth taking."

Jade held her breath.

"Well, if nothing else," Hailey said in an impish tone, "you can tell yourself that you're just sleeping with him to take the stress out of the equation, right?"

Jade laughed. "You know me too well."

But her mind was already working—and for once, her body was agreeing with her.

JADE AND DREW SAT in the well-appointed office of Ty Reardon, oil magnate and one of Robson's richest clients. They had driven through New Mexico and were now in Texas…this was the last stop before they headed back toward San Angelo. Outside of the Reardon headquarters, it was hot, dusty, and one of the most desolate places Drew had ever seen. Inside, the place was like a palace in the desert…and Ty was obviously its undisputed king. This sale would be a good one, Drew thought. An important one.

He tried to discreetly stretch out the kinks in his neck. He was prepared, at least. He'd been working toward this for the past few days. In fact, working on this was *all* he'd been doing.

"So how's it going?" Ken had asked the last time Drew had called in. "Looks like you're racking up some serious sales."

"Yeah. But I'll be glad to get home," Drew said. "Next year, no more of this big road trip crap. I don't care what kind of Robson tradition I'm breaking. From now on, we stagger it out during the year. All this travel is killing me."

Although, to be perfectly honest, it wasn't the travel that was killing him. He strongly suspected it was the sexual frustration that was tying his mind and his body up in knots.

And the amazing thing was, Jade was able to just buckle down to business. It was as if she didn't even feel the tension buzzing between them. They still worked hard, and they still had a good time talking over dinner, joking in the car. But the heat was always prevalent, just under the surface. At least, it was to him.

He was beginning to think that his plan to convince her that she wanted him was one of the more stupid ideas he'd come up with.

Now, he supposed it made sense. He'd managed to learn the techniques she was talking about, and better still, they seemed to be working. If he could just keep Robson financed, they'd have a banner year next year...they had that many orders lined up. And this order would push them over into the black. It was a make or break point.

He turned to Jade. She was wearing a skirt, a shorter one than usual. Maybe she was running low on clean clothes, he thought, or maybe the heat prompted her to. Still, he hadn't seen her in a skirt that short since his smart-ass remark the first time he met her. Just as he'd noticed then, she had luscious legs, and the heels she was wearing only accentuated it. There was something different about her today, he thought. Almost predatory. Maybe she'd been working on another client file or on the presentation or something.

He wished absently that she'd focus that much attention on him.

Company first, he thought. He'd worry about her later, when this was taken care of. In fact, when the Inesco business was taken care of and he had more time, he'd definitely put a lot more effort into convincing her that she wanted to spend more time with this.

"You okay?" He studied her face. She was wearing her hair pulled back, and it framed her face, emphasizing the heart-shape sharpness. "You're quiet today."

She stared back, her glance downright sultry. "I'm just fine."

He swallowed. "Uh...good."

A secretary stepped into the office and said, "If you could proceed to the twenty-third floor," she explained. "Mr. Reardon will be waiting for you in the executive conference room."

"Great," Drew said. Jade simply smiled and they headed for the elevator. Was he just imagining things, or was there an extra swing in her hips this afternoon? Or was he finally snapping under the pressure?

He stepped in, and the doors slid closed. He turned to her. "This is it. After this, it's home to California...and the big game."

"Mmm-hmm." She let out a vague noise of assent, her eyes never leaving the flashing LED sign that showed the floor number. The numbers rose as the elevator did.

"Today's sale is a big one, but I think we're more than prepared." He was babbling now. She just looked so good—and she was acting so strangely. He was used to her being a rock during these things, and now she was...

Without warning, she moved forward and hit the

stop button, bringing them to a jarring halt. "What are you doing?"

She didn't answer. Instead, she dropped her portfolio, pinned him against the wall of the elevator, and pressed her body against his.

Her eyes were wide and her breathing was shallow, and she moved on him before he could blink. Next thing he knew, her mouth was ravishing his, her arms curled around his neck, pulling him to her. Her tongue, that wonderfully wicked tongue of hers, was slipping between his lips and teasing him. His body reacted instantly—he'd been tensed with sexual awareness for a week, and now he sprang to life, groaning as he dragged her body along his. She moaned, and he couldn't help it...he reached down to that short skirt of hers, only to find that her stockings were thigh-highs, a fact barely concealed by the hem. He groaned as his fingers sought her out...she stood on tiptoe, tilting her head back. He ignored the fact that they were in an elevator, in one of his most important client's office buildings. Just before his last big sale of the road trip. All he could think of was her—the taste of her, the feel of her beneath him. The dampness of her panties beneath his probing fingers, the silk of her throat beneath his lips.

He found her mouth again, kissing her deeply. She stroked against the bulge in his pants, and her mouth stifled the groan he uttered at the feel of her. Before he could do anything about it, though, she pulled away, out of his reach. After her warmth, the air-conditioned elevator felt like an arctic zone.

"You're probably wondering about my timing," she said unevenly.

''For a start,'' he said with a grimace, trying to get his raging blood under control. ''I thought you said...''

''I know.'' She was leaning against the opposite wall. ''I didn't really mean to do this...now, I mean. I meant to do this today. I just...''

He waited. ''You just what? Have always had this thing for elevators?'' He glanced around. He doubted he'd look at elevators the same way again, either.

''I've wanted you,'' she said with quiet conviction. ''Even when I said that it was a bad idea. Even when I told you we shouldn't. And it's only gotten stronger.''

She looked at the ceiling for a moment, as if gathering her thoughts. Then her green eyes trained on him, solemn and dark.

''I've never felt this way about anybody. I enjoy spending time with you, but I always want more. I have trouble sleeping...and when I do sleep, I dream about you. About us. About you making love to me...''

He closed his eyes, her words doing as much to him as her body had. He'd felt the same way—but hearing her, in that husky-rough voice of hers, talk about him moving inside of her, feeling her surround him, only made the memories of him making love to her more vibrant.

''Jade,'' he said, his body throbbing, ''I want to do all of those things to you. Just...I can't. Not now.'' He looked at her. ''You understand, right?''

She smiled wistfully. ''I know. And I really thought I could hold out until after the meeting. I'm sorry.''

He didn't want her to be sorry. In fact, the last thing he wanted to do was to switch gears and focus on business. For a brief, foolish moment, he thought about doing just that...restarting the elevator, taking it back to the first floor, and heading right back to the hotel room. Forget about the meeting, about Reardon, about the whole thing. They'd make love all night and all the next day, and worry about California and the Inesco project some other time. Maybe not ever.

But Robson Steel is depending on this.

Like it or not, she was right the first time—they couldn't screw this up. "Just one more meeting."

She smiled. "Okay."

"I'll get through it quickly."

"Do what you have to do," she assured him, straightening her skirt and taking several deep breaths.

What he had to do, he thought, was bury himself in her. As soon as possible.

After the meeting.

She got the elevator started again, and he clenched his teeth, staring at her…wanting her.

Ty Reardon would never realize exactly what sort of sacrifice he had made to offer him this deal today, Drew thought when the doors opened on the twenty-third floor and he and Jade stepped out as if nothing had happened. But by God, he'd better make it worth it.

"Drew?" Jade said just before they got to the conference room.

He turned to her. "Yes?"

She leaned up, and he could feel the breath tickle his ear as she whispered, "I don't suppose you could hurry."

He glanced at his watch. "This will be the quickest meeting you've ever seen."

THEY DIDN'T MAKE IT three steps into his room before she had her arms around his neck, pulling herself to him. She sensed blindly that he shut the door behind them even as his mouth searched out hers.

"That *was* one of the quickest meetings I've ever seen," she said, laughing as he reached for her.

He kissed her, hard, then pulled back to reveal a grin. "I made a few concessions. I think he realized what a hurry I was in." He smiled at her. "I told him it was an emergency, and we had to get back as soon as possible. That it was very, very important."

She registered a warmth radiating from her chest, all the way out to her extremities. He was like a warrior, capturing her mouth fiercely. Her tongue mated with his, and she thrilled at the taste of him. She worked on the buttons of his shirt, needing to feel all that hot, smooth skin beneath the cotton Oxford. Their arms tangled as he went to work on her blouse, and they wound up bursting into ragged laughter.

"I've wanted you so much," he said, kissing her between words as he worked at a button.

"I know. I know," she said, finally tugging his shirt out of the waistband of his slacks and pulling it off of his shoulders. She was stopped by the fact that his cuffs were buttoned. She didn't even pause to unbutton them. She leaned up, feeling the heat coming off of him in waves, and bit his shoulder, gently. "Take me, Drew."

She registered the sound of cloth tearing as he pulled his shirt off of his wrists, impatiently. He was barechested, just as she remembered him from the first time she'd knocked on his hotel room door. Then, he'd looked devilish. Now, he looked ravenous...and he was staring at her.

"I'll buy you a new shirt," he said just before taking her blouse into his hands and literally tearing it off of her. It should have incensed her, but all she could think was he was delirious, fierce for her. She wanted him to. She wanted to tear things off of him. Her hands flew to the fly of his pants, taking only a moment to rub her palm over the hardness of his cock as he closed his eyes and took a quick, gasping breath. Then she had his pants undone and was pushing them impatiently open, undoing the boxers. She was still wearing a skirt, and he was pushing it up on her hip, backing her up against the wall. Next thing she knew, she was being lifted, propped up.

"Drew," she gasped. She wiggled as he tugged at her thigh-highs, kicking off her shoes as he pulled the impeding stockings off of her. Her thong panties were soaked, and his fingers pushing the bit of cloth out of his way was almost her undoing. She moaned, rubbing against his probing fingers.

"Condom. Damn it."

She wrapped her legs around his waist and he groaned. He carried her to the table, propping her up on it. His cock brushed against the damp curls between her legs, and she whimpered, instinct pushing her against him before sanity pushed her away, breathing hard.

"Hurry," she said, tugging at him as he got the foil packet opened and rolled the condom on. Then he plunged into her, and she gasped. She was already wet and ready for him, but his size filled her, plowing into her. *"Drew!"*

He didn't move her to the bed, although it seemed as if he would. Instead, he pressed her back against the wall, the animal-like frenzy of his entering her making her even hotter. She wrapped her legs around him, pulling him deeper into her, leaning back. He cupped her breasts, still cased in her bra, as he moved into her with strong, steady strokes. "That feels so damned good," he said between gritted teeth as his body moved into hers.

She held him, biting him gently at the base of his neck even as she raised and lowered herself onto his erection. He gasped, gripping her hips, tilting her, grinding against her. She kissed him, feeling his tongue in her mouth even as the length of his erection stroked hypnotically inside of her. She almost passed out from the sensation of it.

"I don't want to hear," he said as he pressed into her, "about how this is wrong. How I feel about you isn't wrong."

"No," she said as he plunged inside of her, the coldness of the wall a counterpoint to the heat of his body. "No. It's not wrong. Oh, please, harder."

"Yes," he said, leaning his forehead against her collarbone and driving into her. She whimpered from the feel of him, rolling her hips to feel the delicious friction of him. "Jade, I want you."

"Uh…Oh, yeah. Oh, Drew, *yes,*" she moaned as he started moving faster, feeling the hard heat of his erection sliding against her clit. She was clutching at his shoulders, gripping at him with her thighs, even as he continued driving against her, endlessly stoking the sensual fire inside of her.

"Drew!" she shouted, feeling her body clutch him. Her climax roared through her like a train.

"Jade…Jade!" He slammed into her, and she felt the aftershocks of another climax as he pressed her there against the wall.

After a moment he shifted their weight, angling toward the bed. They collapsed on top of it with a soft bounce, and she gasped…then started laughing, weakly.

"We're going to kill each other one of these days," she muttered, then kissed him lightly…lingering over it.

"But we're going to keep doing it, right?"

There was weight to that question, she realized as he peered down at her, his bangs sweaty…his heart in his eyes. He wanted no more rationale of client ethics. No more reasons. No more barriers. No more regrets.

"Yes," she breathed. "We're going to keep doing it."

8

JADE WAS LYING SIDEWAYS on a large, luxurious king-size bed. It was a far cry from the small, tacky motel rooms that they'd stayed in for the past three weeks.

"I can't believe this is our last night on the road," Drew said.

"I can't believe you got this incredible hotel room," she said. They were in Las Vegas, and they'd be driving back to San Angelo the next day. He'd indulged in a large room at one of the more expensive hotels on the strip. The place was sumptuous, but still tasteful. The room was decorated in cream and gold, with understated decorations. The only really decadent thing in the place was the spa tub, deep enough for four people, a nod toward the city and its preferences.

"I figured it's the least I could do." They'd checked in that afternoon, intent on seeing the sights...but hadn't managed to leave the room yet. He was wearing a terry-cloth robe, matching the one she was currently wrapped up in. "After all those hours in the car, all those lumpy, wretched beds...Robson Steel can shell out for a little R and R for two of their hardest-working proponents."

She laughed as he popped the cork from the bottle of champagne he'd ordered. "I figured you'd wait to celebrate until after the investor meeting," she said, stretching out. They'd be hitting that spa tub pretty soon. She could almost feel the hot water on her aching muscles.

His smile was hot, a mix of pure sunlight and sex appeal. "I thought we could celebrate both times."

She sat up, revising her reverie. She could almost feel the hot water, and *him,* together.

They were *definitely* going to hit the spa tub.

She was about to make that suggestion when her cell phone rang. She'd been charging it, since she had let the battery go dead that week. She glanced at the small display, then groaned.

"What?"

"It's my boss."

He nuzzled her neck. "Don't answer it."

"I haven't checked in all week. She probably thinks I'm dead." Still, she couldn't help but feel the beginnings of arousal as he kissed the hollow of her collarbone, nipped at the sensitive skin at the base of her throat. "Why don't you fill up the tub? Then I'll get her off the phone, and we can, uh, soak a bit."

"Like the way you think, lady." Reluctantly he pulled away. She watched him head for the bathroom as she clicked the phone on.

"This is Jade."

"Where have you been?" Betsy's voice was high-pitched, a little frenetic. Unusual, for her usually collected boss. "I've been trying to get a hold of you for days."

Jade winced. "Sorry. This week has been crazy. What's wrong?" She felt a little knot of panic in her stomach. She'd been checking e-mails. Had she missed something? One of her regular clients had some kind of crisis she wasn't aware of? She'd never been out of contact with the office for an entire week before…

''No, nothing wrong. But there's a new client that we're trying to land. I need your help, Jade.''

Jade quickly moved to the desk, grabbing the hotel stationery and a pen. ''Shoot.''

''I need you to brainstorm some approaches for a personal digital assistant thing. You know, one of those hand-held electronic jobs. How would you make that press worthy?''

''Personal digital assistant thing. Press angles. Got it.'' Jade realized that her mind was a complete blank. ''Um...let me think about it. I'll e-mail you some ideas.''

''I need them by tonight, Jade. I know you're working on your little pet crusade, but it's time you got back to work, especially if you still want that promotion. At least, that's my assumption.''

''Of course I still want it,'' Jade said, reacting to the testiness in her mentor's voice. Jeez. She'd been out of the office for three weeks, and this was the reaction? She felt her warm cocoon of relaxation start to fray around the edges. ''I'll come up with ideas tonight and e-mail them to you. Do me a favor and e-mail me anything you have on the client themselves—maybe there's an angle there.''

''That's my girl,'' Betsy said, her voice a little more smug. ''I'll keep an eye out for your e-mail. I was starting to think you were losing your edge, there.''

Jade didn't even answer that one, even though she felt her blood burn a little at the accusation. ''Trust me, I haven't lost my edge.''

''Good. Well, finish up. We need you here in the office.''

''I know, I know. I'll talk to you later.'' Jade hung

up, then shut the phone off. She didn't want to talk to Betsy again.

She didn't notice the tension creeping over her as she frowned at the paper. What was press worthy about something people bought to keep track of their schedules? Not very sexy, she thought, doodling. Ordinarily she would have five ideas jotted down before she'd hung up the phone. This was some of her bread and butter—that was what had helped her get as far as she had. That was why Betsy asked for her to be on her team. She'd helped Betsy land more clients, and she'd even worked on a few of them.

All of that will change once I get the promotion. She'd be working from anywhere in the world, for one thing. She wouldn't be doing lackey work for Betsy. Of course, she wouldn't be home a whole lot, either.

And she'd be nowhere near San Angelo. The thought disquieted her, more than she wanted to admit.

"Jade? You okay?" Drew's voice sounded amplified from the echo of the cavernous bathroom. "The tub's almost filled."

"Right." Was she losing her edge? Of course not. Well, she'd been on the road for three weeks, for pity's sake. That was enough to…

No. She wasn't losing her edge.

She wrote the words "organizer," "electronic" and "Assistant" down, then halfheartedly started to cluster word associations. She was so intent on her task that she jumped when Drew kissed her on the back of her neck.

"The water's ready…and I've got to admit, I'm pretty ready myself." He glanced over her shoulder. "What are you doing?"

"Betsy needs some help tonight." She almost

flinched when his hands came down on her shoulders. Then she groaned as he started to knead the tension out of her sore muscles. "I just need to brainstorm some press angles for this hand-held electronic organizer thing. And send her an e-mail tonight."

"How long is that going to take?"

She leaned her head back and closed her eyes. His fingers felt like heaven. "I don't know. At this rate, it's going to take hours. I feel like my brain's on autopilot."

"Why don't you just relax," he suggested. "You're pretty fried. Get in the tub with me. I've got some patented relaxation techniques that might help out."

The rumble of his voice sent sensual shivers through her. "You're trying to get me to avoid work," she said, trying for sternness and failing miserably.

"Damned right," he said, then leaned down and kissed her—a slow, lingering, serious kind of a kiss. "I mean it, Jade. You're too stressed out. Let it wait for a couple of hours. You'll be better for it."

She put up a token resistance. "But..."

He tugged at her hands and she let him lead her to the bathroom. "Shh," he said. "I know your work is important to you. But you need to let it go for a little bit. You're under too much pressure. Let me help you out."

She sighed. When was the last time someone had offered that? Or for that matter, had noticed that she needed a little tender loving care? With that in mind, she let him reach for the sash of her robe, tugging the knot undone and letting the robe fall open, revealing the naked skin beneath. She smiled.

"Since you ask so nicely," she said, and leaned in for another mind-blowing kiss.

DREW PARKED in the lot of Robson Steel, staring at the old gray building as if he'd never seen it before. It had been three weeks, but he felt as though it was even longer...and he meant that in a good way. As cliché as it might sound, he felt like a different person. Sure, he had several serious sales under his belt, and that helped his confidence. He'd learned a lot, he'd accomplished a lot. But that wasn't what put the spring in his step as he got out of his car. He looked over to where Jade was climbing out of the passenger seat.

Jade. She had made all the difference. He'd never met another woman like her—and he doubted he would again.

"You ready?" She stepped close to him. "It's probably going to be a jungle in there."

"I'm ready." He started to lean in to kiss her, since she was looking simply kissable in the late-morning sunlight. But he remembered at the last minute their agreement—they weren't going to advertise their relationship.

That is, he was calling it a relationship. He wasn't sure what she thought about it.

She'd spent the past week waking up in his arms. He damned well was calling it a relationship.

"Come on. Let's see what the mice have been up to while the cat's been away."

She was smiling, a confident sort of grin. He watched as she strutted toward the factory as if she owned it. Since he did own it, he wondered if he'd ever come close to such a sure attitude. He imagined once the investor meeting was landed, he would. And now, thanks to her tutelage, he was more confident that the investor meeting would go smoothly than he was about anything. She was incredible, sexy, devastating, gorgeous, flirtatious, fun. But more than any of that, she was good at what she did—both in sales, and in teaching. He had no doubts.

Well…almost no doubts.

They walked into the building together, and several of the factory workers were nudging each other, saying hello to him, asking him how it went. He gave them a thumbs-up, smiling broadly. They seemed heartened. However, they also seemed a little…

"Thank God you're back."

Mrs. Packard hadn't changed a bit since the last time he'd seen her—not that she would, he supposed. "And good morning to you, Mrs. P."

"The place has gone to hell in a handbasket," she said without preamble, "and Ken's about ready to jump off the roof."

He sighed. "I see not much has changed."

"I've got a pot of coffee going, and there are reports on your desk. We've been fighting off creditors, we've been denied shipment on supplies, and the delivery trucks are threatening to sue us," she said, standing and escorting him to his office, frowning at Jade as she did so. "What are you going to want to do first?"

"Get my bearings," he said, feeling his stomach start to tighten as he surveyed the chaos of paperwork that now littered his desk. "Jesus. I'm gone for three weeks, and the factory does everything but catch fire."

"Oh, did Ken tell you about that?" Mrs. Packard looked at him with a solemn expression.

He blinked at her.

"Just kidding," she said, her voice never even changing inflection. "Do you want me to send Ken in?"

"I'll call him when I'm ready. Thanks, Mrs. Packard,'' he said, the bravura he'd walked in with waning quickly. He sat. Jade sat across from him.

''Wow,'' she said, looking around. ''Just...wow.''

''This is insane,'' he muttered, sifting through the paperwork. There were a lot of official-looking letters, stuff with red stamps of Cancelled on it. He swallowed hard.

She stood quickly, walking over to him. ''Don't.''

''Don't what?'' He could barely register what she was saying. It looked like the factory was on the brink of bankruptcy. The success of the sales he got suddenly meant nothing. Less than nothing. He'd been deluding himself. He might as well throw in the towel on the thought of the investor meeting. With this? How was he going to...

To his surprise, she grabbed his face, angling him toward her. ''Listen to me,'' she said, her voice low and impassioned. ''You're going to be fine. This is all temporary stuff. I know you. I believe in you. You can do this.''

''Jade, have you looked at...''

''Shh.'' She leaned forward and kissed him gently. ''Yes, I saw. But remember what I told you? Nobody screws up on my watch. You'll be fine.''

He sighed. ''I wish I had your confidence sometimes.''

Her green eyes glowed. ''You do have my confidence, Drew.''

He smiled, and would have leaned up for another kiss, but Ken walked in, ruining their moment. ''Drew! Thank God you're here.''

''When did people stop saying hello and start saying 'Drew, thank God you're here' instead?'' Drew muttered.

Ken ignored his little joke. "I've got about twenty fires to put out, the most important being the suppliers. If we don't get some more ore, we are hosed. We have *got* to get more materials in the pipeline!" He stopped, midtirade. "Oh. Hello, Ms. Morrow."

"Jade, please." She smiled. "I imagine you've got a lot to talk about with your boss. Do you have an empty office anywhere that I might use? I want to work on your presentation slides a little bit before I call it quits."

"You'll still be around, though, right?" Drew knew Ken was probably wondering about his attachment. A blind man could have seen that there was something between Drew and his sexy consultant from the minute he walked in the room. But Drew didn't care.

Jade smiled as she got up. "Yes. I'll still be here."

Ken pointed her to a tiny empty office just down the hall. Actually, it was more like a supply room with an old desk in it, but she didn't complain. Drew wasn't surprised. The woman was a fighter.

Well, so was he.

Nine hours and about a million phone calls later, Drew was rubbing at his eyes, feeling the tension between his shoulder blades like a massive vise. The good news was that he'd managed to get their next shipment released with some fast talking and only a few personal favors. The bad news was, it was the last time he'd be able to. He'd used up all of his good grace in one day.

"Drew?"

He looked up, blinking at the darkness. He only had his desk light on. "Jade?" He immediately felt guilty. "I'm sorry. I didn't know you were still here."

"I know." She smiled. She looked tired, too. "I

would've stopped in to see you, but you looked like you were on a roll."

He nodded. "All the fires are put out. Damn, I'm exhausted."

"I can tell." She paused. "Ken just went home. I think it's just us."

"Just a couple more things and then I guess I can go home, too." He looked at her. "And you, too, if you want."

"I was thinking about it."

She sounded serious—and a little hesitant. "I'd love to have you at my house, Jade."

"I know," she said. "But...well, you've got one week until the investor meeting. And it's obvious that you've got a lot going on here."

He frowned. "Well, yeah."

"So I thought I'd go home." She paused. "To my home."

He felt surprise like a belt. He was used to seeing her. He was used to being around her. Hell, they'd spent almost every waking moment, and lately most sleeping moments, within four feet of each other. "You're going back to L.A.? Tonight?"

"You're going to be here for a few more hours, Drew." She squared her shoulders. "I am not asking for sympathy here, but you're not going to know I'm alive until you take care of this factory."

He sighed. "I can't help it, Jade. That's the whole point—that's why I've done all this work. Why *we've* done all of this work."

"I know," she said quickly. "But honestly...what do you think you're going to manage with me tonight? You're going to go home, hopefully eat something, and collapse." She shrugged. "You don't need me there."

He felt a tugging at his chest. The thing was, he wanted her there. She was comfort, and strength.

He wasn't quite sure how to say that, so he said, "Are you sure you're going to be okay driving? It's two hours. Maybe you could just..."

"It's not that late," she said, "and you've done most of the driving for three weeks. I guess I ought to try just to make sure I remember how." She laughed a little. "And don't worry, I'm not abandoning you."

"I wasn't thinking that," he countered quickly. Probably a little too quickly.

She shrugged. "I'll be back on Friday. I figure we'll be able to work more on the weekend, when most of your people are gone and you're less distracted."

He nodded. "Okay," he said, trying to sound nonchalant. "Well, drive carefully."

She grinned, and a little gleam lit in her eyes. "I will be. Oh...and, Drew?"

"Mmm?" He was trying to turn back to his paperwork. He had to focus. She was right, he had way too much work...

She was in front of him in a blink. He only had time to look up before she was straddling his lap, kissing him with fervor. He drank her in, getting drunk on the taste of her. One hand moved to her hip, moving her against him, and the other hand threaded through her hair, pulling her to him even as she clung to him of her own will.

After long minutes, she tugged away, both of them breathless. "I wanted to make sure you didn't forget me in four days."

Four days? He doubted he'd forget her in four lifetimes.

"Just get your stuff taken care of in L.A.," he

rasped, stroking the denim of her jeans as she pulled away. "And hurry back here."

She gave him one last lingering kiss, then strode out of the room and into the dimly lit hallway...and, he noticed she never even looked back once.

"JADE. It seems like forever."

Jade glanced up from her desk, her eyes blurry from staring at her computer screen for hours. "Betsy. Hi. I thought you were at meetings all day."

"Just stopped back to follow up on a few things."

Jade's gaze fell on the clock she'd received after five years with Michaels & Associates. "Jeez. Is it eight o'clock already?"

"Time flies, huh?" Betsy laughed. "Welcome to the fast track."

Jade laughed with her, albeit weakly. "Yeah. Well, I finished up that digital organizer stuff you asked for. It's waiting on your desk."

Betsy's perfectly outlined lips pursed in a moue of disappointment. "I was really hoping you'd be a little more timely with that," she noted. "I could have used more time to go over the notes."

Jade bit back a retort. It was on top of her other duties, and she had the Inesco stuff to worry about. Still, she kept silent, simply shrugging. "I'm sorry about that. The Robson account..."

"I will be so glad when you're off that account," Betsy said with a huff of impatience. "I certainly hope you're bringing this one in. The partners are pretty dubious—especially after this whole road trip business. I mean, what if everybody here decided to work remote?"

Then they'd probably be twice as productive, Jade

thought rebelliously. But she was tired, and cranky. She'd been in the office for twelve hours. And worst of all, she missed Drew. More than she thought she'd miss anybody. She'd tried burying herself in work to forget about him for a little while, and it wasn't working.

She wondered if anything would.

"Jade?"

She realized that Betsy had continued talking and that Jade had been so deep in her thoughts of Drew, she'd ignored her boss completely. "Sorry. I blinked out there for a moment," she said, truly apologetic now. "I'm a little worn down."

"You've got to stay sharp, Jade," Betsy said. "In this business, there's always somebody younger and hungrier who's bucking for your job. If you don't stay sharp, you get pushed aside. Remember that, Jade."

Jade nodded. Her parents had proclaimed similar advice from time to time…when they were home. "I'll work on it."

"Great." Betsy nodded. "I'll be going home in about half an hour. If I have questions on the organizer stuff, is it all right if I call you?"

"My cell phone will be on," Jade said automatically.

"Great. It'll either be tonight or tomorrow morning—my meeting's at eight."

Which meant that any call would be either after nine o'clock or before seven, Jade thought as she watched her boss walk away.

And all this can be mine, someday.

She closed her eyes, rubbing at them with the heels of her palms. She was stressed. She had too much going on. It was funny—when she was with Drew, the hard work and long hours didn't seem to run her down as much. Maybe that was rose-colored glasses, but when she was able to vent to him, it was like being able to vent to Hailey. He made her feel comforted. He could either make her laugh about it or he'd listen sympathetically.

And, she thought with a grin, he usually had a way of making tension just melt out of her body.

Her body responded with a zing, and she quickly redirected her thoughts. She'd only been away from him for three days. In a way, she was glad…if she was having this much trouble away from him, what would she do when she was on the road for weeks or, worse, months at a time? How would she manage to do her job if all she could think about was Drew and how much she wanted to be with him?

What's worse…did he feel the same way? And when all this was done, what if he decided he didn't want to see her again, ever? What would she do then?

She groaned, leaning her head back and feeling the tension in her shoulder blades like a vise.

She clicked open her e-mail, and smiled to see a note from Hailey.

"Hey, there. Hope things are going well. I'll be down in L.A. in a week or two," Jade read. "I've still got your key, so keep an eye out for me. I'll be expecting a full report. Hope you're feeling better."

That was Hailey—always thinking of her. Then she saw another e-mail—from an address she didn't quite recognize. She almost deleted it, until she read the subject. Steel Man Seeks Expert.

She opened it, and laughed, delighted.

"When you read this, I hope you realize that I'm

miserable. I'm neck deep in slides, and without you here, I've discovered they aren't half as fascinating."

She grinned.

"The hard thing is—I've discovered few things are. Get back here as soon as you can. Drew."

It wasn't a love sonnet, or anything really romantic, she thought. But her heart still melted and she felt warmth seeping through her. She smiled, a goofy, foolish smile, she felt sure.

He missed her. Suddenly she felt better.

DREW WALKED INTO his apartment like a zombie. It was finally Friday night, and only seven o'clock. He walked mechanically to the small table by the door, dropping his keys in a bowl of marbles. He couldn't have been more exhausted if he'd been pummeled by a gang of lead-pipe-wielding accountants. Every other night that week, he had been at Robson Steel until eleven o'clock at night. He usually had just enough energy to nuke a microwave dinner before collapsing into bed. Worse, every night he'd dreamed up new nightmares. He gave his investor's presentation in the nude. He faced hordes of angry, unemployed workers as they surrounded his apartment with torches. He'd also had nightmares involving Jade, he remembered. Not that the dreams themselves were nightmares—at least, not at first. Normally the dreams themselves were pure pleasure, seeming as real as if she were there in his apartment. As if she were really in his bed, gasping beneath him as he moved into her. But inevitably, before they got close to climax, she would stand up, gloriously naked, denying him her body to go over presentation slides. He'd wake up, tangled in his sheets, sweating profusely, his body throbbing like a toothache. He was six feet five inches of sexual frustration, and the added pressure of work only made things worse.

He was dangerously close to going nuts.

He peeled off his jacket, dumping it on the back of his couch. He was hoping he'd see Jade this weekend. Unfortunately he'd only been able to steal enough time from his workday to snatch five-minute conversations with her…and her cell phone had been dead, as usual, for the rest of the week. He was panicked enough about the presentation to want her advice, but he had to admit, the dreams made him want some other kind of help from her, as well.

No wonder she said this was going to be complicated, he thought with a humorless grin. He wanted to make love with her, but odds were good that if she was there, he'd be thinking of the investor meeting—and when they were prepping for the investor meeting, he'd probably think of getting her naked. He then thought of her naked, her high, full breasts, the smoothness of her stomach, the curves of her long legs.

Well, maybe it wasn't *that* complicated.

There was a knock on his door, and his heart did some quick double-time beats as he crossed his living room to answer it. *Please be Jade. Not Ken, not Mrs. Packard, not anybody from the factory. Please, please be Jade.*

He opened the door, and his wishes were answered. She was standing in her customary dress—black jeans, a snug T-shirt, her hair tumbling across her shoulders in coppery waves.

"Good. I was hoping you'd be home this time." She walked in, a compact rolling suitcase by her side and a sizable brown bag in one hand. He waited until she'd put the bags aside and until he'd shut and locked the door before walking to her and enveloping her in his arms. He didn't say anything. He just savored the heat coming off of her, the soothing feel of her against his body.

"Hey, you," she breathed, rubbing his back in soothing circles with her palms. "That bad a week, huh?"

"Worse," he muttered, nuzzling the top of her head with his chin. Her hair smelled like flowers...roses, he thought. "But I'm feeling better now."

"That's nice." She pulled away enough to look in his face. "Anybody ever tell you that you work too hard, Drew Robson?"

"What do you think?" He laughed. "Doesn't anybody ever tell you that?"

"Not lately," she said, laughing ruefully. "At least, not in my office."

All at once, he felt a pang. If he didn't nail the investment meeting, Robson went under. If Robson went under, Jade wouldn't get paid. If she didn't get paid, she might be really good at what she did, but maybe she'd lose her job, right? That was a pretty big screw-up.

Damn. He felt the tension in his muscles kick up a notch. What was a little more pressure on an already loaded situation, right?

She'd been watching his face, stroking his jawline with her fingertips, so she must've seen his expression change. She pulled a step away from him, her expression stern. "Knock it off. Right now."

"Knock what off?" He heard the surliness in his voice, scowled. "Damn it. I didn't do anything."

"My work problems are just that, okay? Mine." She

crossed her arms. ''It's sweet that you're concerned, but let me worry about it. You can't solve everybody's problems and you're not responsible for everybody's well-being. You've got enough on your plate.''

He might have been surprised at her perceptiveness before their three week road trip. Now, he just dug in his heels. ''What's on my plate directly affects you,'' he pointed out.

She looked for a moment as she had when they'd first started out, her mouth drawn in a mutinous line. Then her expression softened and she reached up and kissed him, her lips coaxing away the frown on his face. When her tongue traced his lips, he parted them willingly, groaning as he tasted her. When she pulled away, his heart was trip-hammering in his chest and his body was tense for an entirely different reason.

''Drew, I think you're one of the most caring, amazing men I've ever met,'' she said, her eyes shining. ''But, sweetie, you have to take care of yourself right now. If you don't, you won't be any good to anybody.''

He knew she was telling him the truth, but it was hard not to worry about her.

Especially feeling the way I do about her.

He let her lead him to his kitchen table. ''All right. So first off, we feed you.''

He smiled as she pulled out to-go containers, obviously from Grady's. ''Woman, you are too good to me,'' he said, then groaned as he sat. ''Man. I'm a wreck.''

Her eyes had narrowed at the noise, and she scooted around behind his chair. Before he could reach for the food, she started kneading the knotted muscles at the base of his neck. He groaned again, this time in pleasure.

"If you want to do that for...I don't know, a year or two," he said, feeling the strength of her fingertips start melting away some of the stored tension in his shoulders, "I won't complain one bit."

"You are possibly the most stressed-out guy I've ever seen," she muttered. "Don't you ever relax? Do yoga, tai chi...breathing exercises? Anything?"

"Um...I play basketball," he said with a chuckle. "We're not big on yoga here in San Angelo."

"Did you play this week?"

He grimaced as she hit a sore spot, both literally and figuratively. "I'll relax next week, after this is all over."

She sighed impatiently. Then, he felt her tugging on the chair. He helped her by scooting away from the table a little bit. "What?" he asked innocently.

She stared at him for a moment...then a slow, naughty smile spread on her face. "You know, I have ways of making resisters like yourself relax," she said.

The sexy look on her face, combined with a week's worth of frustration for her, made him go hard in a rush. "Really?" he said, his voice challenging. "Well, I don't know..."

He stopped when she straddled the chair, putting her arms around his neck. "Are you going to cooperate?" She nipped at his neck.

"Never," he breathed, nipping her in return then inhaling sharply as she rotated her hips in a sinuous, sensual motion. The friction of her jeans against his groin elicited a groan.

"Well..." she said as she got off him for a second, making him almost whimper. "We'll have to see about that."

He was seeing about that. In fact, he thought as she

kicked off her shoes and reached for the fly of her jeans, he was riveted.

She inched the zipper down, tooth by tooth, smirking at him. Then she eased the material off of her hips, exposing a pair of thong-cut panties. She smiled when his eyes widened.

"Boy," he said on a strangled whisper, "you take no prisoners, huh?"

She shook her head, then pulled her jeans off one leg at a time, leaving her only in the T-shirt and the panties. He started to get up, but she stopped him.

"I'm the one in charge here," she murmured, cupping his cock through the material of his slacks. He leaned his head back, closing his eyes.

"Okay," he replied, then let out a small noise as she undid the fly of his pants, moving the zipper down tooth by tooth. "No complaints here."

"I'm going to relax you to within an inch of your life," she said. The zipper was finally all the way down and he could barely feel the air hitting his sensitive erection through the opening in his boxers. She went directly for him with knowing fingers. When he felt the barely there touch of her fingertips stroking him, his hips jerked reflexively.

"Did you miss me?"

He groaned as she pulled him out of his pants. "You have to ask?"

She straddled him again, gently. "I missed you," she said, pausing to kiss him thoroughly. He felt his cock brush against the silky fabric of her panties, and pushed up to meet her. He felt dampness against his flesh and kissed her harder, his hands jetting up to her hips, trying to tug her down to meet him more snugly.

"Uh-uh," she said, pulling away a little. Then she

reached for the edge of her T-shirt, pulling it over her head. He held his breath. She wasn't wearing a bra, and her breasts were right in front of him. She leaned forward, smiling. He didn't need more invitation, leaning forward, sucking gently first on one nipple, then the other. She arched her back and he was treated to the dual sensation of her breasts pressing more firmly into his mouth as the hot heat between her thighs cuddled his erection. His groan was muffled by her, and he was gratified by her responding sound of pleasure as he teased her nipple with his tongue and then his teeth.

"I missed you so much," she repeated, her hips rubbing against him. He felt the fabric of her panties move a little to the side and he wanted nothing more than to press into her. "And I wanted you."

"I want you now, Jade," he said, circling her nipples with his thumbs. He raised his arms as she pulled his shirt over his head, throwing it onto the floor. They kissed again and he reached down, stroking her clit through the now soaked fabric, feeling the head of his cock probing her, frustrated by the material between them.

"Condom," she muttered. Her lips were swollen and her nipples puckered. She moved just enough to grab a condom from her purse. She ripped through the foil packaging, then rolled the condom onto him. He gasped first at the coldness of the latex compared to the heat of her, then again at the firm feel of her palm stroking him with knowing pressure. He lifted his hips enough to let her tug off his boxers and pants, then watched as she pulled her own panties off. They were both naked, in his living room.

Thank God there aren't any windows in this room,

he thought briefly before she straddled him with purpose this time, lowering herself, impaling herself on him. Then his rational thought blinked out. Her body gripped him and he felt her breasts against his chest as she pushed him fully into her. He gripped her hips, pulling her against him, and she let out a small gasp of pleasure, her head thrown back, her eyes closed.

"Drew," she whispered, her breathing turning quickly to small, uneven panting. "Oh, yes."

He raised her a little, still raining kisses on her collarbone, the hollow between her breasts. She was moving her hips in a small rolling motion, and the friction and pressure was driving him wild. She'd pull off of him enough to make him crazy, then drive herself onto him with enough force to leave him breathless. He closed his eyes as the feel of her exploded through him.

"Jade," he said, pulling her to him, as if he wanted them to become one person. She kissed him hungrily and their tongues twined as she ground against him, bringing him as deeply into her as she could. She bucked against him and he arched his back, meeting her stroke for stroke.

Their pace was increasing now, quickening. He could feel the pressure mounting in him, as she rode him, her stomach rubbing against his, her body tightening around him. The heat of her was incredible. He thought he'd die from holding off, waiting...

"Drew," she breathed, and he felt it: her grip like a vise as she wrapped her legs around his waist and drove him into her. He didn't wait. He succumbed to the feel of her, letting the orgasm rip through him like a bullet. It seemed to go on forever, her twisting against him, clutching him, his pleasure spilling out volcanically. Finally she collapsed against him, each tiny

movement of her pelvis sending aftershocks of pleasure through him.

Long moments later he nudged her up, pushing sweaty curls away from her face. She looked dazed, her mossy-green eyes dreamy, a small, smug smile haunting the corners of her lips. He had to say, she looked pretty sated.

"So," she purred. "Tell me you're not relaxed."

A mischievous little part of him caused him to grin. "Well," he drawled. "It was a hard week, you know."

Her eyes widened, then narrowed as the fires of battle lit.

"Well now," she replied, and he felt her thighs tighten almost imperceptibly. "Why don't I get some food into you…and then we'll see if I can't do a better job."

9

THIS WAS IT. Game time. The big deal. The whole enchilada. This would make or break both Robson Steel and Jade's career in one fell swoop. They got the investor backing, Drew cut a check to Michaels & Associates, and she got the promotion. If not, Robson Steel went under…and Jade was given her walking papers.

She sat at the table, next to Ken Shimoda. Mrs. Packard had coffee prepared. The investors were huddled at the other side of the table, talking among themselves.

"Now, don't worry," Ken said to Jade, although it was evident that he was just trying to convince himself. "It'll be fine. You've been working hard with Drew. It'll be fine. Everything will be fine."

"Ken?"

He looked at her, his eyes ever so slightly frantic in his hound-dog face. "Yeah?"

"Switch to decaf." She got up when he sent her a weak smile, and walked over to where Drew was, going over his slides. "How are you doing, chief?"

He looked up at her, and all she could think about was the lazy way he'd held her that morning…the look of slumberous pleasure in his eyes before he'd moved on top of her and said good morning as only Drew Robson could. She could still feel her toes curl slightly just at the memory of it. "I haven't gotten any complaints yet,'' he said in a low voice, his eyes gleaming. Obviously he remembered, too.

''Well, keep your eye on the ball. I don't have any doubts, you understand.'' She leaned in a little. ''But let's just say once you get through this, and you can finally relax, I'm going to do things to you that most men only dream of.''

''Don't tease when I'm just about to step into a meeting,'' he murmured back, but there was humor as well as sensual warmth in his eyes. ''Oh, one more thing.''

''Yes?''

''I love you,'' he said simply. ''In case I get distracted later.''

She felt her heart stop for a beat, then resume at twice its normal speed. ''What?''

''Shh,'' he said, and his grin was devilish. ''Gotta do this thing now.''

And with that, he stepped toward the table. ''I think we're all here now. Let's get started.''

Jade remained rooted where she was for a second, stunned. He loved her. He actually said it.

He actually said it just before the biggest meeting she'd ever been involved in. When she couldn't say anything in return or ask any questions or have any time to really process it.

She sat in her seat.

When this is all over, I am going to kill him.

She glanced at the head of the table, where he was sitting. He just grinned at her.

''What we're here to discuss is Inesco's possible investment in Robson Steel. After today's meeting, you should be able to see why investing in our plant is the best move for Inesco...what we can offer, what sort of flexibility you'll have, and what a relationship in Robson Steel will do for you."

Not too fast, Jade thought. He was casual, and he sounded relaxed, confident. That was important. He wasn't stressing. His speech was slow and easygoing. Great, she thought. He's doing great.

He loves me.

She shook off the thought. Not that there was a lot she could do now, since she wasn't going to be an active participant in the meeting. Still, she was going to monitor how he was doing, and nudge Ken if she had to. She'd helped orchestrate the presentation. She knew every single bullet point, every anecdote, every argument. She now knew more about steel than she ever thought she would in her life.

He loves me.

If she could just move past that point!

He looked great, standing there. He looked like a man in charge of millions, not a desperate steel mill on the brink of bankruptcy, asking for money hat in hand. It was exactly the right thing.

He looked good enough to eat, on top of it.

He loves me. And I love him.

She hadn't anticipated this, she thought as she watched him move into the presentation, fielding questions like a pro. She hadn't ever thought she'd open up to someone and trust them enough to love them. But he was quite possibly the best man, one of the best people, she'd ever met. When she was hurting, he did something about it. He listened to her opinions. He trusted her with his business, which these days was the closest thing to trusting her with his life.

He loves me.

She was just a little bit terrified of what was supposed to happen next.

Does he want me to stay with him? What if I have to travel a lot? Will he be all right with that?

This wasn't helping in the short term. Short term was all they had.

"If you invest in Robson, you get the following benefits..."

He was focusing on benefits. That was good. What was the benefit of her staying with him?

He was an honest man. He was loyal. Look how sincere he was about the community. He genuinely cared about it. And he was...ethical.

She wasn't going to go into the ethics thing. Not now.

The head of Inesco was a dark-haired man who didn't really speak much—he left the speaking to his second-in-command, who was shorter, had a spiky blond haircut and the tenacity of a pit bull. He kept cornering Drew, but it was Drew's show. She sat there next to Ken, stopping her toe from tapping or her fingers from fidgeting. Stopping herself from leaping up and starting to talk.

It's Drew's show. He has *to take care of this himself.*

Still...it was hard to just sit there.

Especially when you love him so much.

The blond pit bull was conferring in a low voice to his boss, then he looked at Drew, steepling his fingers, just like a bad guy in a movie. He was going in for the final question. They'd been there for an hour and a half. They knew everything there was to know about Robson, about steel, about San Angelo. About Drew. What was he planning?

"Mr. Robson," the guy said smoothly, considering

the attacks he'd been lobbing all afternoon, "we've just got one last question."

"Fire away," Drew said, as if he were fielding one last pitch from a questionnaire or something.

"Give us one reason...one *good* reason," the guy tacked on, "why we should go with you over any of the three competitors we've spoken with."

She could feel Ken tense up. They hadn't mentioned the competitors up to this point. This was it. The go-for-the-jugular question. The defining moment.

She looked at him.

To her surprise, he looked at her, not at the Inesco guys. She barely noticed that the blond guy especially noticed this, too. His blue eyes were as always intense. Just like always, she felt like holding her breath.

Game on, Drew!

And then, slowly, he smiled.

He looked back at the Inesco guys.

"Let me make sure I've got your question down right," he said, his voice slow but sure. "From what we've gone over, in all our past dealings, ending with this afternoon, I've gotten the impression that Inesco is a company that's growing, that's looking for partners to grow with."

Even though he wasn't looking at her, she could still feel as if he were talking to her. She nodded, slowly, silently cheering him on.

"Your company has a lot of history, and you feel a lot of the newer companies don't share that vision."

She felt the smile tugging at her own lips. That knocked out one of their newer competitors. The dark-haired guy was still sitting there, stock-still, and blond guy was still frowning.

"You're also having trouble finding a partner with the same commitment to quality, I believe."

She clasped her hands together under the table to prevent herself from doing a high five. One of their competitors had trouble with quality control...it was well documented. He wasn't calling it out, he was putting it in terms Inesco themselves had said. Yes! Yes!

"And you're looking for a partner who is just as strong as Inesco, who has the same strong beliefs concerning progress, innovation and streamlining. Did I get that right?"

He'd just showed his ideas on those very subjects. She kept her poker face on, even as she scrutinized the Inesco table.

Slowly, Mr. Inesco, the dark-haired gentleman, smiled.

"Mr. Robson," he said, his voice deep and very slightly accented, "I think you've covered what we're looking for perfectly."

"Mr. Inesco," Drew replied, "I think that Robson Steel covers what you're looking for. Perfectly."

There was a minute of silence.

Then Mr. Inesco laughed.

There was a general sound of applause, cheering, and Mr. Inesco and Drew shook hands. Everything else turned into a blur for Jade. The bottom line was, they landed the sale. Drew *nailed* the sale. Slam-dunk. Game over. We were the champs.

She stood, using the chaos as cover.

Her job was done, she thought. It wouldn't quite process. She had been part of the Robson world, so deeply lately, that she simply couldn't believe it was over.

Before she'd gotten too far, Drew walked over to her. "There you are!"

She turned back to him. "Wait a minute. Shouldn't you be back in there? You just landed the investment deal. You should be celebrating!"

"Mrs. Packard is pouring champagne," he said, taking her hand and tugging her toward his office, "and Ken is entertaining them with some stories of the old days at Robson. Mr. Inesco's being charming and his watchdog guy is obviously figuring out what he needs to do as far as paperwork. We're covered for a few minutes."

"But..."

"But nothing," he said with finality as they entered his office and he shut the door. "This is more important."

"Drew," she said, even as her heart fluttered, "this is *no* time for a quickie."

He looked at her. "Well...if you insist. But first things first."

He tugged her to his desk, putting her on its surface. "Drew!" she squealed.

He wiggled his eyebrows...and then, to her surprise, he put his speakerphone on and started dialing.

"Drew, what are you doing?"

He put a finger to his lips, hushing her. The phone rang through, and then a female voice answered. "Michaels and Associates."

Jade shot a look at Drew.

"I'd like to speak to..." He paused. "What's your boss's name, Jade?"

"It's Betsy Diehl," she said. "Hey, wait a second..."

"Betsy Diehl, please," he said, putting his fingers over Jade's lips.

Jade watched as he grinned, waiting for Betsy to come on the phone.

"Betsy Diehl."

"Ms. Diehl, this is Drew Robson. I'm the owner and president of Robson Steel. I've got one of your account execs working with me."

"Ah. Mr. Robson." Jade hadn't heard Betsy go into client mode before. Her voice sounded like drizzled honey. "What can I do for you today?"

"You've already done enough, by sending me Jade," he said, winking at Jade. Jade could feel the heat of a blush start creeping over her cheeks. "I just wanted to let you know that I'll be sending that check for one hundred thousand dollars to Michaels and Associates, as promised."

Jade let out a little gasp, but it went unheard behind his palm.

"I also wanted to say, for the record, that I wouldn't have been able to without Jade Morrow's help," he said, and she felt her chest warm with pride. She had to blink hard against the moisture in her eyes. This was not what she had expected.

He knew how much it would mean to her, she thought. She hadn't realized he was so perceptive.

"That's fantastic. We've got a reputation to uphold here at Michaels and Associates," Betsy said, although her voice was a little flat. "Could you get her a message for me, then?"

He grinned, leaning forward and pressing a silent kiss on Jade's neck, causing her to shiver. "I think I can manage," he answered loudly.

"Wonderful. In light of her work there, she's more

than earned what we promised. She'll get that promotion to account supervisor.'' Betsy paused. ''Not to say that she wouldn't have worked just as hard on your account anyway, Mr. Robson. But there was a certain...well, let's just say there was a test involved in this one. And she passed with flying colors.''

Drew looked at the phone, nonplussed. Jade, however, froze.

He's not going to understand.

''I'll, uh, tell her,'' Drew said, looking at Jade with puzzlement.

''Wonderful. We here at Michaels and Associates look forward to working with you more,'' Betsy said, her voice going back to that persuasive pitch. ''Perhaps we could extend a further contract...''

''I'm sorry, I've got to run, Ms. Diehl,'' Drew said. ''It's been nice talking with you.''

''Of course. Goodbye.''

He hung up, and looked at Jade, pulling away a little. ''Account supervisor, huh?''

''It's not...oh, crap,'' she said, standing next to him and reaching for him. ''It's really not as bad as it might sound. I didn't...you can't honestly think that I...''

Ken burst into the room. ''Drew! Come on, man. The champagne's poured and Mr. Inesco has some questions for you. We also need to schedule a few conference calls. Come on!''

''Okay,'' Drew said, then turned to Jade. ''I have to take care of this stuff.''

''We'll talk later,'' she said, feeling a miserable lump in her stomach.

''Sure.''

She watched as he left, shooting her one last look before disappearing back into the conference room.

He doesn't believe me.

She had to make him.

OUT TO DINNER. Thank God the Italian restaurant had reopened. The new decor was a big step up from the old, red-and-white-checkered-vinyl tablecloths. He guessed they were aiming for more upscale. At any rate, the Inesco people were pretty happy at having the decision finally nailed down, and obviously he and Ken were happy. Ken was actually more cheerful than he'd seen in years. He was certainly more happy than he'd ever been since Drew had taken over the helm of Robson Steel.

She was in it for the promotion.

"So there Drew was, only seventeen years old, and sitting in the rig of one of our delivery trucks..."

Drew tuned out the story that had the Inesco gang guffawing and making peanut gallery comments. He tried grinning, but it was an effort. Even though he'd made one of the biggest deals of his life today, the thing that would save his plant, he still couldn't quite get in the festive mood.

She finally got what she wanted: the promotion.

It wasn't as if it was a huge shock, he thought, pushing the salt and pepper shakers around on the new white tablecloth. She was a businesswoman, he was a businessman. They happened to be doing business with each other. And she'd tried to warn him that this would get messy, the intersection of business and pleasure, as it were.

It just seems convenient, damn it. She keeps me happy, I get the deal, she gets the promotion.

He shook his head as Ken hit the punch line of his

anecdote. "And Drew says, 'Don't look at me, officer, I'm just here for the ride!' I'm not kidding!"

The Inesco guys laughed. Ken laughed. Drew forced a chuckle.

I'm just here for the ride.

"Say," one of the men at the far end of the table said when the laughter subsided, "who was the young woman with the red hair? And why isn't she here?"

Ken looked at Drew quickly, to see if he wanted to field it. When Drew didn't say anything immediately, Ken took over. "That was Jade Morrow. She's a sales consultant and public relations expert working with Robson Steel, sort of on a short-term basis."

Drew braced himself for the inevitable questions—how long had she been there, what did she do exactly, and even worse...was she, you know, available? She was attractive, and a lot of these guys weren't married. It was, he supposed, a reasonable question.

The real question being...is she available?

They'd only known each other for a matter of weeks...had only had a few encounters, if you were going to be grossly technical about it. They hadn't talked long-term commitment. Hell, they hadn't even talked about where she was staying that night. He didn't know what he had a right to.

It could've just been business. Not that it didn't mean anything to her, but the business is over, the contract is closed. Where does that leave me?

"Is she the one that pulled together the presentation, then?"

Drew blinked. That wasn't one of the questions he had mentally steeled himself for. "Uh, yes. I mean, yes, she worked on the graphics and the layout and helped us get it organized."

Ken was frowning a little—Drew figured he didn't want to divulge just how much outside help they'd had with the presentation. But that wasn't the point here. Besides, they knew that Drew's strong point was his knowledge of the steel business, not his dog-and-pony-show skills.

"Impressive," Armand Inesco said with a nod. "Is she a freelancer, or does she work with a firm?"

"She's with Michaels and Associates," Drew replied, and was surprised to see the look of recognition go across the Inesco team's faces.

"That explains why your presentation was head and shoulders above any of your competitors," Armand said, sounding impressed. "She's worked with steel companies before, then?"

"No, not to my knowledge." Drew frowned. "Why?"

"You're going to be doing a lot of improvements over the next year," he answered. "And you're going to want a lot more sales to give us the return on investment that we're looking for. So we were thinking of putting in a provision—you'll improve your sales team and your marketing department. That would include advertising and P.R." He smiled gently. "We figured that you got some outside help, and when we didn't see her at the dinner, we assumed she wasn't really a Robson employee."

Drew nodded with respect. The guy was on the ball. This wasn't about "who was the hot redhead we saw earlier," as he'd stupidly assumed. They knew she was talented.

He was getting hung up on Jade…and he obviously was letting it blind him to business. She'd warned him that might happen, as well.

"Michaels and Associates might be a good place to start, but they focus primarily on public relations. We'd like to suggest a marketing consultant."

Drew shrugged. "I'm sure we could..."

"In fact," Armand said, "you might want to think about letting Inesco help you with that."

Drew shot a quick glance at Ken. Suddenly what the guy was doing made sense. He was trying to change the deal a little...and make Robson even more a part of Inesco's house, rather than just invest money.

"We'll work out something," Drew said with a cool smile.

It wasn't personal, Drew reminded himself as Ken launched into another story and a guy from the Inesco side responded with some humorous tales of his own. He was so fixated on the fact that Jade might've been using him to get what she wanted, that he had blinded himself to the fact that she had helped him, above and beyond the call of duty. She had tried nothing tricky or underhanded. She hadn't been looking out for number one, as it were. She had kept him in mind, what he believed in...and she had believed in him. She didn't need to do that to get her promotion. She certainly hadn't needed to sleep with him to guarantee it. In fact, sleeping with him had jeopardized what she'd wanted. It could have ruined his focus, just as she'd warned. It could have sunk her. She'd risked a lot to get close to him.

Why was he getting suspicious of her motives? And why wasn't he talking to her about it and clearing it up?

He glanced around the table. It looked like the Inesco guys were settling in for a long night of partying, right here at the restaurant—it wasn't as though a little town like San Angelo had a strip joint or a night-club for them to frequent. He smiled, then got up, motioning Ken to join him. Ken left them talking to each other, and accompanied Drew to an alcove that held the public telephones. "What's up, Drew?"

"How long do you think these guys are going to be going at it?"

Ken glanced back at the table. "These guys look like they're in it for the long haul. I see another couple of hours at least."

"And you? How are you doing?"

Ken grinned. "No problem. I can handle these guys with one hand tied behind my back."

"Great," Drew said with relief. "I hate to do this to you, but I was wondering...do you think you could finish up with them, make sure they get into a cab okay, and take care of the bill?"

Ken's grin slipped. "Where are you going?"

"I've got some things I have to handle," Drew said.

"The deal's done. Everything's settled but the signatures," Ken countered. "Why don't you take a night off, just enjoy the moment?"

"It's not..." He took a deep breath. "It's not really Robson Steel related, Ken."

Ken looked blank for a moment. Then his eyes narrowed. "Tell me this doesn't have to do with a certain tall redheaded woman who didn't come with us to dinner."

Drew shrugged. "Let's just say it's personal, and leave it at that?"

"I can't believe this," Ken said in a low voice. "You've just landed the biggest deal of your life. You have to stay here and do this. These are the investors.

You have to represent Robson. For Christ's sake, your sex life can wait a few damned hours!"

Drew felt anger pulse through him. "Watch it, Ken."

"No, Drew, you watch it," Ken answered with a flash of temper of his own. "This is important. I know you've been with this woman twenty-four-seven for the past three weeks, and I know she looks like God's gift to horny bachelors, but this is about the *plant.*" His expression was disapproving. "Think with the big head for a change, Drew."

"When haven't I put the plant first?" Drew shot back.

"Since you first laid eyes on Jade Morrow," Ken replied. "A few hours. Then you can patch things up with her. But you have to nail this first."

Drew knew what he was saying made sense, even though the anger wouldn't dissipate. Ken was right—the plant came first, had to come first. Jade would understand.

He hoped.

"Okay. I'll be back at the table in a second," Drew said.

Ken nodded. "We'll talk more later," he warned, then headed back to the table, putting a big smile on before he got there. In so many ways, Ken was more a Robson than Drew himself. The plant, always the plant, before anything else.

Drew pulled out some change and got on a pay phone, pulling Jade's card out of his wallet. It had her cell phone number on it, but when he called, he got her voice mail. Chances were good it was either shut off or the battery was dead. He knew she had a habit of not charging it.

He decided to leave a message. "Jade...if you're still in San Angelo, or even if you're not, I want to see you as soon as possible. I'll drive to L.A. if you've already gone home. But we need to talk, and soon." He paused, wanting to add more, but unsure of what exactly he wanted to say. "Just...call me at home. We really need to talk."

He hung up, frustrated. There was a burst of raucous laughter from his table. The last thing he wanted to do was to sit there, swapping stories with the guys, under the watchful, crafty gaze of Armand Inesco. Or deal with Ken's forced joviality, knowing that he was blaming Drew for not staying focused.

Just another few hours, Drew thought without enthusiasm. Then he'd get to the bottom of the Jade thing. He only hoped he'd have the chance to make things right.

JADE STRETCHED OUT. She'd been sitting in the hallway of Drew's apartment building for the past—she glanced at her watch—four hours. She'd checked her messages when she first got there, but her phone had characteristically gone dead since then. She didn't know how long Drew was planning on being gone. He was so angry, and puzzled, when he'd put the call through.

She frowned. And what was the deal with Betsy? If she hadn't known better, she would've thought her mentor was angry with her. Or angry in general. She didn't know what was going on with that. Of course, maybe she was being paranoid. She'd come so close to getting promoted in the past, and something had always seemed to come up to stymie her progress. Maybe she was just trying to throw hurdles in her own way, she thought, grabbing her organizer out of her backpack and opening it. Maybe she was just trying to keep things complicated. It sounded like her. She'd just scored a huge coup, and she should be happy. Why wasn't she?

She glanced at her watch again, then closed her eyes. *Because of Drew.*

She'd known that sleeping with him was going to complicate things. What she hadn't counted on was falling in love with him.

She closed her eyes, leaning her head back against the wall. It was ludicrous to think that she was in love after less than a month. They'd only slept together for—what?—two weeks. Not that that was any kind of indicator of love, she supposed. But even if they'd never had sex, she would've known that what they had was special. He was everything she'd ever looked for. He was passionate, attentive. She grinned, foolishly. He was quixotic. She'd never met anyone quite like him, especially not in her line of work. He was the real thing.

She liked that reality.

"You haven't been here long, have you?"

She opened her eyes. "Drew," she said, rising then almost toppling over as the stiffness in her muscles from sitting on the floor for so long made getting up difficult. "I was hoping you'd get here."

"If I'd known you were waiting here," he said, helping to steady her, "I would've tried to get here sooner. If I had been thinking, I would've given you a key."

"You didn't know," she said hastily, "and you were pretty upset with me when you left today." She took a deep breath. "Which is what I wanted to talk to you about, Drew. I didn't—"

He put a finger on her lips, stopping the stream of words that was trying to tumble out. "It's okay. I understand," he said. "Come on inside. You must be exhausted."

"I really need to talk to you, though," she protested when he uncovered her mouth. "I wasn't just sleeping with you to..."

"I know." He smiled, opening the door. "Really. You don't have to talk about it."

She huffed impatiently. "I've just detailed a whole speech in the four hours I've had to wait for you. If you think you're off the hook without hearing some of it, then you're out of your mind."

He laughed as he walked into his apartment, shutting the door behind her and putting his keys in the bowl. "Okay. Far be it for me to deny you a well-thought-out speech."

She paced, working the kinks out of her system, and took her jacket off, draping it on the back of his couch. Just looking at his living room brought back a flood of sensual memories. "I wasn't just sleeping with you to keep you happy. I wasn't just trying to satisfy the client, as you so artlessly put it when we first met."

He winced. "I know better."

"I slept with you because I..." She thought about what she was about to admit, chickened out. Tempered it. "I cared about you. I still care about you. A lot," she added.

"I...care about you, too," Drew said. "You really don't have to go through all of this. I understand."

"I don't think you do," she countered stubbornly. "You don't know what I went through. I've never slept with a client before. I like keeping my life simple, and you were anything but."

She thought about it, getting agitated, walking around at an ever-increasing pace. "In fact, I told you that sleeping together was going to complicate things. I tried to keep it casual once we did it, but you wouldn't let me. I've done more for you than I have for anyone I've been involved with."

"Are we involved?"

She glared at him. "What do you think?"

His eyes glowed. "I'd like to think we are," he said, disarming her immediately. "But it didn't occur to me until I was at dinner that I didn't know what you thought."

She paused. This changed things.

"I've already said I cared about you," she said, backpedaling a little bit. "And I got together with you for reasons that were anything but business-related."

"I'll admit," he said slowly, walking up to her and taking her hands in his, "I was...well, I was ticked off when we spoke with Betsy earlier. I didn't know how much you had riding on all of this. And yeah, I'll admit that I thought maybe you were sleeping with me as a guarantee, to try to get me to succeed so you could succeed."

"You know," she said as realization dawned on her, "I've spent the past four hours worried that you might be thinking that. Now that I hear you say it, I realize that I shouldn't have been worried. I should be ticked off." She frowned at him. "Okay, now I am. You believed that I just slept with you to get what I wanted? What's wrong with you?"

He chuckled. "Now, now, don't get upset. I thought about it and I realized that I was wrong. No...that I had to be insane to believe that you'd think sleeping with me would actually increase my chances of success.''

She blinked. ''You're confusing me,'' she complained.

''I know. I'm confused myself. But I will say one thing.''

''What?'' she finally prompted when he just stared at her.

He rested his forehead against hers. ''I think I'm falling in love with you. How's that for complicated?''

She held her breath.

Love.

She leaned up, kissing him gently, tenderly, with all the emotion she was scared of saying out loud.

After a long moment he held her in his arms, in a warm, crushing embrace. ''That's why I asked if we were involved,'' he said, and she felt the words through her more than just heard him. ''I wanted to know if you might be feeling the same way.''

She froze. ''I...well.''

''I know it's sudden,'' he said when she'd fallen quiet for a moment. ''I'm not asking you to change your whole life. I'm just asking you to make some room in it for me.''

She didn't know what to say to that. ''I know that I care about you. And I might...'' She took a deep breath. If she admitted she loved him, or thought she was falling in love with him, what happened if she was wrong? Or worse...what if he realized he was wrong, and she didn't? They barely knew each other. It was more than a long shot.

''Shh. I shouldn't have crept up on you with that,'' he said, stroking her hair. ''Will you stay with me tonight?''

She nodded, grateful at the reduction of pressure. He leaned down and kissed her, and she tickled his tongue with her own. He laughed into her mouth. The two of them made their way toward the bedroom, shedding clothes slowly on the way there.

"I wanted you," he said. "If it hadn't been for that stupid dinner, I would've left. I was dying to see you."

"You did what you had to," she discounted, ignoring the hours of waiting. "I would've probably done the same thing."

"I'm glad you waited," he said, taking off her shirt and smiling.

"I'm glad I did, too," she said. "Now, anyway."

10

JADE STEPPED BACK into the office of Michaels & Associates for the first time in a month. It felt strange, surreal. She'd already had to fight Los Angeles traffic to get to the office, so she was running a little bit late. Still, they'd been so pleased with the outcome, she knew they weren't going to be pointing out her slight tardiness. Of course, she probably had a pile of work on her desk that was taller than she was, but that wouldn't matter much. She was looking forward to it. She wondered if they were planning on putting her in an actual office, now that she was an account supervisor. Of course, there was a chance she wasn't going to be in the office much anyway. Or in the country, for that matter.

I wonder if that's negotiable?

After all, there were still plenty of clients that she was responsible for. And just because Michaels & Associates wanted to expand internationally didn't mean that *she* necessarily was the person for the job. Maybe it was still up in the air. But if they did think she was responsible enough to handle working on the road, maybe they'd be up for her telecommuting. Say, from San Angelo. Assuming, of course, that she'd be there often. She could just go there on weekends...even though the weeks apart from him were excruciating, surely that would wear off, right?

Hell. I haven't even broached the subject with Drew.

She'd spent a wonderful weekend with Drew. She got the feeling both of them realized that after that weekend, they'd both be buried in work...her from her new promotion, him with his new improvements and renovations to the factory. Still, it didn't feel like a last weekend for either of them. On the contrary, she felt more hopeful than she could remember feeling in years. She didn't want to ruin it, maybe, by talking about plans for the future.

"Promise me you'll call me tomorrow night," he'd said, sealing the promise with a long, involved kiss before she reluctantly got into her car for the two-hour ride back to L.A.

She would be calling him tonight, she thought as she made her way back to her cubicle. Maybe then, after she saw how he was going with the factory, she'd start broaching how they were going to handle their relationship.

She didn't know when she'd gotten so careful, she thought with a wry grin as she put her laptop case down on her desk. It was so unlike her, the woman used to leading with her chin.

Maybe it was because this time, she was leading with her heart.

"Jade? That you?"

Jade looked up to see one of the other account execs, Bob, peering around the muted fabric wall of her cubicle. "Yup. How's it been around here with me gone? Pretty quiet, I imagine."

"Well, you certainly liven up the place," Bob said, "but the bigwigs are getting pretty lively themselves. Something big's coming down the pike. Something involving your boss. We haven't seen Raw Diehl running around like this since she got here."

Jade fought to keep her grin contained. "You don't say."

"Honestly, we've been pretty freaked out about it." Bob studied her carefully. "You've been out of the office, but if you knew what was going on, you'd spill, right? Do you know what's going on?"

Jade sighed. This was one thing she hadn't missed. It was like spy vs. spy, every day. Funny that she hadn't noticed it as much. "I've got an inkling of what it is," she said honestly, causing his eyebrows to rise. "I don't think it's a bad thing. Chances are, we'll find out soon enough, right?"

"You're holding out on me, Jade," he reproached.

"Give it half an hour. Keep your pants on," Jade said with a wink.

Grumbling, he retreated back to his own work area.

She wasn't sure how they were going to announce her promotion, she thought, sliding her laptop into its docking station and starting it. Probably something small, like an e-mail. She was hardly expecting fanfare. Still, it was going to feel good to finally reach that bar. In fact, she'd probably ask Betsy out for a drink to celebrate. The woman was the one who set up this opportunity. With any luck, the two of them would become a force to be reckoned with at Michaels & Associates.

Suddenly, Betsy showed up at her cubicle. "Jade, I need you to come with me."

Sooner than she'd anticipated. Jade couldn't help the feeling of nervous butterflies in her stomach, feeling people's gazes watching her as she followed Betsy to the main conference room where a few of the partners were sitting. They all looked pretty solemn, she noted as Betsy closed the door behind her. Maybe they didn't want to offer her the promotion, Jade thought with sudden panic. No, that was silly. They sounded happy enough on Friday when they told her officially that she'd landed the job.

What was going on here?

She sat. The partners looked at each other. Then Dean Michaels, the man who started the firm, stood.

"Jade, it's come to our attention that there might be some problems with the promotion we just offered you."

"I beg your pardon?" Jade glanced around wildly at the partners, who all seemed set in stone. "What sort of problems?"

"Ethical issues." Dean's voice was mournful.

Jade felt her heart start pounding, and her stomach clenched. "I didn't do anything fraudulent. All the paperwork is well documented. I didn't violate confidentiality. I did everything I could. Now, Michaels and Associates is getting paid the first installment of a very sizable contract."

"Now, Jade, we're not attacking you here..."

Like hell you're not. Jade forced herself to take several deep breaths. "What exactly do you think I've done?"

"You've slept with a client, for God's sake," Robert Duncan, an older partner, said with a nasty edge to his voice. "What, did you expect a medal?"

Jade froze.

They'd found out. She wasn't sure how, but they'd found out. And it was hardly something she could lie about. Rather, she would not lie about it. Drew meant too much to her. She'd known it was wrong at the time. Now she'd just have to brazen it out.

"Do you even deny it?" Robert's face was turning a splotchy red.

"May I ask who's accusing me of this and what proof they have?" She was amazed she could keep her voice even.

Dean fielded this one. "We've got some rather incriminating photos of you and Mr. Robson of Robson Steel." He looked embarrassed to even have to say this.

"Photos?" She blinked at them. "You spied on me?"

He actually winced at that one. "They were provided to us by a concerned party. In light of this, you can understand why you can't possibly be made account supervisor."

Jade gaped at him. "But..."

"In fact," he said, not quite meeting her eyes for any length of time, "you have to understand...we don't think we can continue your employment here at Michaels and Associates."

Now Jade jumped to her feet. "What?"

"Come now," Robert said sharply. His thick white eyebrows were beetled together, so deep was his frown. "You honestly can't expect to sleep your way to the top in a respected establishment like Michaels and Associates! We're a family organization!"

"We're a public relations firm in Los Angeles! We've represented everything from professional politicians to actors, back when we were really raking in profits. Do you really think we were worried about our image as a family organization then?"

She knew she was blowing her stack, but the whole

thing was so incredible...after all this time, after coming so close, she was losing on an ethics issue. She took a deep breath, looking at Betsy. Betsy was looking back at her, her expression inscrutable. She was not jumping in to help or defend. Why wasn't she helping?

It looked as though Jade was on her own.

So what else is new?

She put her hands on the tabletop, feeling the cool wood beneath her palms as a sort of support and source of strength. "I will not deny that I have gotten involved in a relationship with Drew Robson," she said slowly, and saw that many of the six partners were muttering to each other while Betsy continued to stare at her with that fixed gaze. "I am not ashamed of it, nor will I try to hide it or downplay it. However, I can say that the relationship has nothing to do with the contractual agreement Michaels and Associates has with Robson Steel. I did not get involved with him in order to get him to honor the contract and pay us. I can prove this."

"The fact of the matter is," Dean said, almost apologetically, "you slept with a client, while you were working with said client representing Michaels and Associates. It's an ethical breach. You have to know that."

"So you're firing me?" Jade felt nauseous.

"I don't know that we have much choice."

"Is there a policy on this?" She studied the woebegone look on his face. "Is there some kind of ethical code on the books?"

Robert was turning a rosy shade of red. "Have you no shame? You're actually going to try to use some kind of...some kind of bureaucratic nonsense to save yourself? This is an honorable establishment! We've been in this business for the past fifty years, young woman, and I'll be damned if I..."

"Michaels and Associates has been steadily losing revenue for the past four years, Robert," Jade interrupted, and he actually spluttered. "While I respect the tradition and mission and vision of the company...*I didn't do anything wrong.* I made a mistake in judgment, perhaps, but it was a personal decision that had nothing to do with this firm. My personal life is just that. *Personal.*"

"That personal life of yours," he replied snidely, "stops when you cross the line and convince a client to pay by sleeping with him."

Jade's heart clenched painfully. She could picture herself getting up, walking over to the older man and punching him one square in his fat, jowly jaw. "Careful," she said instead, in a whisper that cut through the room like a razor.

Dean Michaels held up a hand, obviously trying to get things back on track. "Jade, you've been an asset to the firm," he said awkwardly. "We were hoping you would understand our position and honor our decision."

"Tell me something," she said, looking over at Betsy...who was staring back at her, not saying anything. Why wasn't she saying anything? "If I'm such an asset to the firm, why wasn't I made account supervisor before now?"

Dean let out a heavy, weary sigh. "I think that was an oversight on our part. But there were some, uh, factions," he said, and she noticed he shot a quick glance over at Duncan and, to Jade's surprise, Betsy, "that were against the idea. Didn't feel like you really went in with the firm's philosophy. Too much of a maverick, too independent.'' His tone gentled. ''Honestly, Jade, I was surprised you haven't hung up a shingle for yourself.''

It was bad enough that she was getting the promotion ripped away from her, she thought as she looked at the ceiling for a quick moment and blinked fast to stop the traitorous tears from rushing in. It was even worse to know that the head of the firm believed in her—and that others didn't, cutting her career off before it had a chance to really grow. He thought she was good, but hadn't said anything. What a stupid waste.

''I don't want to leave Michaels and Associates,'' she said, focusing on Dean because he was the only one she could trust herself to look at without screaming. ''And I don't think you have the grounds to fire me.''

He blinked. ''You don't want to...''

''Tell me you're not thinking of a wrongful termination of employment lawsuit of some sort,'' Robert bellowed. ''Just tell me you're not that much of an idiot!''

''That's the sort of thing lawyers love to hear,'' Jade said in a cool voice. *You jackass.*

Dean frowned at Robert. ''Jade, we'll have to convene a special meeting with all the partners. If you can convince them that what you did was not ethically questionable and did not go against the corporate policy, human relations policy, or our own firm's mission and philosophy, then I don't see why we couldn't keep you on.''

''With my promotion,'' she added.

His eyes gleamed. Robert's eyes, she noted, bugged out as if he were going to explode.

''Of course,'' Dean said with a nod. ''I'll have my

secretary call the meeting up. In the meantime, I think it's prudent if you treated this as a suspension and went home."

Jade nodded, feeling her stomach churn. "Of course."

They all left, and Jade noticed that everyone outside in the office was pointedly absent, hiding in cubicles or anywhere else out of her eyesight. Instead of heading for her cubicle or the door, she waited a few beats, watching Robert mutter loudly to Dean, who kept walking to his office. Then Jade saw Betsy head for her office and she followed, shutting the door behind her.

Betsy made a face. "There isn't anything I can do to help, Jade. You'd best just go home."

"You knew this was coming," Jade said. "What do you think I should do?"

"Honestly?" Betsy sat behind her desk. "Dean was on to something. You're good. Start your own firm. Robson Steel could even work with you…well, no, they're still under contract with us. But I'm sure Drew Robson has other customers and a client base that you could work with."

Jade blinked. "Just like that? Give up?"

"Yes." Betsy's voice was firm. "Here, anyway. The party's over, Jade. Just call it a night and leave with dignity."

"You can't believe that," Jade said, feeling numb. She sat in an opposite chair, ignoring Betsy's frown. "You're a fighter. I've heard about the coups you pulled, at your previous firms…"

"I'm sure you did," Betsy said, and for the first time, Jade noticed a shade of smugness in the woman's voice. "Let me see if I remember the rumors—I was one of the most bloodthirsty, ambitious, ruthless P.R. women in Hollywood before switching from show business to real business.''

''Exactly.''

''I'd stop at nothing to get what I wanted.''

''That's it, that's it exactly...'' Jade suddenly stopped, and it was as if a wheel suddenly clicked into place. ''You. You sank me.''

Betsy remained silent, but Jade knew, just as certain as she knew her social security number.

''Why?'' Jade couldn't help it. After all this time...she should've expected it, she cursed herself. Mentor, indeed. ''Because I might make partner, too?''

''I told you,'' Betsy said, and her voice took on a little edge. ''You reminded me of me, when I was your age.''

''You thought I'd gun for your job.'' Jade felt dazed. ''So you...what? Made up some stuff? What was the deal with that photograph crap?''

''It's a simple thing to hire a private investigator, Jade,'' Betsy said, ''and before you embark on a tirade of self-righteousness, it was stupid for you to sleep with a client. Even more stupid to let me figure it out—you weren't exactly discreet about it. They're just clients, Jade. The sooner you learn that, the sooner you'll get ahead in this. But frankly, I don't think you'll ever really get ahead. And do you want to know why?''

Jade stared at her. ''Please. Enlighten me.''

''Because you lead with your heart and not your head.'' Betsy's voice rang like steel with finality. ''You're too sensitive for this business. Maybe you should find something else to do.''

She stood, walked over to the door and opened it.

"And while you're at it, maybe you should find somewhere else to do it."

Jade stood, anger pulsing through her like white-hot molten steel. "I've got a few ideas of what I can do, and exactly where I can do it," she said.

"Tacky," Betsy said, but to Jade's satisfaction, her cool facade cracked just enough to show she was a little nervous.

"See you at the hearing, *boss,*" Jade said.

Betsy said nothing, so Jade stalked down the hall, past a few curious onlookers, and out to her car.

I'm going to go home, she thought. *Go home, and call Drew.*

She never thought about going to someone for help before, she thought as she started the Mustang. Now his voice was the only thing she wanted to hear.

And all I want to hear him say is everything is going to be all right.

She was dialing on the cell phone as soon as she got the car started, barely able to hear the ring of the dial tone over the roar of her engine. She drove through the streets like a madwoman.

"Robson Steel, Drew Robson's office..."

"Mrs. Packard," Jade said, "please put me through to Drew."

She could almost hear Mrs. Packard's face scrunch up. "Mr. Robson is very busy..."

"This is important!" Jade couldn't help it. She was in no mood for Mrs. Packard running interference.

Mrs. Packard paused a minute, then said, "Fine. I'll just put you right through."

Jade heard the lame-o hold music that Robson Steel still used. *I'll have to talk to him about that,* she thought absently, zipping from one lane to the next.

Later. She'd have plenty of time to talk to him about it. Right now, her whole being-fired thing was just a little more important.

She heard the hold music shut off as she was clicked over to Drew. "Jade? Is that you? What's wrong?"

"Drew," she said, feeling the tears well up in her throat. "I've just had the shittiest day…"

"Where are you? In your car? I can barely hear you."

"Yes," she said, yelling, then cursing as someone cut her off. She responded hard with her car horn as the guy started yelling obscenities at her. "You son of a…"

"Jade? What's going on?"

"Sorry, some idiot in an SUV just tried to…"

"Honey, I really don't have time."

Jade paused, almost slamming on the breaks. "What?"

"I am hip-deep in the legal that the investors sent over," Drew said with a heavy sigh in his voice. "They're trying to pull all this stuff we didn't talk about. I'm working with the lawyers right now. Can I give you a call later tonight?"

"Later tonight?" She said the words in a monotone, feeling numbness crawl over her.

"That would be great," he said with relief. "I'll call around…hmm. How's eight? Is that okay?"

"Uh, yeah." This wasn't happening. This couldn't be happening.

"Great." His voice went a little lower. "Love you."

Just like that, he hung up.

She stared at the phone, then clicked it off and put it on the seat next to her. She drove back to her apartment as if on autopilot.

That didn't just happen.

She'd just gotten fired. Betrayed by her mentor. And the man who loved her really didn't have the time to talk about it.

IT WAS CLOSER TO NINE when Drew finally got a chance to call Jade. He was tired, and cranky. And knowing that he was going back home to an empty bed wasn't helping matters one bit.

"Good night, Drew," Ken said from the doorway.

"'Night, Ken," he replied, rubbing at his eyes.

Ken paused. "It's going to be an uphill battle, but the important part is, we're that much closer to saving this place. As long as we stay focused, nothing bad's going to happen. It's a tough time right now."

"I know," Drew said. "Believe me, I know." He stopped, pensive. "Ken, does it seem to you like there's nothing *but* tough times, lately? Seems like if I breathe wrong, the whole place is going to go under."

"That's what comes with the territory," Ken said with a laugh. "No, really, I understand. It's just...give it six months, Drew. That's all. When the investment money is guaranteed, when we've got the new processes started and the renovations going, then you'll have a little breathing room. Trust me. It'll get better. But right now, we need everything you've got. We're not out of the woods yet."

"Six months." It seemed like an eternity...but at least there was an end date. "Okay."

Ken waved, then left. Drew could hear his footsteps growing fainter down the corridor. Yawning, Drew picked up the phone and dialed Jade's cell phone number.

She answered on the third ring. "Drew."

"Hi, sweetie," he said, feeling the little rush of comfort just from hearing her voice. "I'm sorry I couldn't talk before. Inesco's being a bit tougher than we thought, but I'm pretty sure we'll do fine. It was just ugly earlier...and it's probably going to be uglier before it gets better. You wouldn't believe what their second-in-command is trying with the legal department..."

Jade made a noncommittal noise. Abruptly he realized that there was something amiss.

"So," he said, wondering if it was because he wasn't paying enough attention, "how was your first day as an account supervisor? Did you get a new office?"

"Actually, the promotion didn't go exactly as planned," she said conversationally.

"Really?"

"Yeah." She paused. "It actually strongly resembled getting fired."

He laughed. Then realized that she wasn't, and stopped. "You're not serious."

"I'm very serious," she said, and he heard it...the little catch in her voice. He'd bet anything that she was fighting back tears.

"What the hell did they fire you over? That's outrageous! That's..."

"They fired me," she said, her quiet voice stopping his tirade, "for sleeping with you."

He stopped, then took a deep breath. "Oh, no."

"Unethical behavior. Sleeping with a client. There were some veiled insults about the only way I was able to land a sale, et cetera. Then I was given the boot."

"You're going to fight it, right?"

"You're damned right I am," she said, and the fire

in her voice heartened him. That was the Jade he knew. The woman would kick the Devil himself right in the teeth before she gave up on a fight. "They're wrong about this. I'm good at what I do. And we…well, that didn't have anything to do with it."

"Exactly," he said, wishing she were in the room so he could hold her. Tough or not, she needed some comfort. He could see past the tough act.

"So that's why I'm going to need you here."

"Sorry?" His thoughts tripped over themselves as he finally registered what she was saying. "You're going to need what?"

"Drew, I insisted on having, well, I guess you'd call it a hearing," she said slowly. "I thought that if you went in front of them and spoke with them, that they'd understand. We did have a physical relationship."

"We *do* have a physical relationship," he corrected, then added, "more important, we have a *relationship.* Right?"

"Right." She sounded relieved. "I guess that might be our best plan of attack. I've got all weekend to come up with my defense. Between the two of us, I'm sure we can come up with something."

His mind raced. "Ah, Jade…"

She stopped. "What?"

"This weekend…this coming week…" He sighed. This was going to hurt. "I promised Ken and the lawyers that I'd focus on ironing out the clauses in the contract with Inesco."

She was silent for a long few moments.

"It's not that I have a lot of choice," Drew said to fill the growing gap in their conversation. "You know how important this deal is for me. You were the one who helped me get it. If it weren't for you, I wouldn't even..."

"It's just one weekend and one day," she said. "I thought...hell. I don't know what I thought."

"I'm sorry," Drew said, then stood. "You know what? Screw Michaels and Associates. You don't have anything to prove. If they're going to have that kind of stuff against you...if this is how they're going to treat you, then they don't deserve to have you."

She didn't respond right away, and he was about to launch into another round of reasoning when she said, "So. If they really wanted me to work with them, they would have shown more faith in me, right?"

"That's it." He felt his stomach settle as the tension left. She sounded so upset. This was better. "That's it exactly."

"In fact, if they gave a damn about me, they wouldn't be putting me on the block like this," she said, obviously warming to the topic. "If they really cared at all, they wouldn't be hanging me out to dry."

"You're absolutely right," he enthused.

"So tell me, Drew," she said, in a low voice. "How the hell is what they're doing different from what you're doing?"

He stopped dead. "What?"

"I did everything I could to help you," she said sharply. "I gave up three weeks of my life and put a lot on the line to help you. And then I fell in love with you, and I made love with you. And *I lost my job for it.*" Her voice shook, with anger, with sheer agony. "And your answer is to just walk away from it?"

"Wait a second, here," he interjected, but she rolled right over him.

"This job was everything I wanted, Drew. You

know what it's like to want something like that!'' Her voice was just this side of pleading, and the tone of it tore at him. ''I'm just asking for a little of your time. A little help. I know how busy your life is right now, and I know how important the Inesco deal is. But this is my life. I just need a few days.''

He sighed.

She stopped, and her voice was as cold as a snowdrift. ''No, don't tell me. If it were any other time than this... I understand.''

''Jade, I'm sorry.''

''Don't be sorry,'' she said. ''At the risk of sounding very, very drama...you're not the first.''

''Damn it, I'd be there if I could.'' He didn't like this. ''And you didn't just do all of this altruistically. You were getting a promotion out of this. Don't try to...''

''You're right, Drew. I was just in it for me. And now you're just in it for you, is that it?''

''Don't twist my words,'' he said, gripping the receiver as though it were a club.

''I'm not. I'm just pointing out. I thought I loved you...I still think I love you. But that doesn't necessarily mean anything. What would you have done? You wouldn't have moved to L.A. You've got the plant. That's the most important thing for you.''

''You know how important it is.''

She laughed, and it was a bitter sound. ''I understand. And I also understand that, despite my relatively massive ego, I really believe one thing. I deserve a man who puts me first. Who cares enough about me to put me first.''

''That's not fair.''

"I know," she said in a quiet voice. "Drew, this isn't going to work."

He felt a queasy wave of panic warring with the anger that was bubbling up in him. "Damn it, don't do this."

"Just like you, Drew...*I* don't have the time for this," she said. "Good luck with the Inesco deal."

"Damn it, Jade!"

"Damn it is right," she said. "Goodbye, Drew."

And hung up.

11

JADE DIDN'T KNOW what was worse—the phone ringing, or the phone not ringing. Either way, she felt as if she was reading too much into both the fact that Drew might be calling or the fact that Drew wasn't calling. At first she'd tried screening her calls with her message machine, but after three telemarketers and a rather nasty-yet-polite message from the lawyer at Michaels & Associates she'd finally said screw it and disconnected the phone completely. She'd also shut off her cell phone, not that it mattered since she'd let the battery die. If this kept up, she thought, pacing her living room, she might stop collecting her mail.

She couldn't believe that it had only been a month since she'd been home—that it had only been a month since all these things had happened to her. Her apartment felt strange. Probably because the toilet hadn't been sanitized for her protection and the television wasn't chained to anything, she thought, fighting back a wave of nervous laughter.

She refused to think what else was absent from her life that had currently filled up a nice, six-foot-five space.

Finally, after the strangeness of her apartment and her loneliness for Drew made her start to climb the walls, she did the only rational, calming thing she knew. She got into her car and headed for the Pacific

Coast Highway. Between the crash of the waves and the aggressive roar of her engine, she might not find serenity, but she'd definitely be able to get her mind off of things. She had the window down, and her hair whipped frenetically, barely restrained by her ponytail. She had sunglasses on, the warmth of the sun on her arm, and a long line of black road stretched out in front of her.

She'd keep driving until she felt better, she thought.

She didn't feel better, but she did feel more reflective as she tore down the highway. She thought about the last two guys she had been involved with. Her last serious relationship had been one year out of college. He'd been a senior partner, cool, aloof, sophisticated. She'd stolen an account from him for an opposing small boutique firm, and he'd asked her out to dinner as they left the client's lobby. She'd been with him for two years, before realizing that they never really saw each other...they were both too busy working and their scheduled meetings together seemed more like business than pleasure. It was a pity, too...her parents had liked him on the one occasion that they'd met him. Before that, it had been a bad boy, back in college, a bruiser she'd met at a sports bar. After about six months of delirious sex, she'd tried to bring him home to meet her parents, only to discover he really didn't do commitment—and he certainly hadn't been that exclusive with her. She'd been hurt with that one, heartbroken with Tom the Businessman. But the thing was, she hadn't really trusted either of them with anything important. Sure she'd slept with them, spent some time with them. But her heart hadn't been in it.

With Drew, for the first time, it had. Of course that was the problem. Of course it hurt.

She passed a cruising minivan ignoring the driver's envious stare, and paced a Mercedes-Benz before getting bored and dusting it, tearing up the pavement with a quick shift of gears.

So she was hurt with Drew. Big deal. In a way, she should've been expecting it—should have been warned by what she was feeling for him. Business and pleasure. For some people, business *was* pleasure. Better to leave sex out of it altogether.

But Drew was more than sex.

After a few hours she finally forced herself to turn around and pulled into the parking lot of her apartment building. When she climbed out of her car, she rolled her shoulders. She had a bit of a tan, her body was sore and tired, and her problems hadn't really lightened much at all. She had hoped for clarity, or at least a respite. Now, she dragged herself back up to her apartment, fumbling the key in the lock.

"Hey, you. I've been waiting for hours. Where have you been?" Hailey greeted her from her couch. Hailey's black hair was cut in a spiky gamine style and her pixie-delicate face puckered in a look of disapproval.

Now *here,* Jade thought, was somebody she could count on. Without saying a word, she walked over the to the couch, tugged Hailey to her feet, and hugged her, engulfing Hailey's five-foot frame with her own five-nine one.

"Boy, I'm glad to see you," she said, and realized the words came out watery. She let out a hiccupy sob.

"Whoa, whoa, whoa," Hailey said, hugging back fiercely. "Come on, it's not that bad."

"I got fired for sleeping with a client that I'm in love with who doesn't love me," Jade said all in a rush.

Hailey paused. "Okay. It is that bad. This calls for ice cream. As it happens, I bought some on the way here."

Jade pulled back and smiled, rubbing at her eyes with the back of her hands. "Chocolate-chocolate chip?"

"Of course."

Jade smiled. This was comfort. If Hailey couldn't help her feel better, than nothing could.

"MR. CLARK, it's getting close to one in the morning." Drew stood, rubbing at the back of his neck. "We're not getting anything else done here."

Mr. James Clark had been the lawyer for Robson Steel since Drew was a little kid. Consequently, Drew had difficulty calling the man "James," even though Drew was now president and CEO, and James worked for him.

Mr. Clark rubbed his eyes, putting the paper off to one side. Then he glanced at his watch. "Good grief, you're right. I think we got a lot accomplished. Still, I'll be back in the morning at eight, if you like."

"I'll be in, but I can work on other stuff if you'd like to come in later," Drew said. There was always plenty of work at Robson Steel to fill up the time…and it wasn't as though he had any reason to stay at home. He tried unsuccessfully not to think of his last call with Jade. "Whenever works for you."

I miss her. I miss the hell out of her.

"Just six more months," Drew reminded himself out loud.

Mr. Clark paused in the act of packing up his leather briefcase. "Beg your pardon?"

Drew looked at him, with a small half grin. "Six months. It'll calm down in six months."

Mr. Clark laughed. "If you say so. I've noticed that it's always something, if you stay on long enough." He shook his head. "Still, that's the nature of the business. If you own a business, if you're dedicated to something, then you work hard."

"I know that."

"Your father didn't."

Drew looked at the elderly lawyer. Mr. Clark didn't usually badmouth Drew's father, even though Drew knew that he had been the man who cleaned up most of his father's messes. Of course, Drew basically agreed with those sentiments, but he didn't necessarily feel comfortable with the older man making the statement.

"Your father," Mr. Clark said, stretching a little to work the kinks out of his back, "was a brilliant salesman. But he was probably the worst thing that happened to this plant."

Drew kicked around possible responses. "He had a lot of mitigating factors," Drew finally said, unsure of why he was defending his recalcitrant father. "The economy..."

"Come on now," Mr. Clark scoffed. "The economy doesn't force you to steal a million dollars and take a hike to the Bahamas."

Drew kept quiet. He really didn't have an answer for that one.

"Your grandfather and I used to talk all the time about it." Mr. Clark shook his head. "I was a lot younger then. I wanted to be a lawyer—your grandfather helped me get a scholarship. Then I went on to law school. He was my first client. I've worked with

Robson Steel ever since. He once said…'' He cleared his throat. ''He said that I was as close to him as his own son. Wished that I *was* his son.''

''I didn't know that,'' Drew said, at a loss for words.

''It's not all that important now, I suppose.'' But Drew could tell from the tone of the older man's voice—it was just as important now as it was the day his grandfather had originally said the words. ''The bottom line is, your father had it all going for him. Great education, his father's trust, the steel plant in the palm of his hand. And he threw it all away. He never really cared about it. Not the way I would have, in his place.''

Drew felt uneasy. At any other time he would have agreed with Mr. Clark. Hell, he probably would have taken it one step further. But tonight, something wasn't ringing quite right.

Maybe it's because it's so late. I'm tired.

''I know I probably haven't said it enough,'' Drew said slowly, ''but I really do appreciate everything you do for Robson Steel.''

Mr. Clark's expression lightened. ''Well, at least it's working for you, Drew. Your father didn't appreciate this company. Oh, he started out strong enough—put in the hours, had the dedication. But he just couldn't handle the responsibility.''

Drew thought back. He hadn't seen his father from the time he started school, from all the hours his father put in at the plant. Then, after his mother finally divorced the senior Mr. Robson, he'd only seen his dad on special occasions.

He'd been at the plant.

''You know,'' Drew added, ''hating him for the choices he made isn't going to change anything.''

"No, it's not," Mr. Clark agreed, "but making the same decision he made isn't going to change anything, either. If you don't put Robson Steel first, everything will suffer. Just like before. Now, we're all paying for it."

Drew watched as Mr. Clark stepped out the door, briefcase in hand. "See you tomorrow morning."

Drew nodded absently. It was one o'clock in the morning. He'd be back in here by seven. The process would repeat itself.

He didn't know what prompted him, but he pulled open a desk drawer and took out an old framed picture...one he'd stuffed in the desk when he'd taken over as president. It was one of his father and himself. He was about six. He was sitting on his father's desk, his father mugging it up for the camera. His desk was strewn with papers.

Drew glanced from the picture to the desk itself.

Not much had changed.

His father had worked hellish hours, at first, when he'd inherited Robson Steel. He hadn't had any sort of feel for the way the plant ran, or for steel itself, but he had been a brilliant salesman, and he had been pretty well liked by the workers. Drew hadn't hated the plant for taking his father away—he hated his father for simply not being there. Now he wondered if his father himself had hated the plant for what he'd been forced to lose. Even if it had been, ultimately, his father's choice.

Am I willing to do that?

He had gotten the investment money. He still felt indebted to the plant, and to the town. But they were in less danger now. Hell, if Inesco took over the plant, as he feared, the workers would probably still have jobs. What was he fighting for?

He thought back on Jade, about the time he'd spent with her. Even as his body tightened with the memory, he thought about what she'd said one night, just before their passionate culmination.

You can't solve everybody's problems and you're not responsible for everybody's well-being.

He loved Robson Steel. But he also loved Jade. He had done everything he could to save the plant, the town, and everyone around him.

Right now, he thought, it was time to save his own future...with the woman, he knew, whom he loved more than anything.

"SO DO YOU LOVE him?"

Jade was curled up on her couch, cocooned in a flannel throw, with a special Hailey's Hot Toddy warming her hands. The remnants of a yellow cake with chocolate frosting littered a broad platter on her coffee table. Hailey was sitting in her wing-backed chair, looking like a dark-haired sprite, staring at her with concern.

Jade frowned. "I don't know. I mean, can you really fall in love with somebody in just a couple of weeks? This isn't the movies or anything," Jade said. "I cared about him."

"He had to mean a lot to you to get you to sleep with him even though he was a client."

Jade winced. "That wasn't love. That was stupidity."

"Bull." Hailey got out of the chair and sat next to Jade, nudging her with a fist. "You might be impetuous, but you're not stupid. And I know you. You might talk big, but you're intensely loyal, and you've got a stricter code of ethics than pretty much everybody I know."

"You work in a bar, Hailey," Jade reminded her. "What kind of scruples are we talking about?"

Hailey obviously chose to ignore the gibe. "The point I'm trying to make here is, you chose to enter into a relationship with this guy, for good reasons or bad. And I know you. You've had some, uh, recreational interludes," Hailey said diplomatically, "but I've never seen you go crazy because of one."

Jade sent over a wistful grin. Trust Hailey to focus on the real danger signals. "I've never been fired because of a recreational interlude, either."

"We're getting nowhere." Hailey stood, paced. She was still the same little ball of energy...and idealism. "Okay. Let me ask you this. If you got your job back tomorrow, and your promotion, and the only condition was that you could never see Drew Robson again..."

"Oh, come on," Jade protested. "What sort of company would make me..."

"Shut up. This is my scenario," Hailey said. "If you could have your job but not Drew Robson, would everything be all right?"

Jade started to respond, then thought about it. *Never see Drew again.*

The pain was overwhelming.

"No," Jade said in a quiet voice. "No. It wouldn't be all right. Not at all."

"All right," Hailey said smugly. "Now we're getting somewhere."

"But the fact of the matter is, I don't have that choice. I have to fight for my job tomorrow, in front of a bunch of partners who aren't going to give a crap that I fell in love with one of my clients. They're just going to know that I unethically slept with someone who owed the firm money, and got him to pay up."

"I understand you get a certificate of recognition in some companies for that sort of behavior," Hailey quipped.

"The bottom line is, what do I tell them?" Jade tugged at her hair in frustration. "It's not like they're wrong."

"Did you sleep with Drew to get what you wanted?"

"No, of course not."

Hailey leaned back, smiling. "Did you sleep with him because he was your client."

"Hailey..."

"Don't 'Hailey' me. You fell in love. It had nothing to do with your job. You did everything you could to help him both because you cared about him and because he was a client of Michaels and Associates. It was a special circumstance, it is a personal relationship, and it's bottom line none of their business. Period, end of sentence."

Jade leaned back, too, staring at Hailey. "Wow. Maybe I should just bring you tomorrow."

"Maybe you should," Hailey said, obviously still riled.

"I thought bartenders just listened to problems," Jade said, nudging Hailey with her foot and smiling warmly. "I didn't know you went in and solved them."

"You're a special case. So, are you going to give them hell tomorrow or what?"

Jade thought about it. "You know, it occurred to me today, while I was driving, that maybe—just maybe—I spend too much time at my job."

Hailey blinked at her for a good minute, then smiled

broadly. "Thank God for Drew Robson. I've been trying to get you to see that for *years!*"

"Yeah, well, if you're so interested in me taking it easy and getting balance in my work life," Jade pointed out, "then what difference does it make if I show up to this hearing and fight for a job at a company I'm not even sure I want to work for anymore?"

"Look at it this way. They're trying to tell you who you can and can't fall in love with. They're accusing you of being unethical, after years of looking you over for promotion. They're railroading you." Hailey paused a beat for dramatic effect. "If this were happening to someone else, like me for instance, would you just roll over and tell me to make the best of it? Or would you tell me to get the lead out and kick some ass?"

Jade thought about it…a bureaucratic group telling Hailey she was fired for falling in love. Hailey was so not cut out for corporate life, and she had a habit of…oh. "Gotcha. I see your point."

"So…what's it going to be? Rolling over or kicking ass?"

Jade grinned. "What do you think?"

Hailey grinned right back at her. "I think I'm proud of you," she said.

"Game on," Jade replied, and hugged her.

12

DREW SHOULD'VE BEEN used to driving by now. He glanced at his map again. Just take the Five, get off at the Ten, off at Santa Monica Boulevard. Now was that big Santa Monica or little Santa Monica? For a city that big, you'd think they could have the imagination to come up with different names for their streets, he thought, honking hard at a minivan that was threatening to cut him off. He was in rush-hour traffic. It had been a full year since he'd had to deal with something as annoying and mundane as rush-hour traffic.

It's for a good cause.

His cell phone rang and he hit the on button. "Drew, here."

"Hey, boss." Ken's voice rang unmistakably through the static. "It's about eight in the morning. I thought we were going to get an early start before the call to Inesco this afternoon?"

He took a deep breath. "I left a message with Inesco. We're rescheduling the call to Wednesday."

"Um...okay." Ken was obviously puzzled, and Drew couldn't blame him. On any other day, Drew would be in the office, hashing it out.

"I'm taking today for me. I'll be back in tomorrow. I'm not shirking my responsibilities."

"Nobody said you were," Ken pointed out.

Drew sighed. "Sorry. I had sort of an epiphany the

other night. I sorted out some things...about the business, for one thing. And the deal. And...well, a lot of other things."

"Like a certain tall, redheaded business coach?"

Drew smiled. "Yeah. And my father."

Ken whistled, low. "No kidding."

"I guess I sort of figured out I can't do anything for Robson unless I get some balance. Otherwise, I'm going to snap and do something rash, something stupid."

"That's not good," Ken said, laughing nervously.

"Don't worry, I'm not going to steal a million dollars and make a break for the Caribbean," Drew answered with a laugh of his own. "But I'll tell you one thing. For the first time in my life, I have an inkling of why Dad did it."

"Wow. That must've been some epiphany."

"You have no idea. So. Can you hold down the fort until I get back?"

"No problem. Handle your business. Robson Steel will be here when you get back."

Drew smiled. "That's just what I wanted to hear."

"Oh, and good luck...on whatever, you know, personal business you have to take care of."

"Thanks," Drew said, glancing at the map one more time and thinking of Jade. "I'm going to need it."

THE EXECUTIVE conference room at Michaels & Associates would probably work in a pinch if the U.N. needed an extra meeting place in Los Angeles. The room was cavernous, to start, and there was a lot of dark wood and brass accents. It was swank, and intimidating. Usually they brought clients here that they were trying to impress.

That wasn't the point of today's exercise.

Jade sat ramrod straight in her chair, her legs crossed. She forced herself not to fidget with the gold pen she held tightly in her right hand. She was wearing her power suit, trying hard not to shiver in the overly air-conditioned atmosphere. She had a leather portfolio in front of her with all the arguments she could brainstorm the night before.

"You're going to have them begging for mercy," Hailey had predicted, giving her a hug goodbye that morning. Jade only wished she could have smuggled Hailey in somehow. She could use a friendly face. The eight faces flanking her on the opposite side of the mahogany table were distinctly unfriendly. They were all wearing clothing that could only be described as Business Somber, and they were staring at her as if their glares were glass shards, cutting into her.

Jade glared right back. *Game on.*

Dean Michaels cleared his throat. "Well. This is a little unusual for us, so I guess we'll just get started." He looked at Jade with an expression of pity and extreme discomfort. "I, uh, see you don't have a lawyer with you."

She nodded. "I don't think I need one," she said, pausing just enough to let them relax, then adding, "*yet.*"

"Yes, well, we're hoping it won't get to that," Dean said. Still she noticed that as he shuffled the papers he had in front of him, he looked over at two new people entering the room. Ah. That would be Michaels & Associates' lawyer and human resources expert. Apparently they were bringing out the big guns. Jade refused to feel nervous about that, deliberately ignoring the sudden churning in her stomach. "Today we'll be going over the decision to terminate your employment.

We're giving you the opportunity to explain yourself and your actions, and see if we need to, uh, reevaluate our decision."

Jade looked over. The partners, the lawyer and the human resource expert stared back. She noticed that Betsy had almost no expression, although her gaze kept moving from Jade, then tilting over to Dean, then back to Jade.

"Betsy, since you're the one who brought this to our attention," Dean said, obviously eager to pass the ball to somebody else, "why don't you go over the details?"

Betsy straightened, getting her game face in place. "Jade had been on the road for the past three weeks with a client that we frankly were not expecting to pay us. That would be Drew Robson, from Robson Steel." She paused. "Honestly, it was a loser client. We had all but written it off…apparently the previous owner's claims of giving us a big account were completely blown out of proportion. So when Jade pressed so hard to work with this client, to the exclusion of picking up new clients, I was needless to say curious of what was motivating her."

"I wanted to help Robson Steel and the town of San Angelo," Jade said, her temper almost singeing her hair. "And you never…"

"Please," Dean said. "You'll have your chance for rebuttal."

Jade acknowledged his point, seething silently while she kept her face composed.

"As I was saying, I did some research. Mr. Robson, that would be Drew Robson, is the owner of the steel plant. He's also young. From what she described to me, it was obvious that she found him rather attractive."

And what does that have to do with the price of tea in China? Jade only blinked a few times, keeping her mouth drawn in a tight line. *She told me that one of the account managers she was working with had the tightest ass she'd ever seen! I didn't report her!*

"When she said that she was going on a three-week road trip, with this same client, I was more than surprised. I was shocked. It was a completely unprecedented request."

Jade's face must have registered her ire at this comment, because Betsy shook her head. "Think about it, Jade. Three weeks on the road with a client? Does anybody else at this firm do that?"

"There were reasons," Jade said...but she felt her rock-hard resolve start to weaken a little.

Betsy's face was the picture of sympathy, which made her next sentence that much harsher. "I think we all know what those reasons were, Jade."

Jade gasped at the injustice, then looked at Dean. He shook his head, gesturing to Betsy to continue.

This was one of my dumbest decisions, she thought bitterly. At this point she wasn't sure if she meant Dean or this "hearing."

"She had called in regularly, but by the end of the third week, she wasn't calling in at all, just e-mailing her clients and giving me little generic updates. I knew something was wrong. Considering her previous bizarre reaction to Mr. Robson, I suspected the worst and decided to try confirming it. I called his secretary and found out where he was planning to stay."

Betsy produced a piece of paper from her leather portfolio with a flourish. "I have here a copy of an invoice from the White Sands hotel in Las Vegas. Two occupants. Mr. Drew Robson and Ms. Jade Morrow."

There was a general gasp at this, as the paper made its way down the table. Jade felt heat flush her cheeks.

"I realized at this point that she was sleeping with a client. It completely goes against the ethics of the firm. She had started showing aberrant behavior, she was ignoring her regular book of business, and now this. I brought it to Dean's attention, he discussed it with the rest of you, and the decision was made to terminate her."

Betsy gestured to Dean, as if to say, *All right, now you nail the coffin shut.*

Dean squirmed in his executive chair. "Well, Jade," he said in a tone without hope, "what do you have to say for yourself?"

Jade stood. She thought it gave her a bit of an advantage, evening out the ten-to-one odds she was currently facing. "I only have one thing to say for myself."

She waited a second, taking a deep breath. They watched her, expectantly.

She straightened her back. "I could give you a lot of explanations and excuses, but the fact is that I did sleep with a client. I take full responsibility for that action."

They gasped. Betsy let out a triumphant, catlike smile before realizing she'd let the expression slip and slapped on a look of shock that mirrored everyone else's.

"Do you have any idea what sort of liability you've put the firm in?" Dean goggled. "You have an affair with him, he sues us...Good God, what were you thinking?"

"I was thinking I was in love with him," Jade said quietly.

Now they were more than shocked. They were openly aghast.

"And that's supposed to make it all right?"

"I wasn't in love with him when I started the job. There was no intention of ever getting involved in any non-professional way," she continued. "I know it seemed like a losing proposition, but the town and the plant touched me. Do you have any idea how many clients we represent, who carry on grossly unethical practices, and we paper it over because they're paying us gobs of money? Or how many times clients have tried to proposition me, in really ugly and mercenary ways, and I've said no? Robson Steel was a special case," she said, and at this point her voice broke. "Drew Robson is a special case."

"I appreciate your emotion, dear," Dean said, and his kindness made her eyes moisten with tears, "but you have to understand—emotion or not, what happened was wrong."

"No," Jade corrected. "What happened was unethical and definitely ill-timed. But I can't look at falling in love with Drew Robson as wrong."

With that, the door opened. She turned and her mouth dropped open.

Drew was standing, resplendent in a navy pinstriped suit and gleaming white shirt. His tie was crimson silk. He looked as if he'd just stepped off a model's runway.

"I'm sorry I'm late," he said without any other preamble, as if it were the most natural thing in the world. "I'm afraid my map was a little misleading."

She gaped at him.

"Excuse me, who are you?" Dean looked bewildered. "This is a private..."

"My name's Drew Robson, and I think this meeting affects me as well as Ms. Morrow."

Now the partners were riveted, as though they'd somehow accidentally stumbled into a daytime soap opera. Betsy, Jade noticed, paled a little.

"I understand that Ms. Morrow is getting fired because of her relationship with me." He stood next to her, his eyes like glacial ice. "I want to get the details on this."

"Well, uh, you are our client, and it is unethical for her to...er, get involved with you. While you're our client."

"The job is finished," Drew said. "I'm no longer your client, so she shouldn't have—"

"The thing is," Betsy interrupted, "she got involved with you while you were still a paying customer." She put emphasis on the term *paying*. "That's unethical."

"I see." He sat, and Jade followed suit, still numb from the unreality of the whole situation. "So...she wasn't able to get work done because of her involvement with me?"

"Yes," Betsy said.

"That's not true," Jade said. "I was able to maintain my normal book of business."

"You weren't working up to par. What you were turning in was completely substandard."

Jade thought back to her night in Las Vegas and Betsy's frantic phone call. "You mean, I wasn't able to help you with the new sales pitch that you wanted me to."

Betsy hissed, then her eyes narrowed. Now some of the other partners weren't looking at Jade...they were craning to look at Betsy.

"You slept with the man," Betsy said in a frigid voice.

"But she wasn't neglecting her work?" Drew's voice, on the other hand, was completely calm. "I see. And what brought the fact that she was involved with me to your attention? What is the proof of this?"

"You two shared a hotel room," Betsy said. She looked vindicated. "There's proof of that."

"And that's proof that we were romantically or otherwise unethically involved?" His voice was mild, but his face was stern. "I see. Just how did you obtain a copy of my hotel bill, Ms. Diehl?"

She blinked. "That's not the point here."

"It is the point. Or rather, it will be the point after I speak with my lawyer."

Dean went a few shades whiter. "This is what we were afraid of," he said, looking at the Michaels & Associates' lawyer. "I knew that a lawsuit would result from this!"

Drew sighed. "I see. So your main concern regarding the ethics of her behavior isn't so much how you feel it will reflect on the firm...but the kind of trouble the firm will be in?"

Jade looked at him. Where was he going with this?

"We don't want to see this go to court," the lawyer said, his voice rumbling and low. "Perhaps I ought to speak to..."

"What if we draw up a contract, an agreement if you will, saying that I won't sue Michaels and Associates for sexual harassment, or anything similar, now or any time in the near future?"

Dean blinked. "That...would work well." Then he paused. "And what would you want in return?"

"I'd like you to reinstate Ms. Morrow, of course,"

he said, and Jade felt her heart stop. "It wasn't her idea...in fact, she vehemently protested getting involved with me because I was her client."

"Obviously that didn't stop her," Betsy added.

He turned his attention to Betsy. "It didn't stop either of us," he said calmly. "Because I fell in love with her."

Jade felt her heart start again with an explosion of speed.

He turned to her. "I'm sorry I wasn't here earlier," he repeated, but she knew this had nothing to do with the map or his tardiness. "I want you to know you can count on me."

"I do," she said softly. "But I could've handled it on my own."

"My point is, you don't have to. Not anymore."

She felt her chest warm.

Dean cleared his throat again. The poor man sounded as though he had laryngitis. "Now, let me get this straight. You fell in love with one of our account executives...and you're willing to sign a contract if we keep her on? Am I getting that right?"

He looked at Betsy. "That's right. Although if you're so interested in ethical issues, I'd suggest you look into the ethics of getting someone's hotel bill. That's got my credit card information on it. Technically, there could be some other ethical and legal issues hovering around."

Dean looked at Betsy, who immediately looked nauseous. "Oh, don't worry. We'll be going into that immediately after this meeting."

Jade did a little internal dance at that announcement.

"Well. Then we don't get sued, Jade gets her job back, and that's all settled." It sounded as though that was what Dean had wanted all along. He brushed his hands together, as if washing his hands of the matter.

"Actually, there's just one more thing," Jade said.

They all looked at her.

"I think that, having said all this, you won't need to sign anything, Drew," she said, giving in to her instinct and taking his hand.

He smiled. "I won't?"

"Nope." She smiled back. "I quit. I hear you've got an opening for a marketing person."

He gave her a look of blank surprise... Then he grinned.

"Besides, I think I'd rather freelance, anyway."

He leaned down, kissing her cheek. "Are you sure about this?" he whispered. "You went through the trouble of facing them..."

"Have you ever known me to walk away from a fight?"

He stood up straight, grinning. "In that case, I guess this meeting is over."

LATER THAT NIGHT they were in her apartment, in her bed, twined around each other. "I can't believe you came to help me," she whispered against his chest.

"I can't believe you told them that you loved me, and that was your defense," he said, pulling her on top of him and kissing her throat. "What happened to tough-as-nails Jade Morrow, the one who tells me I lead with my heart and my chin?"

"I guess you rubbed off on me," she said, kissing him back. "I thought I had everything I wanted, going exactly the way I'd planned. Then I met you, and...well..."

"I know what you mean," he said, nuzzling her. "I

thought I knew exactly what I wanted. I thought my whole life was Robson Steel. Until I got stuck with this incredibly sexy, incredibly *bossy* sales coach…"

"Bossy!" She wrapped her legs around him, grinning when he groaned. "I prefer the term 'assertive.'"

"Assertive, then," he said, lifting himself a little. She let out a soft gasp as he entered her, slowly, with maddening gentleness. "Anyway," he continued, his voice a little tighter. "You turned my world upside down, Jade. You not only taught me how to save my plant—you taught me how to save myself. I never would have figured out what I was doing wrong until I burned out. Until I lost my plant and any chance at happiness in my life."

She smiled down at him, even as her hips began to move in response to his gentle invasion. "I wasn't planning to do any of that," she murmured, leaning down and kissing him, her lips brushing over his insistently. "I thought you were going to be just another job. I didn't think I'd fall in love with anyone. And I didn't think I'd fall for anybody who made me feel the way you do."

He turned her over, flipping her gently to her back. "I don't expect you to stop working. That's part of what makes you what you are. But we're definitely going to put each other at the top of the priority list. Right?"

"Are you kidding?" She grinned at him, nipping at his shoulder. "Just *try* to ignore me and be a workaholic."

He grinned back at her. "Same goes for you, lady. If you even try to work an eighty-hour week and leave me alone in bed…"

"No problem there," she said as he wrapped his arms around her. "You're still my favorite client."